SHADOWS
on the MOON

SHADOWS
on the MOON

A NOVEL BY

Bracha
Goykadosh

ISRAEL BOOKSHOP
PUBLICATIONS

Copyright © 2009 by Israel Bookshop Publications

ISBN: 978-1-60091-115-6

Cover design by: David Yaphe
Page layout and design by: Eden Chachamtzedek

Published by:
Israel Bookshop Publications
501 Prospect Street
Lakewood, NJ 08701

Tel: (732) 901-3009
Fax: (732) 901-4012
www.israelbookshoppublications.com
info@israelbookshoppublications.com

Printed in Canada

and it's you are whatever a
moon has always meant

and whatever a sun will
always sing is you

— *EE Cummings*

To Yo, Fred, Beanzul and O

i carry your heart
(i carry it in my heart)

Acknowledgements

THOUGH ONLY MY NAME APPEARS on the cover, many people played significant roles in the production of this book and it gives me great pleasure to express my thanks to them.

Foremost, I would like to thank the many readers who took the time to write to me. My efforts would be incomplete without your feedback and I am continually appreciative of your insights and care for the characters I have created.

This novel was originally serialized in The Jewish Press, and I must extend my gratitude to their stellar staff, in particular my editor Chumi Friedman whose encouragement and optimism enliven the editorial process.

Israel Bookshop has become a home for my novel. I wish to thank the entire superb Israel Bookshop staff for their professionalism and unflagging commitment to this project. I am especially grateful to Malkie Gendelman, an editor nonpareil, for her patience, warmth, and thoughtful editing. I also thank Liron Delmar for her guidance through the editorial process and production.

Though writing is an organic process, every garden could use a little watering. I am continually appreciative for the advice of my many writer friends whose names here would be too many to include. I wish to express my gratitude to Sarah Shapiro — not only a writing mentor, but also a role model — for her generosity with her time and her continued encouragement.

What fun is a good book without a good friend to share it with?

Before this book was truly born, I first showed the scraps of a manuscript to Miriam Ehrenpreis-Felder, who has patiently and quietly been waiting for it to be published these past three years; I am indebted to her for her initial support and constant enthusiasm.

My sisters, Yocheved, Eden, Bina, and Orah, to whom this book is dedicated, are continually teaching and inspiring me. Without their love and zest, nothing would be worth happening. They are truly the best friends a girl could ask for. I wish, in particular, to thank them for their constant readings and re-readings of this manuscript through its many stages and their always-helpful suggestions and ideas.

I cannot even begin to express my thanks to my parents for their unwavering support. Their faith in me has made this — and so much more — possible. I am forever grateful.

Bracha Goykadosh
Rosh Chodesh Cheshvan 5770
New York, NY

TO MY READER:

I wrote this novel three years ago as a senior in high school. Those days now seem far away — almost like figments of my imagination. What I remember clearly, though, was the extreme highs and lows associated with every high school event; everything was either *amazing* or it was the end of the world. Shabbatons, Chumash tests, and telephone calls all seemed to be momentous occasions: happenings that needed to be understood, analyzed, and captured.

Ella's story, I have realized, captures this dimension. Her story is told in a confessional narrative, meaning that you, the reader, are privy to her innermost thoughts and emotions. Though Ella is a fictional character and certainly isn't purposely based on anyone I know, I hope you readers will be able to relate to her and understand her struggles.

Ella's story is not a story about rebellion. It is a story about growing up, accepting our struggles, and realizing how very lucky we are: an intrinsic element of human life.

As always, I am most appreciative for your comments and feedback. These characters in this novel cannot exist without your reading! I would love to hear from you.

Sincerely,
Bracha

I PUT MY PEN DOWN, AND rubbed my temples. I had forgotten something. Was it the pre-calculus test? No, I had somehow forced synthetic division into my head — and trust me, it wasn't easy. I had done most of my homework. What could I have forgotten?

I sighed. Sometimes, I just lose it. My mind, my memory, my temper, my sanity; everything's evanescent with me. Except losing in general — that seems to be permanent. You'd think if it was important — and because my mind was sending me these SOS signals, I knew it was — that I'd actually remember. But, noooooo. I pulled down the shade in front of my desk and then shrugged. The neighbors already think I'm crazy. Shrugging to myself would not help the situation.

I started to lift up my pen again; the tantalizing story of "The Princess and Delilah" was on the tip of my…pen. Have I mentioned I love acting? I love everything about it. I love performing, I love writing plays, I love painting scenery, I love picking out the music for scenes; I love it all! Sorry, scratch that — I wouldn't want to sell tickets. Way too much math involved in that for my taste.

I love it so much, that this year little ol' me even went and begged our principal if we could have a drama club, and she… agreed. Of course, *I* couldn't be a head, since I'm only a Junior (but thank goodness my Freshie days are over; I shudder when I think of the horrors…), and you know, the Seniors have seniority and all that kind of status stuff. But I guess just acting isn't too bad. I'd like to lord over everyone like Ahuva and Chanie do, but I'll get my chance next year.

Suddenly, there was a wretched banging on my door. Goodness! Some people in this house have absolutely no sense of delicacy. It had to be my youngest brother, Ari. Who else would pound on the door like that?

"Whaddya want?" I yelled. Why did he always have to disturb me when I was in middle of something important? I once took a personality test; I forgot the exact term, but I'm one of those people who don't like to be disturbed.

Tova, my sister, barged into my room, a wild look in her usually calm hazel eyes. Her thick black hair was wet and in a messy bun on the top of her head. Droplets of water were pouring down her face, and if I didn't know her too well, I would think she had been crying because her eyes were a teeny bit red. But since she's my twin sister and I've known her from, like, the second we were born, I knew that she wasn't. Tova *never* cries.

"Can I help you?" I said with a sigh, as I pushed my play to the far corner of my desk. Tova usually doesn't barge into my room, either (that special privilege is reserved for Ari), so I assumed it was something important. Or maybe she just wanted me to, I don't know, bake a cake for dessert or something. She did that once before. "Is this important?" I added as an afterthought.

"Oh, no," Tova answered. She rubbed her eyes as if she couldn't believe the scene she was witnessing. "Don't tell me you forgot, Ella. Please don't tell me you forgot."

"Forgot what?" I whined. Couldn't she see I was *doing* something? Here I was, in middle of writing my magnum opus, the next great Shakespearean play of this century, and all Tova could do was blabber about something? I probably had forgotten something. But really, was it *that* important? Talk about overreacting.

"What kind of impression are you going to make?" Tova yelled. "This is really bad, Ayelet. Really, really bad!" I knew it was really bad. She only calls me Ayelet when something is wrong.

"What are you talking about?" I swiveled around in my chair and faced her. Couldn't she get to the point? Was I supposed to babysit for someone tonight? Once, I was supposed to babysit for the Kleins, and I forgot. Needless to say, it wasn't a very happy day for the Kleins or for me. I know it was irresponsible, but it had just slipped my mind. Really.

"The *vort*, Ella!"

Oh, no. How could I have forgotten about the *vort*?

"What am I going to do?" I screeched, jumping to my feet. I could feel my face turning hot and my heart begin pounding. I wondered if I would faint right now. I wondered if that would be good.

"I won't tell Daddy," Tova said, not looking at me but out the window. "But let me tell you, if he found out, he would *so* not be happy!"

"You're telling me," I groaned, flopping back down into my chair. How had something of this magnitude just slipped my mind? It must have been all that synthetic division. It has a way of doing these kinds of things to a person. I put my head in my arms and started to cry. What was I going to do? I was so not ready for this *vort*. Besides the fact that I didn't have any desire whatsoever to attend, I wasn't even ready to go. I was *so* not going.

"Get up!" Tova said. "Ari is ready, and I just have to do my hair. We have to be there in twenty minutes! How are you going to get ready in that short?"

"I don't know. I can't go," I moaned. "Help me, Tova."

Tova sighed and took a deep breath like she had done this one time too many. She had.

"Do you know what you're going to wear?" she said slowly.

I shrugged.

"Honestly, Ella! How could you have forgotten this? What have you been doing all day?!" She yanked my closet open and started to rummage through it for something suitable. I think it would have been easier to find a smudge of dust in a diamond store.

I placed my head in my hands and moaned again. I had nothing to wear.

"Here!" she said, throwing an outfit on my bed. "Wear this, and don't argue with me!"

"But, Tova," I moaned. See, Tova is my sister, my twin sister, and I really, really, really do love her. But she and I don't exactly have the same taste, if you know what I mean. And of course, she had to pick the ugliest little excuse for an outfit — this pink and black thing — out of my closet.

She held her hand up. "Go take a five-minute shower, and don't even think about blow-drying or straightening your hair!"

"But—" I tried to interrupt in my sweetest voice possible. Tova knew how ugly I looked with gelled hair. Although we're identical twins, Tova looks so pretty with curly hair, but I look like I stepped out of some clown shop. Yeah, my hair turns into a puffy Afro.

"We have no time!" she yelled. "I want you downstairs in ten

14

minutes! The sooner we leave, the better! We can't be late!"

She was right. We couldn't be late. What kind of impression would that make? What would they think of us if we were late? What would they think of Daddy?

"Okay, okay," I grumbled, bumbling into my bathroom. Time to get ready. Yay.

Tova and Ari were both sitting at the kitchen table when I got downstairs. Ari looked very sharp in his new suit and pink tie, and Tova looked like an absolute darling in a pale pink sheath dress. We all matched in a sense. I supposed that was good.

"The princess is ready," Ari said sarcastically. "Servant, why don't you go get the carriage?"

"Ha, ha," I said.

"Okay, okay," Tova said. Her voice was calm now, and the expression on her face a lot more mellow than before. "Let's get this show on the road. We have to be at Shaarei Zion at five."

"At five?" Ari asked. "Well, what time is it now?"

"Five after five. Let's go."

She must have noticed that Ari and I weren't making any effort to move. Actually, the kitchen chairs were pretty comfortable; a lot more comfortable, I supposed, than the *vort* would be.

"Come on, guys! We have to go."

Poor Tova. I really did feel bad for her sometimes. She tried so hard. What was the point of trying so hard?

Ari and I glanced at each other. Synthetic division was one thing; life was another, and I didn't think I could do it no matter how hard I tried.

"Listen," Tova said, running her fingers through her hair. "I'm just as *excited*" — she paused momentarily, as if shocked by her own sarcasm. Tova is *never* sarcastic — "about this as you are. But if we

15

don't leave now, we're going to be really late, and that certainly won't help things."

There was silence for a moment. Tova's eyes scanned ours with an urgency I had never seen before.

"Isn't Daddy driving us there?" Ari asked meekly.

Tova shook her head. "He had to go early to help set up. Michal asked him to, since you know, this is her youngest sister's *vort* and everything."

Since when did Daddy *set up*?

"I'm driving," Tova said with a timid smile, as if that was supposed to cheer us up. Have I mentioned that I failed my road test? Twice.

I heard Ari slowly push his chair back. "It's not like I really have a choice," he muttered. He and Tova began walking toward the door. I felt like a mountain sitting on my chair, and mountains don't move. I took a deep breath. Then I took another one.

"Ella, come on!" Ari said. His eyes were tired, as if he had fought one fight too many. He probably had.

I got up, too.

Tova led us out of the house and then locked the front door. We got into the car. Tova backed out of the driveway and began to drive.

A stoic silence filled the car. If someone didn't know better, he'd have thought we were going to a funeral instead of an engagement party.

And he might have been right. Because as Tova drove, I started to remember, and there was a funeral going on within my brain, with mourners shuffling to and fro...

WHEN I WAS FIVE YEARS old, something within me died.

My father always says that I was a lively little girl, and I have no trouble believing him. If you look at pictures, you'll see that there was always a mischievous spark in my eye, just like there was always a serene spark in Tova's.

Shortly after my fifth birthday, Ari was born. I think every little girl has secret notions that her dolly is a real, live baby. So when I was presented with a living, breathing baby-doll, I immediately switched into the cooing, caring mommy. Well, sort of, anyway.

That charade, my father informs me, lasted precisely for a week. After Ari's *bris*, I was back to my usual rowdy ways. The impish spark had been reignited.

Then it happened.

When I was five years old, my mother became sick.

It happened suddenly. After the birth, complications cropped up. Sometimes, complications can be worked out; sometimes, they can't. In my mother's case, it was unfortunately the latter.

The sickness dragged on for two years, taking my mother's

strength and personality along with it. My mother lived to see my seventh birthdayand she lived to see Ari begin walking and talking. But she would not live to see our other milestones. She would not see me graduate from high school, get married, and start a life of my own.

When I was five years old, something within me died. And that was the ability to really love. My mother, the woman who had pampered me, loved me, doted on me, and cared for me, shriveled rapidly into a sick and suffering shadow of her former self, and all I could do was look on and wonder where the sun in my life had gone.

I remember the day my mother passed away. I was only in first grade at the time, but I remember Mrs. Markowitz, who was the grade school principal, coming into my classroom, her face blotchy and red.

She told Tova and me that our Mommy was near Hashem now, and she was so much happier, and that she wanted Tova and me to be good *kinderlach*.

I remember that I didn't get it. I just didn't understand. What did Mrs. Markowitz mean, near Hashem? Could I go near Hashem and see Mommy, too? And why was Mrs. Markowitz crying? I think the real reason I started to cry was simply because I was frightened by Mrs. Markowitz's tears.

With regard to losing my mother, as far as I was concerned, I had already lost my mother two years ago.

Grandma Rose moved in when my mother passed away. She took care of us for the next three years, until I was in fourth grade. I won't deny that it was hard for her. We were three young, wild (well, except for Tova, but she wasn't exactly an angel in those days, either), motherless children. Grandma Rose slowly withered away from exhaustion; she was a sixty-year-old woman doing a thirty-year-old woman's job. When she developed her first hernia, Daddy presented her with a ticket to Florida. Of course, Grandma Rose insisted that she couldn't leave three orphans and a widower all alone to fend for themselves. But Daddy said that it was more important for her to stay healthy. Taking care of us was too much for her. And so, as we kids watched Grandma Rose board the big 747 to Miami Beach, Florida, we felt like we were saying goodbye to our mother for the second time.

Then we got a housekeeper named Mrs. Frankfurter. Tova, Ari, and I (well, it was really mostly me) used to make fun of her and call her 'Hotdog,' 'Hamburger,' and sometimes even 'Knish.' We put slugs on her pillow, mixed up the salt and sugar, and played all kinds of tricks on her. She, in turn, would complain to my father, who would then punish us. No computer, no friends, no dessert, no nosh, no phone calls. But nothing helped. The poor lady didn't last very long in our home. In retrospect, I realize that she was really a very nice person who just didn't understand children, or maybe she just didn't understand *me*. But then again, who did?

After Mrs. Frankfurter, I guess my father realized we needed someone younger, someone who could relate to children. Daddy hired Anita, an au pair from Austria. We adored her. She made Austrian delicacies for supper and took Tova and me shopping. She even gave Tova piano lessons! (Tova still takes lessons and plays the piano.) Then, it turned out that she was stealing my mother's old jewelry, so she was promptly dismissed.

After Anita came Madame Hoch, of whom we all, even my father, were terrified. When Tova and I entered high school, my father asked her to leave. He said we kids were old enough to take care of ourselves, though he did hire Blanca to do the laundry and cleaning.

Things went nicely like that. To tell you the truth, I enjoyed the new sense of freedom. Tova liked cooking supper, and Ari, well, he had never liked any of the housekeepers. He said they all treated him like a baby, so he was pleased with the new arrangements, as well.

Then, a short while ago, Daddy had to go and ruin my perfect little haven.

Okay, so I'm being rude and *chutzpahdik*. I guess I should be more understanding and everything, but it's kind of hard when one afternoon your father suddenly announces that your life is about to undergo a huge makeover, and there's nothing you can do to stop it. Nothing. I guess I'm a control freak. It's a problem. This was especially so when my father made his big announcement.

We all knew that my father was looking for a *shidduch*. That was just a fact of life, like the sky is blue and butter is yellow and roses are red. The end.

At least, we thought it ended there. We never really thought it was anything serious. Just an answer for Grandma Rose when she tried to set up Daddy with one of her Floridian friends' daughters. We thought it was a way for Daddy to spend his evenings. Truthfully, we didn't think much of it at all.

Right before Purim, my father became busy. Suddenly, he was going out all the time, with one woman in particular: Michal. I ignored the foreboding signs; it couldn't be true. It *couldn't* be happening.

But I was wrong.

We, Tova, Ari, and I, met Michal and her two daughters the week before Shavuos.

"Kids," my father said while Tova and I were preparing supper one evening. I was stirring the hot and sour soup, and Tova was doing the stir-fry. The two of us were making Chinese cuisine, my favorite, while Ari was working diligently on his math homework at the kitchen table. "There's someone special I want you to meet tonight."

I took the wooden stirring spoon out of the pot and exchanged glances with Tova. At that point, we sort of guessed that things were going very well for my father and this Michal whom he was seeing, and that he might want us to meet her one of these days. But we still refused to think any further than that.

"She's coming for dessert," my father continued.

"Who?" Tova asked innocently, as if she had no idea who it might be.

"Her name is Michal, and she's the woman I've been seeing for a while," my father said. "And I'm hoping you'll like her just as much as I do, because it looks like we're going to be getting married."

The wooden spoon fell from my hand and clattered to the floor with a thud, sending droplets of soup splattering all around. I felt my world crashing to the floor along with it. Daddy was remarrying? He was *remarrying*? I would have a…*stepmother*?

Tova looked shocked, and Ari looked up from his homework with a pained expression on his face.

There was silence in the kitchen.

"She's very nice," my father said meekly. "I'm sure you'll like her."

"Well," Tova said, taking a deep breath. "Well, well, well. This certainly is quite a shock, Daddy."

"Yes," my father agreed. "I'm sorry it came out so suddenly." Suddenly? *Suddenly?* Humph. He had to be kidding me. I could feel my heart racing. This could not be happening. I was dreaming. I pinched myself and it hurt, but then everything was hurting.

21

Especially my head. This was a bad dream. This was nothing but a very bad dream, a nightmare, and I was going to wake up as soon as my alarm went off. It would go off soon. It had to.

Then, Tova started freaking out and blabbering how she could not serve fortune cookies to her future stepmother! How uncouth was that! And if Daddy had only told her beforehand, she would have made a cake or regular cookies or something! What would Michal think!

Daddy tried to calm Tova down. I think he was a bit surprised. I was usually the one who lost my cool, not Tova. Oh, he didn't know that I still thought this was the most nightmarish nightmare ever. And that I would wake up in a few minutes, and I'd be four years old again, and my mother would put her arm around me, and I would feel safe and loved.

"Don't worry," Daddy said. "Michal'll love whatever you give her."

But I knew she wouldn't.

I saw the way she surveyed Ari, Tova, and me, sniffing her nose almost disdainfully at us. I saw how, in comparison, she smothered her own little girls with devoted affection.

My father was giving us to her as a new family. But deep inside my heart, I knew the truth: Michal didn't *really* love us.

My father and Michal married right before Rosh Hashanah, adding Margalit and Yaffa, Michal's daughters from her previous marriage, to my world. Since then, my life has been nothing more than a topsy-turvy, crazy circus.

Of course, there are some people who would say the entire thing is in my mind.

3

I'M THE KIND OF PERSON who loves parties. The festive, blaring music, the fabulous assortment of nosh, the friends — what's there not to love? I can just lose myself and pretend I'm a carefree little girl again, and that I don't have a care in the world.

There was one party I didn't like, though. This one.

Everything was perfect; that was the first thing I noticed when I walked into the hall. Absolutely perfect. Maybe that's why I was gritting my teeth. Waiters glided around, offering sushi and mini foods galore to all the guests. The guests' laughter tinkled in perfect resonance with the clinking of their wineglasses. My father looked spiffy in his new suit, and at his side stood Michal, my stepmother. I could feel my anger growing.

Why did even *looking* at her make me mad?

Michal was wearing a mauve two-piece outfit which somehow impeccably blended in with the lavender and silver décor of the hall. Her blonde wig was coiffed into an elaborate up-do, tendrils framing her delicate face. As soon as she saw us, she plastered a huge smile on her face and marched over, my father straggling behind her.

I muttered something along the lines of a greeting. Tova smiled, and I'm pretty sure that Ari said, "Hi."

Michal obviously took Tova's smile as a sign of love, because the next thing I knew, she was kissing Tova's cheeks. She was *so* not going to do that to me. I noticed Ari backing away.

Yeah, right. Next thing I knew, I was overcome with Michal's perfume. She gave me a slight embrace as she air-kissed my cheeks. She whispered something in French into my ear. Like I really understood her. For a moment, I wished that my school gave French instead of Spanish, but then I pushed that weird feeling into the recesses of my heart. Why would I wish that? Spanish was much more practical than the language of love! Love, indeed.

"Tova! Ayelet! Ari!" Michal said. Her blue eyes looked like sapphires, and I vaguely wondered if she was wearing colored lenses. "Come see the *kallah*, your Auntie Adele!"

We had met Adele very briefly at Daddy and Michal's engagement, and then again at their wedding. Actually, it might not have been so briefly. At both events, she did try to talk to me and dance with me, but I wasn't really interested, to say the least. I spent most of that happy time in my life sitting on some chair or other and staring at everyone. We didn't really get to talk or anything. It wasn't like I wanted to.

I shrugged noncommittally, and Tova smiled and nodded. Ari wasn't there anymore. I looked around and noticed him by the smorgasbord, filling up his plate. Smart boy.

Michal linked her slender arms in ours and led us to a tall, reedy girl who was wearing a deep plum-colored dress. Auntie Adele.

"Adele!" Michal said, giving her sister two air-kisses. She smiled at me. "Tova and Ayelet, you remember them, do you not?"

She had mixed me up with Tova! I saw Tova blush and I wondered if she'd say anything.

Adele gave us a cursory smile. "Hi," she said in a totally unaccented voice. "Nice to see you again."

I mean, there wasn't a single trace of French in her voice. She sounded like she had grown up in the grand old Land of the Free and Home of the Brave since she was a wee baby.

"*Mazel tov!*" Tova exclaimed. I muttered something that could have been excused as, "Congratulations." Oh, I knew something big.. Michal was nothing but a skinny fake! Her accent was obviously nothing but one big façade, and so was all that air-kissing! I mean, her sister would have a French accent if Michal's family was from France, wouldn't she?

"Why don't you have an accent?" I said suddenly.

I saw Tova's face burning red and slowly felt a warm blush creeping up my own face. Yes, I sure had impeccable manners.

But Adele only laughed it off. "Oh, I'm so pleased you can't hear my accent! It took years to get rid of it."

"Adele went to school in the States, did she not tell you?" Michal said proudly. "She graduated with honors, of course." Of course.

Adele blushed. "Oh, come on, Michal," she said.

I gave them a weak smile. So much for my fabulous theory.

I spent the rest of the evening sulking. I didn't want to be at this *vort*. I just wanted to go home. I frowned at Michal's entire family when they tried to approach me. I barely even touched the delicious food that was served. And I'm sorry to say it, but I made a face behind my stepsisters Yaffa and Margalit's backs after they ran up to their mother with huge kisses.

Okay, so I acted like a spoiled brat. A really, really spoiled brat. But you haven't heard the worst of it yet. I haven't even *told* you about the highlight of my evening yet.

It happened sometime toward the end of the festivities. The

dancing (which I had not joined, but that was okay, because Tova got me off the hook by saying I didn't feel well) was over and the guests were milling around, sampling petit fours and whatever other kinds of pastries that were there.

"Ella, I'm going to show Margalit where the bathroom is, okay?" Tova said, holding Margalit's hand. Why didn't she just *abandon* me?

"Okay," I muttered.

Without Tova at my side, I suddenly felt very conspicuous. My clothes seemed garish, my skin like that of a leper's. And everywhere, there were the eyes. That lady, right over there, in the purple silk dress — she was watching me, I just knew it, and whispering something into her friend's ear. Little children were looking at me in fascination. Who is this person? I could hear the little engines in their minds rumbling. Why is she frowning? Why is her hair so curly and messy? And, with wide eyes and open mouths, they'd tug on their mothers' sleeves and ask them. Then their mothers would quickly "shhh" them. But it was too late, because I would have already noticed...

It was then that I realized I was in a fishbowl. Whenever anyone passed me, I knew they were looking at me and pitying me and thinking how lovely it was that I now had a new stepmother who would take care of me.

And that just clinched my decision: I had to leave. Now.

I got up from my chair and started to walk briskly out of the room.

"Aren't you Michal's new little girl?" an old woman asked me. I ignored her.

"Yellie, your hairdo is frizzish!" I heard Yaffa call out to me. I ignored her.

"Ow!" a girl screeched as I accidentally stepped on her toe. I ignored her.

"Tova, where are you going?" Michal asked me.

I stopped, looked straight into her fakeblue eyes, and said, "For your information, my name is Ella. So please stop calling me 'Tova.'"

I left her standing there, totally shocked.

I stormed out of the hall. Grabbing Tova's coat from one of the hangers in the coatroom outside, I was relieved to see that her car keys were in her pocket, as well as her license. Ironically, I thought how wonderful it was to have such a well-prepared, identical twin sister.

And then, I drove home, illegally.

Away from it all.

W ASN'T LIFE JUST GREAT?

It was two months since Adele's *vort*, and approximately four months after my father's wedding. Life was swell. Fine. As sweet as candy. Absolutely dandy.

Right.

You probably can imagine what happened that night, after the *vort*.

I was exhorted never, ever to do that again. I was accused of being *chutzpahdik* and hurting poor Michal's feelings and making everyone feel embarrassed. Why, after all, did I leave without saying goodbye? Why was I ignoring everyone? Why couldn't I have told Michal in a nicer and more respectful tone that she was mixing me up with Tova? After all, this wasn't the first time someone had mixed us up, so why was I being so rude about it? How could I have stolen Tova's keys and driven home illegally from the *vort*? And I was grounded for a week.

Did anyone think about me? About how *I* felt? About how I didn't know how to feel, for that matter? Did anyone wonder why I just wasn't in the mood of anything? No, only *Michal's* feelings mattered.

I admit, I was extremely immature and disrespectful and I acted like a seven-year-old, embarrassing myself as well as the bazillion people who were there. But even though what I did was wrong, that didn't make everyone else right!

Ever since the *vort*, Tova pretty much ignored me. Tova is just so perfect, that when someone is "bad," for lack of a better word, she immediately feels as if she has to distance herself from him or her. It's nice, I guess, in theory (she doesn't have to worry about bad influences or peer pressure!), but not when your own sister doesn't speak to you for around two months. I mean, okay, it was getting a bit extreme. What had I done already? I had walked out of a party where I wasn't even wanted! There really wasn't such strong reason to treat me like a pariah. I mean, I knew I shouldn't have stolen Tova's keys and everything, but sometimes these situations are inevitable. Why couldn't Tova understand that? Why couldn't she understand that I couldn't stay?

Ari was the only one who seemed sympathetic toward my plight. He gave me chocolate. It helped alleviate the pain.

The only thing I was allowed to do for a whole week after the *vort* was go to school, come home, do homework, eat, and sleep. Basically, all the joy was sucked out of life. I couldn't even go to my dressmaker appointments for my gown for Adele's wedding. Since Tova and I are the same size, she went for me. At first we were going to get similar gowns, which would have made the dressmaker's job a whole lot easier, but after the…*incident*, Tova refused to dress like me. You'd think that I'd at least be able to pick out the *style* of my gown (preferably a straight, satiny gown in the lightest shade of gold — which would look good with my eyes — with a lace trimming and a princess neck), but no, Tova got to pick it out, since I was in a sort of excommunication. She chose this dark gold gown — I would be competing with the ring for brilliance — in chiffon, with a ruffled skirt and a round neckline. Ugh. So, I was joyless *and* a nerd. I was not very excited for Adele's wedding. At all.

I know, I've said it before, my behavior at the *vort* was…well, it didn't set a nice example for the children there, let's put it that way. I was probably the girl about whom parents warned their children. They'd probably say, "Shprintzie, you remember that bad, bad girl? Well, if you don't eat all your vegetables and listen to Tatty and Mommy, you'll be so bad like her." Right. But I still didn't deserve this. Did I have to look like a complete buffoon at Adele's wedding?

But yeah, I supposed that was the deal with having a new stepmother. It put a whole new twist on the phrase "wicked stepmother". And my evil little stepsisters — I don't think those kids found any greater joy than to bug annoy me. My life was just great, really it was.

But that horrible week after the infamous *vort* was thankfully behind me, and now it was a full two months later, and it was Shabbos again.

I have a routine on Shabbos: In the morning, I go to shul. Then after the *seudah*, either my friends come over or I read a book. After that, I take a nap until it's time for *shalosh seudos*. And that's the way it is. Ari is pretty much left up to his own devices, and Tova likes to do *Bnos* or say *Tehillim*. I never even gave a thought as to what my new little sisters would do. I mean, Margalit is six and Yaffa is seven; they'd play dolls or a game or something, right?

Sweet dreams, indeed. Their game was called "Torture Ella," and I am pleased to say that it was quite an enjoyable game for everyone besides Ella.

After the *seudah*, Naomi and Tzippa, two of my good friends, came over. I was really excited. I had baked these scrumptious coffee chocolate-chip cookies and I had managed to salvage a few before Ari had demolished them all. I couldn't wait for my friends to try them. Besides acting, Tzippa, Naomi, and I are into baking and — as old-ladyish as this sounds — knitting!

"Hi, good Shabbos!" I said cheerily as I ushered them in.

Naomi and Tzippa waltzed in and I hung up their coats.

We were just getting comfy on the couch and starting to chat about the upcoming play auditions when Sister Doom and Sister Gloom marched into the room. Oh, great, Yaffa and Margalit.

"Who are these people?" Yaffa demanded as she squished herself between Tzippa and me on the couch.

"These are my friends," I muttered. "And if you don't mind, you're kind of smushing me. Could you move?"

Naomi gave me a weird look. We had never had these problems…before.

"Uh, why don't we go to my room, guys?" I said, standing up. Margalit was sprawled out on the floor. *So* normal.

"Yeah, let's go to your room," Tzippa said. "You can show me your new Shabbos outfit you were telling me about."

We started to troop up the stairs to my room. It wasn't until we had settled ourselves on my comfy bed that I noticed that Yaffa and Margalit had followed us.

"Can I help you?"

"Yeah," Yaffa said. "Could you get me a cup of tea? It's freezing in your room!"

Well, no one had asked *her* to come!

"If it's so cold, you can leave!" I said. I was starting to get a little…annoyed. And believe me, that's *not* a good thing.

"But, Yellie!" she kvetched. That's another thing. Margalit and Yaffa call me "Yellie". Could you believe it? No, not Yellie as in Old

Yeller, but Yellie as in *Ayelet*. I never experienced anything more frustrating in my life. I've explained to them time after time that my name is *Ella*. But they just don't get it! I think they think it's funny to call me "Yellie," like it's *funny* to annoy me!

"Please don't call me that," I said in the calmest voice I could muster, which was of course not that calm at all. Actually, the words weren't quite those words either. I more or less said something like, "Don't you dare call me that, you little brat."

I saw Naomi's blue eyes widen ever so slightly and Tzippa raised an eyebrow.

"Yellie, Yellie, Yellie," Yaffa started singing loudly.

"Yellie is yelling, Yellie is yelling!" Margalit started to chant.

Oooh! They were making me so angry. Okay, that called for deep breaths. I would not scream. I took a huge mouthful of air and swallowed it down. Would not scream, would not scream…

"Yellie, Yellie, *yeller!*"

"GET OUT!" I screeched, and before I realized it, I had shoved them both out of my room. I could feel my features twist into an ugly, angry mask. I felt my eyes blaze and my face burn wildly. I knew that I had scared them.

Margalit and Yaffa looked shocked. Then, tears streaming down both of their faces, they slowly, slowly slunk away and out of my sight.

I slammed the door shut.

"Don't you think you were a little too hard on them?" Naomi said hesitantly as I plopped down on the small couch in my room. "I mean, they're only little kids."

"*Annoying* little kids," I said in a harsh voice. "Who *don't* leave me alone and *won't* even let me enjoy a peaceful Shabbos afternoon," I said.

Tzippa shifted uncomfortably. "Whatever," she said and then she immediately changed the topic. "Aren't you excited for play tryouts?"

"Uh-huh! I cannot believe it's *this* Motza'ei Shabbos!" Naomi said.

I tried to paste a nonchalant smile on my face, but to tell you the truth, I felt a little bit…guilty now. It wasn't only what my friends had said — although that had made me a trifle uncomfortable — it was the look on Margalit's and Yaffa's faces. They kept flashing before me. Those sad, hurt eyes. *Had I really shoved them?* I owed them an apology. Maybe I'd make them ice cream sundaes after Shabbos. They'd love that. Yeah, that was what I would do. I felt a little better now that I knew I'd smooth everything out, so I tuned into the conversation.

"What part are you trying out for, Tzippa?" I asked.

"Oh, I'm definitely trying out for Oscar. You know, the crazy garbage man!"

"Why would you want to be a crazy garbage man?" I asked with a laugh.

"Oh, I don't know! It's a funny part and I like funny people."

"What about you, Naomi?" I asked.

"Well, I don't know…" she said hesitantly, a blush creeping up her face. "I doubt I'll get any part."

"Oh, *come* on!" I said. Naomi is a great actress. She'd probably get any part she tried out for.

Tzippa and Naomi started to debate what part Heidi Brown would get, and I drifted off into my own world. Although I would have never admitted it to my friends, there was only one part that I wanted. And that was Kreindel. The star of the show.

"I can't wait for tryouts!" I said suddenly.

My friends looked surprised, but it took me a second to realize that it wasn't because of my arbitrary comment. I followed Tzippa's eyes to the door.

There stood my father, Michal, and the nightmarish sisters. Together, against me.

I'D LIKE TO INFORM YOU of an interesting phenomenon called Stockholm syndrome. In 1973, there was a bank robbery in a bank in Stockholm. The thieves took a few people as hostages. Even after the victims were released, they kept defending their captors. They weren't like, "Oh, our kidnappers are horrible; you should lock them up." They felt psychologically attached to their captors in a sense! It became a real problem, because the hostages were actually *helping* their captors escape the police and achieve their wicked goals. This symptom develops because of the victim's attempt to judge his captor favorably and relate to him. And you know what, even though this is a rare phenomenon, in 8% of cases, this is what happens. The hostages become sympathetic to their captors!

Basically, I think it's because the captors and the captives spent so much time together, that they came to liking each other. As crazy as it sounds, it does make some iota of sense in my head.

I wish it would happen in my family. I mean, everyone spends all this time with me, and yet I knew that no one felt a drop of love toward me at that moment. The only thing I could see on my father's, my stepmother's, and my stepsisters' faces were anger, disgust, and wicked smiles, respectively.

This was *so* great.

I sighed. "What do you want?" I said to no one in particular.

Michal looked at my friends, and I was almost certain that I could see an evil glint in her eyes. "Girls, I'm going to have to ask you to leave now," she said, her accent more pronounced than ever. The she gave me a long look, and — you know what — I stared right back. She was making my friends *leave*?! What was this? Kindergarten? Were they going to give me a time-out and place me in the corner, too?

Tzippa and Naomi glanced at each other, and then at me. I would have argued. I mean, how much more embarrassing could life get? First my stepsisters were calling me names, and then my stepmother kicks my friends out of the house. It really wasn't right, and I would have argued, except, well, I noticed something.

There was a silhouette behind my father. It was Tova. My heart leapt for a moment, and then plunged straight down into my stomach. Had she joined their conspiracy? Was she with…them? So, really, I would have said something, except that I was wondering why Tova was standing there. And before I knew it, my friends murmured their farewells, and…left. Me. Alone. To face the interrogating mob.

Michal sat down on the edge of my bed with a concerned expression on her face, like caring mothers in plays do. Except that she *wasn't* my mother. And this *wasn't* a play. This was my *life*. The wicked stepsisters stood by her side, and I could see the smiles behind their tearstained faces. My father loomed threateningly by the doorway, his forehead creased. And Tova was there, too.

Have I mentioned that she hadn't spoken to me since Adele's

vort? Yes, that's right, folks. Of course, she'd say things like "pass the salt," and "behave," but the DMCs ("deep meaningful conversations") of the past were nothing more than that — a thing of the past. Ari informed me that she said that I totally embarrassed her at the *vort* and she couldn't believe we're sisters. I couldn't believe it either. I would never be able to ignore someone for more than five minutes (for better or for worse).

"Yellie," Michal said softly. What was *wrong* with her? Didn't she know I didn't like to be called Yellie? Talk about setting a bad example for the children! "I must say that I am appalled by your behavior. Yaffa and Margalit came crying to me. You ruined a perfectly nice Shabbos afternoon."

Michal had obviously never read parenting books. If she had, she would have known that you're never supposed to talk to a child like that. I mean, I wasn't totally sure what I would have done in her situation, but it definitely would not have been what she was doing.

"Well," I said resolutely, "maybe you should tell your children not to ruin my perfectly nice Shabbos afternoon. I was trying to enjoy some time with my friends when they barged in and started to ruin everything!"

I could tell Michal didn't believe that her little angels would ever do such a thing. She opened her mouth to say something when the girls immediately started screaming.

"Ima!" Margalit kvetched. "She was so, so mean to us! She screamed at us *and* pushed us!"

Then Yaffa piped up, only helping the Let's-Ruin-Ella's-Life Campaign.

"Ima, she's always so mean to us! We only wanted to be friendly!" she said sadly, a tear rolling softly down her face and into the corner of her mouth.

Friendly, my foot! All the two of them wanted to do was annoy me. I knew it. And now they were warping the story in such a way that it made me seem like an evil villain.

I remembered how once someone told me that they had gone up with their younger sisters and brothers to a bungalow colony. The colony was already quite close-knit and the younger kids were having a bit of trouble making friends. One day, the little boy, Dovid, was led solemnly back to his parents by another indignant parent. The parent claimed that Dovid had pulled his little girl's pigtails. Dovid's parents were, of course, horrified.

"Is this true?" they asked Dovid.

Dovid nodded.

"But why did you pull her hair? You *know* we don't pull hair, Dovid!" Dovid's parents exclaimed.

Dovid didn't answer.

"Did she do something to you first?" the parents asked.

Dovid nodded again. "She hit me," he said in a quiet voice.

"Why did she do that? Did you tell her something?"

A small tear trembled down Dovid's cheek. He nodded as he solemnly said, "I asked her if she wants to be my friend."

How poignant. We all know that children can be cruel. But for some reason, I felt as if Michal viewed me as the little girl whose pigtails were pulled in this story. Sure, I was hurt *in the end*, but my darling stepsisters were really trying to be nice to me, and if I would only have been nice to them, none of this would have happened.

Right?

Wrong.

Didn't *anyone* understand? Couldn't anyone see behind Yaffa and Margalit's forlorn-puppy façade? What was so friendly about embarrassing me in front of my friends? What was so nice about calling me Yellie? What was so sweet about making fun of me when I asked them to leave?

My father gave me a stern look. "Ayelet," he said in a grave voice, "I think we need to talk. I have a *chavrusa* waiting for me now and then I have Minchah, but immediately after Shabbos, you and I will sit down and have a discussion together. On how to treat your little sisters."

Oh, joy. So now I was in for a long *mussar drashah* from my father on how wrong, immature and selfish I was, and what a horrible example I was setting for everyone.

"And you owe your sisters an apology," Michal said in what I thought was a smug voice.

Self-control. I would practice self-control and not totally lose it and disrespect my father and stepmother. I would politely explain that although my father believed that giving me *mussar drashos* for the next seven millenniums would be beneficial, because it would make me enter the realms of deep introspection, it would actually make me even crazier than I already was. And I did have a life and plans for immediately after Shabbos, thank you very much.

"But Daddy!" I sputtered. "I already have plans for right after Shabbos! I can't just sit home having discussions and — "

"Ayelet, when a person does something, there are consequences. You'll continue with your plans *after* our talk. You have to learn to have more respect for this family."

Why didn't anyone respect *me*?

"Now, apologize to your sisters," my father commanded.

"They're *not* my sisters," I muttered.

I heard Michal gasp, and my father staggered back. Yaffa and Margalit looked absolutely horrified. Well, no kidding. I had just knocked down the careful little family home they had worked so hard to build. I guess they never realized that I wasn't included in the family picture.

"I believe this little talk of ours is becoming more imperative than ever, young lady," my father said, his eyes glinting. His eyebrows were arched and scary-looking, although he kept shooting anxious and protective looks at my two stepsisters. Yeah, yeah, why not, love them instead of me.

Michal slowly slid off my bed and gave me a dark, hurt look. Her forehead was creased, and her eyes were blazing with anger — or was it tears?

Yaffa and Margalit crept out of the room and my father and Michal followed. I glanced at the doorway and realized that Tova was still standing there, staring at me.

She hadn't said a word in my defense. She hadn't tried to help me one bit.

I got up, marched toward my door, and slammed it shut with a resonating bang. Then, I plopped myself onto my bed. What a lovely Shabbos afternoon! What a great time I'd had. The tears were pouring down my face and I could feel my entire body trembling.

I had come to a sad and horrible realization: When I shut my father's new family out of my life, Tova shut me out of hers. It was as if Tova wasn't my sister, either.

I cried and cried and cried.

T HAT NIGHT, HAVDALAH WAS AN affair devoid of any happiness. I watched my father's face over the burning candle. The dancing flames cast eerie shadows on his face, making him seem years older than he really was. Michal stood at his side, her forehead creased, holding the *besamim* in one hand, with her other arm draped lovingly around Margalit's narrow shoulder. I knew she was doing that just to make me jealous, and it was working. Ari stood meekly at my father's right side, looking as if he'd rather be anywhere but there. I didn't blame him. As for Tova, I didn't bother looking at her.

The moment Yaffa excitedly dipped the flames into the wine, I ran up to my room. I couldn't wait to leave. Drama tryouts were tonight and, like I said before, I was vying for the role of Kreindel. I knew I could razzle and dazzle Ahuva and Chanie with my superb abilities, and then they'd probably give me the role of a lifetime. Especially since I had been instrumental in starting this drama club to begin with.

I was counting on my father forgetting about our "discussion". That's how it sometimes was. If I acted like a little angel for an hour

41

or two, the events prior to this would file to the back of my busy father's head. And if I continued behaving, these events wouldn't pop up at all.

I wore my tiered, hunter-green, corduroy skirt with a black turtleneck sweater that had thin, green vertical stripes (to make me look taller) and my suede, black, flat boots. Then I brushed my hair into a neat half-pony, and was ready to roll.

I pounded down the stairs and sprinted into the living room, encountering a special family moment that could have been straight out of a photo album.

My father was sitting on the big purple couch with Yaffa and Margalit sitting next to him. He was reading my old favorite Dr. Seuss book to them in an expressive voice, and I could hear them all laughing together.

With banner flip-flapping,
Once more you'll ride high!
Ready for anything under the sky.
Ready because you're that kind of a guy!
Oh, the places you'll go! There is fun to be done!
There are points to be scored. There are games to be won.
And the magical things you can do with that ball
Will make you the winning-est winner of all.

Oh, The Places You'll Go was always my favorite book. It still kind of is (after Shakespeare, of course!). I could still hear my father reading it to *me* when I was a kid. And now, he was reading it to these… girls, who had waltzed into my life like interlopers.

Michal and Tova were sitting cozily next to each other on the loveseat, chatting. They looked so happy, almost like mother and daughter.

Ari was sprawled out on the living room carpet, completing a crossword puzzle and a Sudoku board at the same time. He always does that. When he can't remember a word for the crossword puzzle, he does the Sudoku puzzle, until the word comes to him. Presently, he screamed out, "Napoleon!" and scribbled furiously on his paper.

I looked at him for a moment. When had the metamorphosis happened with Ari? He had always been almost an equal partner to me in my battle against the "newcomers". But over these past few weeks, it seemed that he, like Tova, had decided it just wasn't worth the fight and that it took less energy to give in and go with the flow.

As I glanced from one family member to the next in this happy little scene, it suddenly felt like *I* was the interloper. It felt like I was the trespasser in my home. Like I had walked into a play before my cue.

I felt so uncomfortable and out of place, and I really wanted to leave. But I did need someone to drive me to Ahuva's house where the tryouts were being held. I hesitantly cleared my throat.

They all looked up, almost confused at what this disturbance could be. That was it. I was nothing but a disturbance, ruining this picturesque family scene.

"I need someone to drive me to Ahuva Zakkai's house," I said, holding my breath.

I could see my father rummaging around in his pocket for his keys. Yay! He had forgotten about us having our little talk! Good, I had to get to Ahuva's house on time if I was to have a good chance at getting my coveted part.

"You are not going anywhere just yet, Ayelet," Michal said, fidgeting with the corner of her blouse. "Daddy wants to speak with you, remember?"

My father stopped rummaging. "That's right, Ella. We need to sit down and talk right now. Don't tell me you already forgot this afternoon's events."

"Okay," I said with a sigh. "I'm *sorry*. Does everyone forgive me now? Can we get on with our lives?"

"I am also sorry," Michal said, sticking her nose in matters that totally did not concern her. This was a matter between my father and me. Why did she always have to intrude in places where she wasn't wanted? "But sometimes, when a person does something wrong, she must suffer the consequences for it, and right now, Ayelet, you have an appointment with your father. It is not so bad; you will do whatever you want to do afterward."

Like I needed her comfort or reassurance. "But I have plans tonight *that are starting right now!*" I said, looking at my father. "The auditions for the school play are tonight, and I have to be there on time in order to up my chances at getting the part I want! Can't we have our talk when I get back later tonight?"

My father looked like he was going to give in. But then, "Well, perhaps you should have thought of that before you hurt your sisters, Ayelet," Michal said.

I had had enough. Really. "Could you stay *out* of this, Michal?" I yelled.

There was a collective gasp, and I could hear everyone holding their breaths. Now I was in deep trouble. No question about it. I doubted my father would overlook this blow.

Michal recoiled, as if physically struck. Slowly, my father stood up. He looked positively mad.

"Firstly, you do not call Michal by her first name," my father said in a strong voice. "You refer to her as Ima."

I could feel my heart stretch in a thousand different directions and work its way up my throat. Ima? *Ima?!* "Ima" was a sacred word, a holy word in my book. It was a word that would never again play on my lips. My Ima was dead. And Michal was not my Ima. She never would be.

"Secondly, I have had enough of your impertinent attitude, young lady. A sixteen-year-old should know how to control herself by now. You are acting like a baby."

I could feel the tears well up in my eyes. *I* was the baby? Not sniveling Yaffa and Margalit who went running to their mommy at any moment?

"Thirdly, you are grounded for this entire week. That includes your play tryouts tonight."

Because he didn't give me that whole 'think-about-your-actions' *shpiel*, I knew my father meant business. He looked at me expectantly, as if waiting for a cheeky reply.

To tell you the truth, I had a lot to say on the whole matter. On how these auditions were practically the most important things in my life after Hashem and breathing, and how I had been practicing for them for months. On how no one every stopped to see how I felt and if my feelings were hurt and if I felt abandoned. On how no one ever took my side.

I had a lot to say. But uncharacteristically, I didn't say anything. Silence is the best answer sometimes.

Everyone was staring at me. I knew it.

"Do you have anything to say?" my father asked, a touch of nervousness entering his voice. Like I said, usually I would spout flaming anger when things didn't go my way, burning everyone badly.

Did I have anything to say? Only something along the lines of, "Thanks for ruining my life." But I decided that I had been way too rude for one evening, and there was, after all, a mitzvah to honor one's parents.

45

"You're not going to let me go?" I asked again. I knew they probably weren't, but sometimes when I repeat something, I get better results. "To the drama tryouts, the only tryouts, the ones I've been waiting for these whole last few months…?"

"No," Michal said.

It would be the perfect time for Tova to intercede. To say something about how I needed to go, because it was a school function, and it wouldn't look good on seminary applications if I wasn't involved in anything. It was the perfect time for her to say something about how she wouldn't mind driving me, and how we should all feel bad that I didn't pass my road test yet. They would listen to Tova. I knew they would.

It was the perfect time, but she let it slide. I looked at her pleadingly. I was practically begging her! But Tova only looked away. I saw her stare stoically at the dove-white curtains. She refused to even look in my direction.

I could feel the tears trickling down my face. I could feel my body start to tremble. How ridiculous would it look if I, the girl who had begged the principal to start a drama club, didn't even bother to show up for auditions?! How silly would it be if I had to beg on Monday to audition for Chanie and Ahuva during their lunch period! This just wasn't *fair*.

"Fine!" I screamed. "Why don't you just lock me up in a dungeon somewhere and slide me food under the door! I think we'll all be happier that way!"

I stomped up to my room and banged my door shut. Then I sat down at my desk, panting. There had to be some way to get out of this horrid predicament. I called up both Tzippa and Naomi, but they had already left. I tried everyone else, but they were all already at the tryouts. I was stuck.

As I sat there, crying and wondering why my life had to be so horrible, I suddenly heard a slight rustling at the door.

I looked and noticed that a piece of paper was being slid under the door into my room.

I picked it up and read it.

Food doesn't fit under the door of your dungeon. –Ari.

I quickly opened up the door, and there was Ari, holding a handful of chocolates.

"All dressed up and nowhere to go?" he said with a smile.

"It's not like I have nowhere to go," I said, ushering him in. "It's that I have no *way* to go, or better yet, no permission." I let the words play bitterly on my tongue. If I was such a young lady, how come I could still be grounded like a three-year-old? Oh, the irony.

Ari sighed and poured the chocolates onto my bedspread. "I'd stay, but I'm afraid you'll influence me negatively."

I knew the comment was said in jest, but it seemed a bit strange coming from Ari. "Where did you hear that from?" I asked.

"From Ima," he said with a nonchalant shrug.

I nodded back to him, like this was a totally normal conversation. But it wasn't, and I knew it. Because he said the word "Ima" with familiarity, easily, as if he'd been saying it all the time. As if he accepted her. As if he'd forgotten his real mother.

I could feel all my emotions, the anger, the bitterness, and the resentment, slowly mixing together in a huge, bubbling, and boiling caldron. All I could think, as Ari sauntered out of the room, gently closing the door behind him, was that chilling line said by Julius Caesar after the ultimate betrayal of his friend Brutus: "Et tu, Brute?"

My only ally had joined my enemies. And the worst part was that he didn't even know it himself.

SHLOMO HAMELECH WAS THE ONE who penned the brilliant words, "This, too, shall pass." He knew that the happiest times, as well as the sad, would eventually pass, and eventually dwindle away to nothing but memories.

But did you ever notice that the happy times always seem to pass faster than the sad ones? Oh, yeah, sure, they both *pass*, in general, but what do you think goes by faster? Your cousin's bar mitzvah where you see Chanie from Ohio to whom you haven't spoken in months and you dance and dance and dance and sample the gourmet sushi? Or a math test? (Scratch that — actually, I always seem to run out of time on those vile things. A math class would be a better example.)

Well, that horrid night passed, as does everything. But it went by slowly.

I was stuck. There was nothing I could do. Firstly, since from now on I had to be the model child (I mean, I couldn't be a…*bad influence*, could I?), that ruled out any option of walking to Ahuva's house. And besides, even if I was going to act like a *ben sorer u'moreh* and leave against the wishes of those older than me, it just wouldn't be *possible*. It wasn't like I could drive (although it was high time I got my driver's license; this dependency issue was starting to bug me ever so slightly!), and it wasn't like it was some pleasant summer day where there was just a lilting breeze in the air. It was winter, and there was slushy snow everywhere, and the wind chill factor was like a thousand percent. In addition to the fact that it just…wasn't *day*. I live in New York City — did I tell you? It's not exactly the kind of place where you take evening strolls by yourself.

I did a lot of thinking that night. (I mean, what else was there to do?) Okay, maybe I hadn't behaved so nicely toward Michal and her bratty kids, although that didn't mean they had been nice to me. But that didn't make any of us right.

I realized that I was stuck. Michal and her children weren't going to leave any time soon, and — you know what — I realized that I actually didn't want her to leave. That sounds so weird, doesn't it? I didn't like her, but my father was much happier. I knew it. He was even singing in the shower these days (which doesn't really make the rest of the family happy, if you catch my drift, but whatever). It was a lot easier to have a woman in the house. Not that Tova and I weren't capable; it was just that we were still teens. Why should we have to always cook and make Shabbos? It had been really hard, I don't deny that, and coming home on Friday afternoon and being greeted with the smell of chicken vegetable soup, rice pilaf, roast, and other Shabbos goodies was actually quite pleasant.

So why was I so against Michal?

Well, for one, it always used to be my father and me. There weren't any other disciplinarians, and my father was always quite tolerant. I don't know, it was just annoying to have this new person to deal with and to explain myself to when I came home.

Also, she always seemed to be smothering her daughters with

49

love and asking them about their day, and I guess that made me a little jealous. The worst part was that she always took her daughters' sides in any situation.

To make matters worse, everyone had somehow fallen into their perfect little family roles. My father was the great Dad who worked from nine to five, Michal was the stay-at-home mommy who did the shopping and made sure dinner was on the table, Tova was the caring older sister, Ari was the funny brother, and Yaffa and Margalit were the two angelic little pixies. And what was I? A third wheel. Nothing but an intruder in this adorable new family.

I was *unwanted*.

And they wouldn't let me join the *only* thing in which I was wanted, the school play.

Why didn't they just stick a label with the word OUTCAST on my head? It would fit just fine. I mean, Kayin got a sign on his head that named him an outcast. Why couldn't I have one? It would make my life easier in a sense. I was where I wasn't wanted, and I wasn't where I wanted to be.

Joy.

If this was a novel, you know what I'd do right now? I'd run away. Far away. I'd be running and running. It would be dark and there would be a foggy mist in the air. The backpack on my shoulder (filled with my plays, a picture of my mother, and food) would feel heavy and for a second I'd wonder if I could rest somewhere. And then, as gruesome as it sounds — you have to forgive me if you're the squeamish type — a bulldozer would hit me.

I'd lie there, unconscious, on the hard pavement, my sticky blood oozing all around, until the morning, when little children going to school would see me and scream for their mommies. The mommies would come, all right, and they'd start screaming, too. Then, one of the daddies who would be there would call the police and ambulance. The police would mark up the entire place as a crime scene, while the crying EMTs would place me on a stretcher.

They'd rush me to the ER, and they'd call my father. He'd come in, fat, salty tears rolling down his face and trickling onto his white shirt. Michal would walk two steps behind him, her eyes downcast and her face pallid. Ari would be *davening* with gusto as he swayed back and forth, his eyes shining with tears and his face red with exertion. Tova would be screaming bloody murder and the doctors would have to give her a sedative. Yaffa and Margalit would be standing solemnly in a corner, twiddling their fingers around their hair. They would all be devastated. They'd wonder how they could have ever treated me the way they did, and they would take sincere vows to make sure I'd always be happy when I hopefully woke up from my terrible coma. They'd be *sorry*.

Of course, I'd wake up after a month, and they'd all be totally blissful, and then, for the rest of my days, they'd treat me with respect, never ground me again, and always let me go to play tryouts.

And we'd all live happily ever after.

Of course, this isn't a novel, or a play, or anything with fantastical elements.

This is my life.

My wretched old life, where I'm stuck in my tower, but there's no one to help me down.

I vowed to be nicer to Michal. Because, after all, even Cinderella was nice to her stepmother, in theory.

Then, I vowed to break my stupid clock because it was only eight o'clock, and that meant I had only been banished to my room for an hour!

Except that I didn't, because right then my cell phone rang.

I fumbled as I answered it. It was Tzippa; the caller ID said so.

"Ella, where *are* you?" she said. She was yelling. There was a lot of noise in the background; I could hear music blaring and people laughing. It sounded like everyone was having a super-fabulous time. Without me.

"Oh, I'm currently vacationing in a villa on the southern tip of Florida, where the weather is a balmy seventy-two degrees," I said sarcastically. "My personal slave, Adriana, has just brought me an icy glass of lemonade, a plateful of double chocolate cookies, and a thick novel which I plan on enjoying for the next few hours. Why do you want to know?"

There was a long pause. "Ella," Tzippa said slowly, "is everything okay?"

"Just dandy," I muttered.

Suddenly, I heard a loud burst of laughter. Tzippa was gasping for air. "Oh, my goodness!" she exclaimed. "You would not believe what Chaiky Cukier just did!" Without waiting for me to make a comment, Tzippa continued. "I cannot believe she just did a handstand, a flip, and a cartwheel all in one. That kid is *crazy*!"

For some reason, I did not find it particularly amusing. At all. Here I was, stuck in my boring old room, cut off from the rest of civilization for, like, possibly forever, and everyone else was out having a great time. Oooh! Life was so unfair. Maybe Tzippa could get me out of this predicament. After all, what are friends for?

"Listen, Tzippa…" I started slowly. I had to phrase this the right way. "Could you do me like a humongous favor?"

"What, what?" Tzippa said to someone. "Oh, Ella, I have to go! The pizza's here! I'll talk to you later!"

I would have said goodbye, except that she had already hung up. On me.

With friends like that, who needed annoying stepfamilies? Or families in general? Who needed anyone? Why didn't I just become a recluse and live in my little room all day. They'd slip me food under the door.

Oh, yeah, we went through this already. The food doesn't fit under the door.

Hmmm.

Argh.

How boring, annoying, horrifying, and weird could this night get already? I was ready to pull all the hair out of my head. I contemplated completing the entire *sefer Tehillim* for the *zechus* of a *refuah sheleimah* for all the sick people in Klal Yisrael and for the safety of *acheinu* in Eretz Yisrael. And then, I realized that if I didn't do something in the next three minutes, I would turn into Tova. I grabbed the mirror. Oh, no. I was already starting to look like her. (At least I was able to find some humor in this horrible predicament, no matter how corny it was, okay?)

Suddenly, I was blessed with one of those moments which I am convinced are Heaven-sent. *Brain-flash!* I was so silly. Why didn't I work on my play?

And so that's what I did. What was this? A blessing in disguise or a silver lining?

I wrote and wrote and wrote for the next three hours. I poured all my feelings and emotions into that play. I was really getting somewhere. Before, it had only been a smattering of thoughts, opinions, and things I fancied as funny. And now, it was real. Now it was turning into a play.

So, ha, ha on everyone who thought they'd be punishing me when they locked me up in my room for the rest of my life and my children's lives and my grandchildren's lives and for all of eternity.

They didn't realize that when I'm given bitter coffee beans, I make aromatic coffee! When I stand in a rainstorm, I pretend that the raindrops are gumdrops! When I'm given lemons, I make lemonade! (Hungry, anyone?)

I didn't realize all this wonderful stuff either. And once I did, the realization didn't last too long. Because then my phone rang again. And then I realized that maybe this punishment of mine had actually ruined my life.

Forever.

THIS IS HOW THE TELEPHONE conversation between Naomi and me went.

"Ella, what's up? Where were you?" Naomi said. For a second, I thought that she cared; that it actually made a difference to someone what I was doing.

"At home. Grounded," I said sullenly. I played with my hair and folded it in half.

"Oh, that's too bad! The auditions were amazing! Ahuva and Chanie aren't giving out the parts officially until tomorrow, but they basically let on to everyone which parts they think they'll give them." Oh, how lovely. Naomi sure knew how to make a person feel better.

"Really? To everyone? Well, what about the people who couldn't make it?" I started to sketch some diabolic figure in the margin of my notebook.

"Everyone was there, Ella," Naomi said pointedly. "Except you."

"Oh," I said. I tried to sound like I didn't care. But I did. What was I going to do now? All the parts had been given out, even if only unofficially? Was there anything left? What about Kreindel? Had they given that part to anyone? Who had gotten it?

"Well, guess which part I'm most probably getting! You'll be so excited for me, Ella! I know it!" She knew it? Did she really? I was going to be excited? That was good, right? That probably meant that Kreindel was still available, right?

"I don't know. Joe Shmoe, the grocery man?" I said. I put down my pen and began staring real hard at a speck on my wall.

"Ella, really!" Naomi sighed.

"How am I supposed to know?" This was ridiculous. I was so not in the mood of a silly guessing game. Couldn't she just tell me? "I wasn't there! Was it Henya?"

"No! Come on, Ella, think!"

"I'm thinking," I said stonily. That dot on my wall looked like a dart.

"Okay," Naomi said. She waited silently on the other end for me to answer. She was actually taking this seriously. She actually thought I was going to answer. I was so not in the mood of this anymore.

"Maybe I'm just not as brilliant as you, Naomi," I said with a sigh as I picked up my pen again and made little horns on my devil. "I thought the part you really wanted was Henya."

"I'll tell you the truth," Naomi said softly. "The part I really, really, really wanted was…"

"Was what?" The suspense was killing me. Truly, it was.

"Well, it was…" Naomi started to say again slowly. "Guess, Ella."

I was ready to throw my cell phone across the room. Why couldn't she just tell me? Why did everything have to be such a huge production with Naomi? "Naomi, are you gonna tell me?" I said, giving my drawing a curly little mustache. "Because I'm not in the mood of a silly little guessing game."

"Okay," Naomi said, as if she was composing herself for something. "I didn't really want to be Henya. I mean, I know I told everyone I did, but it was only my second choice."

I could hear her taking a deep breath.

"So?" I was a bit fazed, really. Why did I need an entire prelude? Why couldn't she just tell me which part she got?

"So, I tried out for Kreindel. That was the part I *really* wanted."

I almost saw the little devil on my paper jump up and grab the speckled dart from my wall. It seemed to dance around in front of me. For some odd reason, I felt my heart palpitating quickly. I almost felt like I couldn't breathe. What was *wrong* with me?

"And so?" I said in a somewhat wobbly voice. I almost felt like I was going to fall off my chair.

"I'm getting the part, Ella! Aren't you excited? Your best friend, Naomi, AKA the new star of this spring's play, got the lead! I'm Kreindel!" Naomi shrieked shrilly.

Maybe I just didn't feel well because I had barely eaten anything all night. I felt feverish and *uchy* and cold, like I had the flu or something. I felt like I was going to throw up right then and there. I grabbed onto my desk. I was hallucinating. I had to be hallucinating; why else would that silly little devil be scribbling on my play with the dart from the wall? Oh, was that my hand? Was I sick?

"Wha — ? Wha-what?" I stammered.

"Did you hear me, Ella?" Naomi said, trills dancing in her voice.

And I was so excited for her that I just didn't know what to do.

I must have slurred something that sounded like "bye" or "gotta go," and then hung up. Because the next thing I knew, the cell phone was lying in smithereens on the floor and just about a billion tears were coursing down my face.

YOU KNOW WHAT GERHARD GSCHWANDTNER said? I bet a lot of people find it sooo inspiring and have a little magnet on their fridge with the following celebrated words on them:

"View a negative experience in your life like you'd look at a photo negative. A single negative can create an unlimited number of positive prints." I'll pause for a moment of silence so that we can all have some time to reflect on the significance, the beauty, of these words.

(pause)

Wow. What a brilliant little quote. Gerhard's mother was probably *so* proud of her son for being the absolute little genius that he was! I mean, it takes talent to come up with something as inspiring as that, folks; it takes real, developed talent. And for someone who has a last name as hard to pronounce as his (there are, like, two vowels there), and was probably picked on in school because of it, it proves that little Gerhard went a long way! It shows that our gifted boy looked at his negative experiences and just created bazillions of wonderful, magical, positive things from them.

Well, bravo! He should go from *chayil* to *chayil*.

The rest of us normal people will wonder if Gerhard was possibly ever treated for insanity, or extremely ecstatic delusions, or if he was drunk or something. At least *I* will. Because I tried Gerhard's nifty idea and guess what came out of it? Nada! Zero! Zilch! (Except that I learned how to say "nothing" in three different ways, but what good is that anyway. It's not like I'm going to go to Mexico one day, and they'll all be like, "Hey, want a burrito? It's *glatt* kosher!" and since I'm so fluent in their language, I'll be like, "Nada!" Yeah, that's so normal.)

Here are my conclusions:

Negative experience #1: I was exiled to my room (by my own so-called family).

Okay. So what were the unlimited number of positive prints that were created because of this glorious event?

(1) I had to miss play tryouts.
(2) Then, my best friend gets the part I've been dreaming about ever since I was born.
(3) I'm relegated to the girl who dusts the stage after everyone walks on it.
(4) I'm starving and I can't ask Ari to bring me up any more chocolates, lest I be a bad influence on the precious children and lest tomorrow I turn into Godzilla the pimple queen.

I mean, tell me the truth here, what positive experience sprouted from this horrible night? Sure, I had finished my play, but then I had scribbled all over it. And that was the good stuff.

Why did I deserve such a life?

So, what did I do? I cried myself to sleep, that's what I did. I don't think I'd had such a good cry in a long time. Since the night of my father's wedding, when I came home and took the silly sparkly barrettes Michal had made all the girls wear in their hair, and snapped each one in half, and realized what a horrible, fake night I'd had, and what a horrible life I was going to have from then on.

I still have those cracked barrettes in my desk drawer.

When I woke up, it was a beautiful winter Sunday morning. The sun was shining brilliantly and it didn't look like there was a cloud in the sky. But unlike the greater population of the world who has off on Sunday, my school doesn't like to waste a moment that can be spent learning. Usually, I hate it. But today, I was happy to go to school.

And it was only for one reason: I got to see the light of day again. I mean, I if I didn't have school on Sunday, I probably would have stayed in my room until Monday morning!

At a quarter to nine a.m. (yeah, at least they have mercy and don't start school until nine-thirty on Sunday. The rest of the week school starts at eight-thirty. Sharp.), the clock I should have broken, but didn't, started to screech. I sluggishly got out of bed and realized I was still wearing my clothes from the night before, including my boots. Yuck beyond yuck. I had to peel the boots off my sweaty feet.

It would have been nice to take a shower, but *no*. Tova was driving me to school like she always does on Sunday, and Tova *always* leaves early. (I mean, we can't be late, *chas v'shalom!*) Which meant I had fifteen minutes to get ready.

I hesitantly peered into the mirror.

My eyes were puffy and red, my skin was a ghostly color, and my hair was an oily mess. I know; I was an angelic vision.

I looked gross and I felt even grosser.

Thank Hashem for uniforms.

I threw on my navy pleated skirt, some crumpled blouse, and the school sweatshirt. Then, I washed my face and brushed my hair into a bun. No jewelry. No lenses (*ich*, I had slept with those on, too, and it felt like I was taking rubber out of my eyes in the morning!) — just my glasses. I slipped on my comfy black moccasins, and I was ready to roll.

In mud.

Ugh! I looked so *nebby*! Like I was competing in the "Biggest Weirdo Who Ever Walked This Planet" contest. And it looked like I would win.

The pounding at my door interrupted my personal beauty pageant.

Ah, my dear stepsisters barged in.

"Tova said to tell you she's leaving *now*," Margalit taunted. The kid actually had her hands on her hips. I half-expected her to stick her tongue out and go *nyah-nyah-nyah-nyah-nyah* in like a minute.

"You look *so* weird," Yaffa said in a prissy voice. Did I mention she was wearing a Minnie Mouse nightgown and her blonde hair formed a messy halo around her head? Really, she should've been a fashion consultant.

"Thanks," I said. "I love knowing how beautiful I look." I pushed past them. The elementary school doesn't have classes on Sunday. And it's really a pity. "You made my day."

Yaffa looked confused.

Whatever.

I grabbed my coat and my loose-leaf from their respective locations (an armchair and the kitchen floor) and waltzed out to the car, plopping myself into the passenger seat.

Tova didn't even look at me.

She just turned on her boring old classical music and drove me to school.

I'd always wanted a chauffeur.

And a sister.

Can humans fly? Because that's exactly what I did when I got out of the car. I flew into school. You'd think I was one of those girls who are all *leibidike* and jump around singing camp cheers and who love school so much.

Yeah, that's me, all right.

Me and my best friend Rochel Black. Who was staring at me like I was some kind of escaped maniac as I barged into the school building.

"Watch it, Ella Sender," she said. I held my loose-leaf close to my chest. Have I mentioned that last week my loose-leaf banged into her elbow and it started bleeding? Apparently, it still hurt. I'd told her I was sorry, and she'd assured me that she forgave me, and I really believed her. Really.

I gave her a wan smile. People think it's bad to start their week on Monday morning. I start Sunday. And sometimes even Motza'ei Shabbos. My life is waaay too fun.

I trudged up to the second floor and deposited my stuff in my locker.

Then I realized exactly how bad my day was going to be.

I mean, last night hadn't gone all too well. And seeing Rochel Black whom I had practically killed last week surely wasn't a good omen.

But the worst part was that there were drama club meetings on Sunday. Which in theory would have been just dandy, except for one very minute detail: the cast list was officially being posted that day, and rehearsals were beginning.

All for the play that I technically wasn't in.

The realization was enough to make me start crying right then and there, but just then, Tzippa appeared.

"Back so soon from your vacation?" she said, coming up to me with an innocent expression on her face.

"Ha, ha," I grunted. She was a riot, really.

Tzippa gave me a look. "Well, I'm really excited about this play. I'm getting the part of Oscar, and Naomi is Kreindel, which is totally super. I don't know about you, Ella, but I totally thought Ahuva and Chanie would take that role for themselves. It's *so* nice that Naomi got that part, isn't it?"

It was so nice. Naomi was one of my best friends, and I was so excited for her! She was going to have the biggest part in the school play! She would be in every scene. She was the star of the show! She was going to have a great time…doing what I was supposed to be doing.

Okay, I was angry. And jealous.

But you can imagine how it would look if I said, "Y'know, Naomi shouldn't have gotten that part. I totally deserved it!"

Real best-friend-ish, right?

So, I said nothing.

Tzippa stared at me for a second, but luckily, Chaiky Cukier, her long, long red hair in a long, long braid down her back, came bouncing over to us just then.

No kidding.

"Hi, hi," she said. "Ella! Sender! Ella! Sender!" she chanted. Chaiky's a real individual. From her round green eyes, to her rimless Ogi glasses, to the smatter of orangey freckles on her milky skin, she stands out in a crowd. And I think she likes it that way.

"Hi," I muttered.

"I was waiting, waiting, waiting for you at tryouts last night!" she said, her green eyes glimmering. "Where were you, Ellalalalala?"

"Don't call me that," I growled. I leaned against my locker. To think I actually *wanted* to go to school!

"So, *nu*, where were you hiding?" Chaiky asked with a wild laugh. She took off her pink jacket and tried opening her locker to dump the jacket inside. Unfortunately, her door was jammed. She gave it a kick. "Cause I seeked you!"

"I was at home," I said, not without rolling my eyes. Chaiky's jammed lockers were notorious. "And there's no such word as 'seeked'."

Chaiky gave her locker another two strong kicks. She was wearing espadrilles (in the middle of the winter, no less) with thick white socks, and I wondered if her toes felt crushed. I mean, people don't usually kick like that unless they're wearing workman boots or at least sneakers. She gave her locker another swift kick, and it banged open. Three textbooks and a whole load of white papers came avalanching out. "Why didn't you *tell* me that you weren't going to be coming?"

Have I mentioned that Chaiky entertains these fantasies that she and I are best friends, that I have to tell her everything I do, that she has to save me a spot at everything, and that she has to invite me to her house every week?

Because that's the way it is.

And she could get really insulted if I hint at anything otherwise.

Sure, I know Chaiky Cukier means well, but she is just a tad annoying and mostly, she annoys me. Why couldn't she pick anyone else with whom to be best friends? Apparently, she thinks we're kindred spirits. She's mentioned it a couple of times.

"She didn't even tell me that she wasn't coming," Tzippa said, and I blessed her silently. "Why would she tell you?"

"Why wouldn't she?" Chaiky shrugged, as if she was surprised that Tzippa would even ask such a thing.

I mean, Chaiky's an interesting individual and everything, but in reality, I don't think we're really meant to be friends. She's a little too…much for me.

Suddenly, I heard the staircase door swing open. I didn't look, but I heard the familiar quick footsteps. I didn't look, but I smelled the peach-mango shampoo. I didn't look, but I felt the soft hand on my shoulder.

"Ella Sender," Naomi said. "Why did you hang up on me last night?"

W HAT'S THE WORD THAT RHYMES with "gray" and that means you're a bad friend?

I'll give you a hint. It starts with a "b".

Oh, you wouldn't know, would you? No one has ever been in the same awful predicaments that I somehow always manage to roll into. Like mud.

Betray. The word is betray. Traitors betray their friends. Traitors tell their friends that they never really wanted to be in a silly little drama club anyway, and that who cares about the stupid roles and the stupid auditions. Traitors laugh when their friends are shocked. Traitors play loud, ugly music when their friend is having a parade. Traitors crash their friend's party.

Ella Sender, Teen Traitor.

Official Betrayer.

I'll have business cards printed and send you ten so you can give them to your enemies.

Because I, Ella Sender, had entered the murky depths of "traitor-hood".

"Why should I hang up on *you*, Kreindel?" I said. "Whoops, I mean, Naomi."

Naomi gave me a weird look and she brushed a strand of hair out of her eyes.

"Yeah," Chaiky Cukier interfered. "Why should you even *call* her?"

Was this kid serious? Here I was, trying to have a conversation with my best friend, and Chaiky Cukier *had* to stick her skinny little nose in and pry. Why couldn't everyone just leave me *alone*?

Honestly, it was like that time when I told everyone that I was sick, and none of them would believe me, and no one would just leave me alone. And they all wanted me to go to some party Ruti Reuben or someone was having, and I kept telling them to just leave me alone. But nooooooo, they made me get dressed up in like this really nice outfit and come and smile and socialize with everyone there. And then, after I had one of those hero sandwiches and a cup of coke and three and a half rippled potato chips, my stomach started to ache really, really badly, and before I knew it, I was racing down the perfect halls in Ruti Reuben's house, past these perfect paintings of spring landscapes where I wished I could be, and I ran into the gorgeous marble bathroom, and everything I had eaten ended up in the toilet bowl, and my body, especially my throat, felt like it was burning on some kind of garbage fire. It was horrible, and so I cried, and then they finally let me go home and be alone. Yeah, like, thanks. And then, when they all got the flu themselves a few days later, they knew that they should have listened to me.

"Just leave me alone," I muttered. Like anyone would listen, though.

Tzippa took one look at the situation and gently grasped

Chaiky's right arm. "Chaiky, come to my locker for a second. I want to show you the latest picture of my niece."

Chaiky shrugged. "Whatever you say, Zipper."

Then she started to sing, "Zipty-zoo-da-zipty-hey, my, oh, my, what a wonderful day!"

And Tzippa slowly led her away.

"So, why, Ella?" Naomi said. "Are you upset that I got the part?"

"Yeah, I'm really, really upset, and I'm going to cry myself to sleep tonight." Since I had already cried myself to sleep the night before, and was probably going to do it again that night, I didn't really think I was lying. Even though I spoke in a sarcastic voice. I mean, everyone could tell what I was really feeling, couldn't they?

Sarcasm is a good thing, I think. It's just such a great way to say the exact opposite of what you mean and get people to think. Plus, sometimes you don't want to say what you mean. I mean, like, I'm not one of those mushy-gushy, lovey-dovey people. What was I supposed to say? "Naomi, I'm so proud of you"? I mean, *puh-leeze*. Who said she even wanted to hear that? Her mother probably told her that enough times last night.

"Then what's wrong?" Naomi asked. She honestly looked worried, and for a second, I felt bad.

"Nothing," I said. "I'm just having a rotten day."

"But it's not even nine-thirty!" Naomi said, tucking her blonde hair behind her ear nervously.

"Make that a rotten life, then," I muttered.

"Ella, could you please tell me what's bothering you and why you're being so cynical?" Naomi shifted her loose-leaf from one arm to the other. I looked at her hands. They were white from gripping her loose-leaf so hard.

Yeah, really, I should tell. I should pour out the story of my entire wretched life and complain to her. If she'd *really* care, she would have at least called me last night before she tried out for *my* part. Because it was my part.

"Come on, Ella," Naomi said, putting her free arm around my shoulder. "Don't be so tough. Loosen up a bit. It's not good to be so angry. You're going to end up hurting yourself." She gave me an uneasy smile, and her eyes were kind of wide, like she was a little confused and didn't know exactly what to do.

Why did life *have* to be so complicated? If Rivky Rhein or some other *shnook* had gotten the part instead of me, I could seethe and properly enjoy my misery. But my best friend had gotten the part. I *had* to be happy for her. I had to plaster this huge smile on my face and assure her that, no, I was really, totally fine with the fact that she stole my part from me and that she was oblivious to the real reason I was angry.

Why did I always have to be the angel? The sweet one? The one who gave in? Why did I always have to act happy when I wasn't? Because I wasn't! My mother was dead. My sister wasn't speaking to me. My father didn't care about me. I had an evil stepmother. I had two annoying stepsisters. My brother was being indoctrinated to the dark side. And I hadn't even gotten the part I wanted in the drama club I had worked so hard to put together. I hadn't even gotten any part. And I was supposed to be happy?

I was *sick* of it. I was sick of wanting something so badly and then watching it wriggle its way out of my aching hands and into the open, delicate hands of my very own best friend, who had no intention of giving it back to me.

The rational little voice in my head started to blab about how that part had never in theory even been mine, and just because I wanted it so badly didn't mean that no one else was allowed to get it, and all the rest of the gibberish that makes a person so much angrier when she is not in one of her rational moods. Which was, like, *always* for me.

"Didn't I ask you to leave me *alone*?" I screamed. "Get off of me!"

Naomi backed away, looking shocked. Her mouth had turned into this perfect little O and her eyes were round, too. She looked a little bit scared. Scared of me.

"Why does something *always* have to be bothering me? Why does something *always* have to be wrong? Why does everyone *always* want to shrink me? Did it ever occur to you that I don't care about the silly little drama club? Maybe that's why I didn't come to the auditions last night! Did it ever occur to you that I just don't care about frivolous stuff like that?!" I could feel my fast get redder and redder as I screamed like a psycho-maniac. Maybe I did need a shrink.

Naomi looked like she was going to cry. "I thought you'd be happy for me, Ella. I thought you'd be excited," she whispered really softly and hoarsely, as if she was having some trouble getting the words out.

And that's when it finally hit me. Right in my face. And it hurt.

Besides for being a bad daughter and a bad stepdaughter and a bad sister (those were all givens), I was also a horrible friend. You know, the bad kinds you read about in books and stuff, but you don't think actually exist. But they actually do. I mean, I was here, wasn't I?

Oh, yeah, business cards were a *real* option.

Just then, the bell rang, but what difference did it make to me? I didn't have to go school anymore. I had this entire business going

71

for me… I was crying. What did it matter, anyway? Everyone already thought I was crazy. Maybe I was crazy. Suddenly, it didn't seem like such a bad label. It would explain a lot of things.

The world became a wet blur, and suddenly I felt someone pulling my arm.

And I didn't say anything because I knew it was Naomi, and I wanted to apologize to her. I allowed myself to be led into the bathroom, crying bitterly all the while. Those racking sobs, you know, when your entire chest hurts and you can't even breathe.

"Okay, Ayelet," I heard a voice say. It was a voice so familiar and yet so distant at the same time. "Stop crying. It's time for us to have a little chat."

I wiped my wet eyes and stared at the outline in front of me.

It wasn't Naomi.

It was Tova.

What was *she* doing here? What did she want? Had I finally reached the level of wretchedness where she decided she had to interfere? I had really needed her these past few months, but where had she been? In some state of Let's-Ignore-Ella-Because-She's-Crazy, that's where.

So, I didn't say anything.

I just started to cry again.

"Shh, shh," Tova said, smoothing my hair as she placed her arm around my shoulder. "It's all going to be all right."

"No, it's not!" I blubbered. "Nothing's ever going to be all right! I have just about the worst life ever!"

I was shaking with sobs, and Tova didn't say anything. Instead of finding her silence annoying like I had found it before, this time I actually found it somewhat…comforting.

"Everything's just so horrible!" I sniffed. "First I had to miss tryouts, and then Naomi got the part I wanted since I was like born!"

"You have to stop, Ayelet," Tova said. "You really have to stop."

"Stop what? Living? Even though I'm already confined to the four walls of my room until the world ends, and you know a prisoner is considered like a dead person, and — " I leaned against the bathroom wall and started to slide down to the floor. What a day. And it was only nine-thirty.

"I mean, stop *losing it.*"

I stopped crying. "What exactly are you *saying*, Tova Sender?"

"Ayelet," she said, looking into my eyes. "You're hurting yourself. A lot. By doing this, by acting this way, you're not only tearing apart relationships, you're also tearing apart yourself."

"Why are you talking to me?" I asked bitterly. "Aren't you afraid I'll tear you up, too?"

"You need help," Tova said simply.

Oh, so that was it. I needed *help*. I mean, I had already diagnosed myself as crazy, so I was probably, like, institutional at this point. I needed serious help, and what was more, I needed the entire world to shrink me, too. Right, right. I always needed help. Tova was the perfect one and I was the *nebbach* case who was psychologically and emotionally unwell.

"Go away," I sneered. I snuggled against the wall. I thought I could stay there in the bathroom forever, or at least for another twenty years or so. Then maybe I'd get married. Or I'd get help. "Just leave me alone." Why wouldn't everyone just leave me alone?

"But — "

"I don't know who you think I am! I'm your sister, not your *patient*! You think you can ignore me for half a century and then tell me I need help? You don't even know me anymore!" I could feel the

73

anger rising up my chest. The pain, tears and frustration that I had smothered for so long were now rising up like a volcano.

"Ella, I —"

"I've had enough of you, Tova Sender! If you were really my sister, you would have been there for me a while ago. You would have realized that I needed someone to listen to all my troubles. You wouldn't have ignored me."

"But —"

I pushed Tova's arm off my shoulder. "I wanted you to help me before, and you stayed away. Now, I just want you to get off my case, and you won't leave me alone."

"But I want to help you *now*," Tova said. And then, all of a sudden, she started to cry.

Tova Sender? Crying? If I hadn't seen it for myself, I would never have believed it.

"I'm so sorry, Ayelet," she said through her tears. "I know how much you wanted that part."

"No, you don't," I said. No one knew how much I wanted that part, how much I needed to shine, and how devastated I was now.

I pushed myself off the floor and away from the wall. I walked to the sink and splashed my face with water. "I've had more than enough of you."

I couldn't believe what I was saying. I wanted to be friends with Tova again for so long, and now here she was, handing me the key, and I was...slamming the door in her face. But something, some little smidgen at the back of my heart, was telling me that Tova pitied me, that everyone pitied me. That my life was a battle I had to fight myself, and I had to get through this alone. The way it had started.

"I'm sorry, Ayelet," Tova whispered. "Could you please forgive me?"

"Listen," I said as I started to remake my hair. Okay, this was almost over. I would calmly leave the bathroom and life would get back to how it was before. Because I was stronger than everyone. I was going to prove to everyone that as much as they crushed me, I could rebuild myself. "I really don't understand why you're talking to me all of a sudden, and frankly I don't really care, and I — "

"Ayelet!"

"Don't 'Ayelet' me! I'm just *not* interested in you!" I pulled the pony-holder against my hand and let it sling back, stinging me.

"I *said* I was sorry."

"Like 'sorry' really helps. Like you can wake up one morning and decide to turn yourself on to me all of a sudden, and begin to organize my life for me, and dictate how I should live it. You wish, Tova Sender."

"Could you stop calling me that?"

"What?" Did she honestly want me to refer to her as Queen Tova Sender, Her Majesty?

"Just call me Tova."

Something in her voice made me stop. I realized that the way this conversation was going, neither of us were getting anywhere. If I wanted to accomplish anything, I had to talk straight.

"Tova Sender," I whirled on her suddenly, "answer me this time without changing the topic."

"But — "

"Why didn't you speak to me for two whole months, and why are you speaking to me now?"

However I imagined Tova to respond to my question, it certainly wasn't the way she actually did.

For a long moment, she just stared at me with her mouth opening and closing, sort of like a fish. Then, she opened the bathroom door and just walked out!

Yes, things were *really* going to get back to normal.

The grand fun, it seemed, had only begun. And my demure twin sister (some sister!) was the ringmaster of this wild, wacky circus that, incidentally, happened to be my life.

TO FOLLOW, OR NOT TO follow? That was the question. Whether 'twas nobler to see what was wrong with my sister who had treated me like a foe for the past two months, or to sit sulkily in the bathroom with my arms crossed.

Angry as I was, I was even more curious what was going on. And I had this absurd feeling that Tova *wanted* me to follow her, that she was leading me to the answer to my question, that when my curiosity was fed, I wouldn't be dead like the proverbial cat which curiosity killed, but rather invigorated. So I followed her.

My footsteps echoed after Tova's in the quiet hallway. We were the only two students who weren't *davening* in the auditorium. I trailed Tova all the way down the hall and then into the stairwell. I was a tad surprised when she walked down the stairs, but I didn't comment.

Then, we walked out of school. That was the clincher. What was going on? Tova Sender, the epitome of perfection, cutting school? This was bad. This was very, very bad. If girls like Tova didn't appreciate the value of school, what about the rest of us? I knew that everyone considered me a teen rebel, but I would never, ever cut school. Except now of course, but now didn't count. Maybe it didn't count for Tova, either?

Tova unlocked the car and slid into the driver's seat. She turned on the engine and turned to look at me. Her face was red and splotched with tears. I had never seen her look like that, because, as I said before, Tova never cried. There was never any reason for it. Now, though, her eyes were watery and seemed to be pleading with me. Slowly, I opened the passenger door and got into the car. I closed the door and heard the sharp click of the car door lock.

There was no going back.

I didn't say anything as Tova drove. I wasn't really sure where we were going, but it looked like a shopping district. Oh, did Tova want to go shopping? Because there were great sales on winter clothes now, and in the tenseness of the situation, I couldn't help but wonder how great it would be if I got a cashmere black turtleneck. That was a real necessity.

Tova kept driving, past all the stores we usually shop at, past all the restaurants. She turned into a secluded street, where there were basically some apartment buildings and old, ugly Victorian houses that seriously needed to be razed down.

She got out of the car and so did I.

Um, where were we going, again?

We walked a little down that block until we came to a small brick house. Tova seemed to be walking to the side entrance.

There was a sign above the door: *Fixler's Photography*.

Right, this was so, so normal. We were going to a photographer. What did she want to do? Take pictures? Now? Tova was an enigma wrapped in a riddle. This was crazy.

"Um, why are we here?" I couldn't help but ask.

Instead of answering, Tova rang the buzzer and I heard the familiar, metallic buzz in my ears. And suddenly, I was transported to another time, to the buzzer of another studio…

BZZZZZZZZZZZZZZZ.

It was a few months ago. Tova and I walked into Halie's Hair Studio for our hair appointment. It was the day of our father's wedding, and suffice it to say, we were both feeling jittery. Only, we didn't show our feelings to each other, because, like, we both really didn't feel so much like talking. We had gotten into a fight the night before.

Michal's girls had had their appointments at Halie's earlier that morning. I couldn't help but wonder why exactly we hadn't scheduled our appointments together and everything, since we were a new family and all.

Monique, the lady who was doing my hair, blabbered about how darling it was that our father was getting remarried, and how darling it was that we, Tova and I, were twins, and how we should have gotten matching gowns. It would have looked absolutely *dar*-ling.

She expertly sculpted my hair into a half-up-do.

Just as Monique twisted the last tendril into place, I caught a glimpse of myself in the mirror. "That's not how I want my hair," I said.

"Well, darling, that's how your momma wanted it, and you know, the customer is always right," Monique said with her irritatingly easygoing laugh as she rummaged through one of the drawers for something.

And what was I, exactly — a bowl of leftover spinach?

"But that's not how I want my hair!" I said again. I mean, really, a half-up-do? Couldn't we get *nebbier*? All I wanted was to wear my hair back with a pretty headband, not with half a bottle of hair spray!

I looked over at Tova. Of course, she was letting her hairdresser do her hair absolutely docilely, but what else was new?

"Darling, you look absolutely bee-yoo-tee-ful! Your momma would be proud."

I gritted my teeth. "I wanted to wear my hair in a headband," I said, scowling at my reflection.

"Ah, well, maybe with this it will be better," Monique said with another trill of a laugh, and I couldn't help but a let a small inkling of hope putter its way into my heart. Maybe she would take out that silly-looking up-do right now.

Monique took her skinny hand out of the drawer, and she was holding a handful of tiny sparkly barrettes. She delicately slid each one into my hair. Oh, my crowning glory. Next thing I knew, she'd be rubbing olive oil on my head and pronouncing me queen of the world.

Right.

"What's this?" My voice sounded high-pitched, even to my own ears.

"Oh, don't you look like a doll, darling! Your momma had the little girls wear these, and she insisted that you big girls also have them in your hair! And my, my, don't you look darling!" Monique's brown eyes sparkled with delight as she sniffed with glee.

Tova was wearing the barrettes, too. What was this? Why were we all going to be wearing these things? It was just about the most ridiculous idea ever, mainly because it was Michal's.

Monique gave my hair another *shpritz* of hair spray and then gave me a dazzling smile.

"All done, darling! You have a nice night tonight, all right?"

I stretched my lips into something that would resemble a smile. "Thanks." For nothing.

I slowly got off the vinyl black chair and walked toward the car. (The customer, my "momma", had paid earlier.)

I opened the door and slid into the passenger seat. Did Tova even look at me? No. I banged the door shut.

As we drove home so we could pick up Ari and our gowns and then head to the hall, I remarked on the irony of the situation. It was a good thing I wasn't wearing any make-up yet. It would have all gotten messed up by now because of my tears.

A good thing, indeed.

A short time later, we were at the hall. I changed into my gown, but I didn't have anyone to zip up the back. Tova wasn't talking to me, and I wasn't going to ask Yaffa, Margalit, or Michal to help me.

I tried to do it myself, but my arms just weren't long enough, and it made my elbows hurt. I sat down on one of the cushy couches in the changing room and tried to control myself. I would not cry. I would not cry. I would...*scream*! I took a deep breath and hoped that everything would be all right and that I wouldn't lose my temper.

But that's not really what happened.

I jumped up from the couch and yanked at that zipper, trying to close it. Then I heard a deadly noise.

Rrrippp.

Great. This was just great. This was the best thing ever. My day couldn't get better. No, no, it just couldn't get better.

You wish. It could get *much* better.

Yaffa and Margalit paraded into my room. Yaffa's perfectly manicured hands were on her waist. She had a prissy look on her perfect little face, and she seemed almost derisive as she looked at me condescendingly.

"Did you *rip* your dress?" she asked.

I could feel the blush creeping up my neck, and my face got all hot.

"Mommy always tells me that if I need help putting on my dress," Margalit said, arrogance tainting her words, "I should always ask her. Why didn't you ask, Yellie? You're a big girl."

This could get better? Could it?

The bride herself waltzed grandly into the room.

"Why didn't you get your make-up done yet, Ayelet?" Michal asked. "Tibby is waiting."

"Mommy!" Margalit squealed. "Yellie ripped her dress! We have to punish her!"

Maybe my punishment would be that I had to go home right now.

Michal surveyed me with what I knew was deep disdain in her eyes.

"That's okay, Ayelet," she said in what I knew was a totally sarcastic voice. "I knew this would happen. Of course, I assumed it would be Margalit or Yaffa who'd rip their gowns, but I guess it doesn't make a difference. The seamstress is coming in a few minutes. And besides, you're not coming to the *chuppah* or *badeken* anyway, so you can just stay put right here, until Tibby and Fergie fix you up."

I wasn't in such a good mood for the pictures.

I didn't really smile that much, even though Ari poked me a few times.

But really, can you blame me? Those silly barrettes, the ugly gown, and the horrid make-up made me look like some escapee from the circus.

I don't think I smiled at the wedding at all.

In fact, I don't think I really ever smiled since I was five years old.

13

TOVA WALKED DOWN THE STEPS and I followed her.

"Hi, Esther!" she said to a tall, thin girl who seemed to be busy filling out forms.

"Hi, Tova," Esther said absentmindedly, not looking up. "The pictures aren't ready yet, you know that!"

"I know, I know, I just wanted to show the proofs to my twin sister." Tova paused and Esther looked up. "Esther, this is my twin, Ella."

"Ah, Ella!" Esther said, a hint of a smile creeping up her freckly face. "I feel like I already know you!"

I gave her a weak smile.

"You're really something! Those pictures have such *personality* because of you. *Halevai*, more people should have such interesting wedding pictures!"

What was she *talking* about?

"Thanks," I said slowly, warbling the word in my dry mouth.

"I know Mr. Fixler usually doesn't like it when I show customers the proofs tens of billions of times, but since Tova's never rude, I'll make an exception. You do want to see the pictures, Ella, don't you? They're hilarious!"

"Well, I'm never one to pass up a laugh," I said in a voice that made me feel like a stodgy old lady. Whoa, I was *serious*.

Esther got up from her little brown desk and ran to one of the rooms in the back. A few moments later, she returned, her hands full of glossy pictures.

"Look at this one!" she said shoving an entire pile in my face. "You look hysterical!"

I looked at the top picture. My father and Michal were smiling happily, excitement playing all over their features. Yaffa and Margalit looked like cute little pixies straight out of a fairy tale, blissful smiles on their sweet faces. Ari looked smart, and Tova looked angelic. I looked diabolic. I had a cross between a scowl and a smile on my face. My eyebrows were all furrowed and angry, but my mouth was stretched, revealing two straight rows of white teeth.

And that was only the beginning.

Because it got worse.

There was a picture where my eyes were crossed. And then another where I looked totally nauseated and, well, I could go on and on, but I'd rather not.

Because I understood why Tova had dragged me here. I heard what she was silently trying to scream to me.

I looked mad.

I looked angry.

And I was being *such* a baby.

Why? Because my dress got ruined? Because two bratty kids laughed at me? Because I didn't want to wear a bunch of sparkly barrettes in my hair? Because I didn't want to guarantee my family happiness?

It all seemed so juvenile, so absolutely ridiculous. It seemed like Tova was right. And I would change. I would have to — if only for the sake of my pride.

We bid our farewells to Esther and left the office.

When we came outside, I was blinded by the dazzling sunlight.

"Tova," I whispered. "I'm sorry."

And when I looked at her, I realized that her eyes were glistening with tears as her body silently shook with sobs.

"I just want everyone to be happy!" she said. "I just want everyone to get along and be happy. Why are you making everything so hard?"

I guess I thought that by making things harder for my new family, I was making things, in some weird sort of way, easier for myself.

"I don't know," I said. "It's so much easier to be bad than to be good."

"But when you're good, things are so much nicer, Ayelet!"

She was right. I finally understood, in the way that only a twin could, why she hadn't been communicating with me for the past few months.

It was because she didn't want to cause more friction. Exactly what I was doing. And friction was bad, because it sparked into a fire. And fires were destructive. Did I want to destroy my family?

Well, to tell you the truth, a part of me hoped everything would just go back to the way it had been before. But I knew that couldn't happen. So, really, all I could do was hope to build a new future.

I vowed to at least *try* to be good, instead of letting everything spiral out of control. And maybe I'd try to treat Yaffa and Margalit like, well, like…humans, instead of like some alien intruders who had to be fought off and chased away. I vowed to be nice. Because nice people are nice to be around. I think I had scared off enough people already — including my own twin sister.

But the nicest thing about this entire episode was that Tova called the school secretary, who just loves her (although not me!), and said we had to take care of something important, which was why we weren't in school now, but that we'd definitely be back in school tomorrow. The secretary said we were excused!

Then, we went out for coffee. Tova ordered a French vanilla coffee with no milk and no sugar, and I ordered an iced latte with cream and mocha and lots of sugar. Hey, if we were going to celebrate, I might as well go all the way!

We had some very deep, meaningful conversations and also some chitchats. We caught up on each other's lives, and I couldn't help but feel as if everything was going to be okay again. I was almost starting to pretend that I was normal and that everything was super and that I, the new-and-improved me, was going to have a great, great life.

Then my cell phone rang.

14

"**S**O, THEN," TOVA WAS SAYING, her hazel eyes shining happily as she sipped her coffee, "Yaffa told me — "

I could feel those familiar vibrations and then a morose tune filled my ears. That was my cell phone.

"Hold on," I told Tova, rummaging around my pocket for my cell phone. It was kind of broken, due to the fact that it had skidded across my bedroom floor last night.

"Hello," I said. There was a lot of static.

"Ella? Is that you?" a faint voice on the other line said.

"Yeah."

"It's Tzippa! Where are you?"

"What do you mean? I'm currently at Chumy's Café, enjoying an icy latte and having a convo with my sis!"

"No, seriously, Ella! Where are you?"

"I'm serious!" Talk about trusting friends!

"Okay," Tzippa said. I could hear the doubt in her voice. "I don't know why you keep cutting drama meetings. Did you know that Ahuva was all like she totally would have given you another part if you were here?"

"So, what did you say?" I asked as I nervously slammed my latte back onto the table.

"I assured her that you were coming, but Chumy's Café is like half an hour away! How are you going to get here in less than five minutes?"

Oh, no. "I'll fly?" I said meekly.

Tova, across from me, had a nonplussed expression on her face and she kept making these "what?" motions. I told her to hold on a second by raising my hand.

"Listen," Tzippa said. "I'll stall for you, but if you want a part, I recommend you make it snappy!"

"Thanks a billion," I said, standing up. Tova stood up, too.

Tzippa was still talking. "Oh, listen, Chaiky Cukier is here, even though she's not in drama. Maybe I can convince her to do that little song-dance thing — "

"That sounds great! Thanks!" I hung up.

"What's going on?" Tova said.

"Well," I answered, thinking how lovely it was to be on speaking terms with Tova again, "you know I missed drama tryouts last night."

Tova nodded.

"Well, I have one more chance. The only problem is that I was supposed to be there," I glanced at my watch, "ten minutes ago."

"Let's go," Tova said, throwing a dollar tip on the table.

Tova drove kind of like me (which, loosely translated, means that she drove like a maniac), and we got there in about twenty minutes.

I almost banged into the doorman as I rushed in. *Gotta get to the auditorium, gotta get to the auditorium!*

I rushed in, and Chaiky was doing this animal dance thing, flapping her arms and chirping like a bird. Her wild red braid swung as she shook her head back and forth, and to tell you the truth, I really felt like I had stepped into the jungle. I guess we all have our hidden talents somewhere.

"Oh, good," Tzippa whispered to me, "you're here! I was beginning to think Chaiky would have to start acting like an elephant, you know, when she uses her braid as a trunk?"

Something told me I didn't *want* to know, so I gave Tzippa a quick smile and profusely thanked her for sidetracking Chanie and Ahuva.

"Hi, everyone!" I said, giving Ahuva a weak smile. "I'm here."

"Oh, the princess is here!" Ahuva said in a sarcastic voice. Ahuva is tall and broad, with a deep voice to match. "I don't know what you were thinking, Ella Sender, but we're not going to reconduct play tryouts because of you."

Okay, I would totally not scream at them. I mean, let's just forget about the fun fact that I started the drama club, but, yeah, they were right.

"Um, that's all right," I said, feeling like a martyr. "I just hope there's a part for me in the play."

"Yeah, you can have the part of Sasha," Chanie said with a smirk.

They were kidding, right? Sasha is Kreindel's annoying little sister. She pipes up at the weirdest times, making the weirdest comments. I was *Sasha*?!

"Okay," I whispered.

"Thank you," Ahuva said gruffly.

I'm glad she understood that she had to thank me for stepping down this once.

I smiled. "You're welcome!"

"No," Ahuva said, her face turning the slightest bit red. "The correct answer is 'thank you'."

To tell you the truth, I really didn't feel like thanking her for giving me the worst part in the entire play. Even though the more I thought about it, the more I realized that she *had* done me a favor. I hadn't come to play tryouts yesterday like everyone else did. It was lucky I got any part.

"Thanks, Ahuva! Thanks, Chanie!" I said, a genuine smile spreading across my face.

And you know what? They smiled back.

I felt a tap on my shoulder.

"Ayelet?" It was Tova.

"Yeah?" I said, turning around.

"I'm going home now, but if you need a ride later, just call me."

I nodded my thanks to her.

"By the way," she said as she started to leave, "I'm going to speak with Daddy and Ima and try to bail you out of your imprisonment sentence. I think they deserve to know that you've decided to change."

"You would do that? For me?"

Tova nodded.

"Thanks!"

It was so nice to have a sister take care of you and everything.

"Okay, everyone!" shouted Chanie, who is petite with brown hair that is always in a high ponytail. "Sit down! We're giving out the scripts!"

They passed out these thick booklets and I started flipping through it. Though Sasha was a small part, she was still in a lot of scenes, doing all kinds of wacky things. I guess it wasn't too bad. I started to really read the script as Chanie and Ahuva reiterated the fact that the performance would be in about three months, so it wasn't like we had an abnormally long time to work on everything.

The weird thing was that the script didn't seem so…*kosher*, if you know what I mean. Like we're a Bais Yaakov school and everything, and somehow I doubted that Rebbetzin Greenwald would allow this play to be performed.

I looked over at Naomi. (I had apologized to her as soon as I settled myself in the auditorium.) "Did they get this script approved?"

Naomi looked surprised. "I'm sure they did. Rebbetzin Greenwald wouldn't have let us start practicing if she didn't approve of the script first, you know."

Something still didn't sit right with me. I mean, I knew Rebbetzin Greenwald, and it just didn't seem like she would approve of this type of play.

"You know for a fact that she approved of it, or you're just assuming so?" I asked Naomi.

Naomi rolled her eyes. "What's gotten into you, Ella? I'm sure everything is fine. Stop being so bitter about the play!"

It was then that I realized that if I did anything, anything at all that Chanie and Ahuva didn't want me to do, everyone would think it was because I was mad that I hadn't gotten the main role.

Well, I was kind of mad, but that wasn't why I thought Rebbetzin Greenwald should have approved of the script. I wanted her to approve of it just for the club's sake. I love this club. Why couldn't everyone understand that I wasn't just complaining because I hadn't gotten my dream role? I mean, okay, some people would do that, but I don't think that should give everyone a right to automatically assume that, hey, Ella's complaining; she's bitter.

"Okay, girls," Ahuva said. "I want everyone to memorize their parts by tomorrow! No one, except possibly Naomi, has the excuse that her part is too big! This is an absolute must!"

I got a ride home with Tzippa. Chaiky did, too. She was blabbering away about something or another. Apparently, she was in charge of costumes for the play — and she was excited.

I stared out the window at the buildings and rushing cars. What was I supposed to do? There must have been a misunderstanding about Rebbetzin Greenwald having approved of the script; I just knew it. Maybe she hadn't gotten around to looking at it, but Chanie and Ahuva just assumed that she had, and because she hadn't said anything about it, they took it as an okay to go ahead with rehearsals. Who knows?

But was it my place to let Rebbetzin Greenwald know about this? People would think I was sanctimonious and everything, but if Rebbetzin Greenwald decided the play wasn't good, she might just cancel the play altogether. Would that be any better?

I TRUDGED INTO THE HOUSE, BUILDING castles in my mind. Okay, I would do this. I would tell Rebbetzin Greenwald tomorrow about the script. The sooner, the better. I took a deep breath. It wouldn't be so bad, right? I mean, it would be a whole lot worse for everyone if after all those rehearsals, Rebbetzin Greenwald heard about the script and then cancelled the play, right? Right? Right? Right. I could most definitely do this. I could speak up. Couldn't I?

Yeah. My pep talks win me over every single time.

It had sure been a long day. Tova was totally right about the whole be-nice-to-everyone thing, but to tell you the truth, I kind of felt like blowing up at someone when I got home. Preferably two little people. I had all this anger pent up inside of me like a volcano waiting to erupt, waiting to spew hordes of red, hot lava, burning everything in sight.

Got home, gritted my teeth a lot, had dinner, did my homework, studied some math (I missed one lesson a few weeks ago and it had all been downhill from there), and spoke to Heidi Brown, Naomi and then Tzippa on the phone. Then, Ruti Reuben called to tell me to be on time tomorrow, because I wasn't there today, and since she was our grade coordinator, she just wanted to tell me that there was something very, very special going on tomorrow that I didn't want to miss. Special, my foot. It was probably some trip to a place where I didn't want to go. Afterward, I watched the *L'cha* music video on my computer for the umpteenth time or something. (It's just a great way to vicariously release energy, watching that guy dance, jump around, and make all those weird faces and everything, and when his friends throw water on him, I feel refreshed. That's not even mentioning when he throws the basketball into the hoop and then sees that there's no hoop. That's like the story of my life. Seriously.) I dabbled a little bit in my play and then started to get ready for bed, when Yaffa and Margalit came barging into my room.

Oh, great. The bed bugs were here to bite.

As much as I tried to think about raindrops on roses, bright copper kettles, and warm woolen mittens (not whiskers on kittens, though; cats just freak me out), when Margalit threw herself on my pink silk comforter, I didn't feel too good. In fact, I felt kind of nauseous. And then, when Yaffa sat at my desk and turned on my MacBook, my teeth gritted so hard against each other that I could almost feel the enamel slowly chipping off. This. Was. Not. Good.

"Why, hello," I said, pursing my lips together as I sat down on my little couch, right near my bookshelf. "Is there anything I could do to help you two?"

"Can you get us some gummy worms?" Margalit said, looking up from the book she was reading. Hey! Where did she get that from? I had just bought *Footprints in the Sand* from the bookstore last week and I had placed it on my nightstand. When it had mysteriously gone missing, I automatically assumed that I had lost it or that I had lent it to Tzippa, who had been begging to read it. Never in a million years would I have assumed that Margalit stole it.

"Where did you get that book from?" I growled.

"Your nightstand," Margalit said.

"Oh?"

She didn't answer me. She just gave me this look as if I was some kind of moron or something. I mean, how couldn't I have known that? She got it from my nightstand. Duh.

I would remain calm. I would remain calm. I. Would. Remain. Remain. Remain. *Remain.* ARGH!

I leapt off the couch and snatched the book out of Margalit's hands. Her eyes widened like a frightened deer. "What do you think you're doing?!" I screamed. "What makes you think you can just parade into my room any old time you like and steal my things like a little *ganav?*"

She gave me a doe-like stare.

Oh, no way. No way was I falling for this whole "oh, please, I'm so innocent" act. These kids were not innocent.

"Um, Yellie?" Yaffa said in a meek voice. "Your computer just made a very funny noise."

"What?"

"I didn't do it, I promise!"

"I'll bet you didn't do it!" I yelled. First they *stole* my books, and then they *wrecked* my computer? "Get out!" I screeched, very well aware that our neighbors could most definitely hear me. "Get out now and leave me alone!"

The two scurried out of my room and must have ended up in Tova's, because a minute later, Tova knocked on my door and gave me the Look. Like I cared anymore.

You know what, I was just tired already. I was tired of pretending and putting on this fake little smile when I so wasn't happy.

Everyone would just have to see me angry! What was so bad about being angry, anyway? I mean, anger *is* a natural emotion, and people are not supposed to suppress their emotions because then they can have heart attacks. And why should I suppress my emotions and have a heart attack because of Yaffa and Margalit? I didn't love them enough to die for them.

Great. Now I didn't need a shrink; I was shrinking myself. Lovely. Vast accomplishment and tremendous milestone. We should get out the champagne and celebrate.

I threw myself into bed and fell asleep. When I woke up later, it was as if the house was slumbering in a dark silence. I felt gross and I at least needed to go and wash my face, which was not only covered in tears but also in, I am so pleased to say, Margalit's gooey putty. See, she has this thing she made in school as a science project. It's this purple goo that reeks of detergent and all kinds of weird chemicals. She loves it and carries it with her everywhere. Including on my comforter. My silk comforter. The one from Milan. That I had begged my father for, for months and months and months. And now, it would smell like Margalit's chemical-filled goo. Yes, memories of Margalit every single night on my bedspread. What was worse was that it was plastered all over my face like some facial mask gone horribly wrong.

I tried to bang open the door to the bathroom Tova and I shared, but it was locked. Tova had locked me out of my own bathroom. This was nice. Maybe tomorrow they'd lock me out of the house. I was already picturing various scenarios in my mind as I trekked to the bathroom down the hall.

Then I heard it.

It was Michal. She and my father were conversing in the dark hall, shadows dancing on their faces. They hadn't seen me and they hadn't heard me. I slipped into the bathroom, but I kept the door open a crack.

I knew it was wrong to listen to a conversation between my father and stepmother, but they were talking about me! I just knew it.

"I'm sure she does not mean it," Michal murmured, tightening the sash around her long satin robe.

Oh, right, Michal was sticking up for Margalit the book thief now. This was so not surprising.

"Well, Ayelet's a big girl. She should be able to deal with it," my father said. "She has to realize that there are consequences for her actions. Do you think we should ground her again?"

Well, no big surprises there either. But still, the bottom of my heart felt as if it was ripping apart, my dreams falling into the pit of my stomach. This was my Daddy. And he couldn't even stick up for me? As melodramatic as it sounds, here I was, the poor little orphan girl, with not too many friends, not much fun, and bitter disappointments hurled at my chest again, and again, and again. And my own father, the man who changed my diaper when I was a baby, read Dr. Seuss books to me, taught me how to blow a bubble and how to whistle, couldn't even take my side for once. I mean, it was so nice that everyone was on Michal's side, but why couldn't anyone be *my* ally for a change? Why did I always have to fight all my battles alone?

"No," I heard Michal say. "Do not ground her."

I gasped.

"Margalit and Yaffa, they do not realize sometimes how they infringe on every boundary Ayelet works hard to put up — "

"Pointless boundaries," my father said. I gasped again.

Michal held up her hand. "Listen, she is a teenager. She reminds me a lot of myself when I was a young girl."

I reminded Michal of herself? That was like Ruti Reuben reminding me of myself. Like, never.

"And," Michal continued, "teenagers build barriers sometimes. She has to realize by herself that when she is closing everyone else out, she is closing herself in. She will see, I know; she is a smart girl."

"Well, you're probably right," my father said. "But her behavior was still unacceptable. Screaming? Shouting? Yelling? We're lucky Yellie didn't traumatize the poor children."

Yellie? Did my father just call me *Yellie*? Was I in some kind of warped alternate universe? I thought I was gonna be traumatized.

"Still," I heard Michal say, "do not punish her. She just started working on that play. And besides, it will have the opposite effect. Punishing her yet again will make her resent me more than ever."

My heart was beating abnormally. It felt like it was break-dancing, and I felt like I was going to faint dead away any second now. I had so suppressed my emotions. I was going to have a heart attack. I clutched my heart and leaned against the wall.

Then I heard Michal sniff. "It takes time. I know it takes time. But one day, maybe she will accept us."

I heard them go into their room. Then I gently closed the bathroom door, scrubbed the disgusting goo off my face, and washed off the tears.

MY ALARM WENT OFF AT six-o-six the next morning. After I pressed snooze six times (I have to do that, you see. I can't just get up at seven. I have to wake up at six, look at the clock, and blissfully sigh to myself as I realize that I have fifty-four minutes to wander around in the world of slumber. Then I doze off, and when I wake up nine minutes later, I have forty-five more minutes to sleep, and by seven, not only am I fully awake because my alarm clock already went off so many times, I also have this smug little feeling that I got extra sleep!), I rolled out of bed and threw on my uniform.

Have I told you about the uniform yet? When my school was small, like ten years ago, they only had a dress code. It was all very preppy, and the girls all wore pleated skirts and Ralph Lauren sweaters in various shades of the rainbow, with button-down Polo shirts and those Anne Klein shoes that everyone has.

Then, the year before Tova and I entered high school, apparently some fashionistas were let loose into our school system, infiltrating the minds and closets of all the girls. No more were Lord & Taylor and Boro Park the places to shop. Oh, no, no, no. Now girls had to go to Fifth Avenue. Where they could spend their parents' credit cards to the max and dress like they just stepped off a magazine. Which was so not something Rebbetzin Greenwald wanted. I mean, *tznius* doesn't mean that one should look ugly, of course, but Rebbetzin Greenwald, a lot of the parents, and even some of the girls didn't really feel that *frum* teenagers really had to dress so à la mode. Because following fashion to such an extreme degree could become *avodah zarah* and such. So they created a uniform.

And, darlings, it wasn't just any uniform. It was possibly the nerdiest thing anyone could dream up. Pleated navy or maroon skirts, and navy and maroon button-down shirts with lines of yellow; there was a matching navy or maroon sweater, but most girls opted for the black nondescript sweatshirt which just had the school logo on the left sleeve. I mean, Rebbetzin Greenwald said that the parents picked this out and everything, but I don't know. I've met most of the parents of the girls in my class. And none of them seem like they would pick such a uniform, with the possible exception of Mrs. Reuben.

Well, I guess I can look at the bright side and be glad that I don't go to one of those Islam schools where they have to wear burkas and those things on their faces that are netted by the eyes. I mean, as extreme and ugly our uniform is, it will never ever be as extreme and ugly as that.

So I put on a maroon skirt, a shirt that was unfortunately missing a button on the bottom, and the sweatshirt. Then I ran downstairs. The nice thing about the week is that, in the mornings, I'm the only one at home who is up. Tova leaves super early so she can study in the library and then *daven*, because she tutors Freshies when we have *davening*. My father and Ari learn every morning at the *beis medrash*, and Margalit, Yaffa, and Michal sleep until eight, because Margalit and Yaffa don't have to be in school until nine, since they're not in middle school yet.

I opened the fridge, searching for something to eat. I mean, I wasn't going to drink milk, and even though I'd have loved to have one of those tantalizing donuts sitting on the counter that were filled with yummy chocolate and covered in confectionary sugar, I knew they were a billion calories. Cereal was out, because cereal is a totally gross food, and I can't understand how people like to pour little pellets of corn or whatever in a bowl, douse them with milk, throw in some fruit, and then slurp it up like it's some kind of cold soup or something. Totally blargh.

So, there was nothing to eat. I mean, there was yogurt, but just the thought of the bacteria that yogurt is made out of was enough to make me gag. I am so not a fan of Swiss cheese like everyone else in my family, either. I could've had strawberries, but they were looking kind of shriveled. There was some kind of food — it looked like leftover dinner — in Tupperware containers, but just the thought of French cuisine made my stomach turn.

When I was a little girl, my mother always made me scrambled eggs for breakfast. It was the only thing I could really stomach. But those days had long gone. Long. Gone.

The only thing that looked interesting was a yellow lemon sitting on one of the shelves. I cut it in quarters and began to suck, the acidy flavor filling my mouth. Well, life had already given me lemons, so I supposed it wouldn't have hurt to eat one first thing in the morning, especially since they had no calories. Maybe I would start a lemon diet and only eat lemons for the rest of my life. After all, you are what you eat, and since I was *so* tart, I might as well suck on lemons. Lemonade was for wusses, anyway.

Then, I heard Tzippa's car beep shrilly. I grabbed my loose-leaf and my bag, and I was out the door. Naomi was there, too, sipping a latte. Nana Zilber, a French classmate who boards at one of Tzippa's neighbors and sometimes hitches a ride with us, was sitting in the front and finishing her English homework.

"Hey, guys," I said as I climbed into the car, lemon still in hand.

"What are you eating?" Naomi asked, giving me a wide-eyed look.

"A lemon," I said, taking another suck. I stared out the open window. The city was already bustling. Vendors were standing at street corners with rainbow-colored flowers. I took a whiff of air; it smelled like a mixture of grilling food, mugginess, and life.

We drove past large department stores, teeny shops that were almost slipped into crevices, and tables set up on the sidewalk with various merchandise on them. Sigh. My heart is in Eretz Yisrael, but as cliché and souvenir-related as it sounds, I love New York!

"You're starting to remind me of Chaiky Cukier," Naomi said wryly.

I immediately stopped sucking my lemon.

"That's not such a nice thing to say," Tzippa said, not taking her eyes off the road.

"Why, look," Nana said in that marvelous French accent of hers. For some reason, the accent is just gorgeous on Nana. On Michal, it totally makes me gag. "Iz zat not ze Chaiky Zuckier you are discussing?"

I glanced at the street. Tzippa slowed down. There, right on the corner, was Chaiky Cukier buying a yellow daisy. Then, as we watched, she stuck it in her hair.

Uh-oh. She saw us and began waving furiously. Tzippa pulled over with a sigh.

Naomi groaned.

"Naomi," Tzippa muttered, "I can't not stop!"

"Hey, Chaiky," Tzippa said in a voice usually reserved for very young children, very old people, or people who are insane. "We're on our way to school. Do you need a ride?"

"Yeah, thanks!" Chaiky said, barging into the car. "I was so worried I was gonna be late, especially since Ruti specifically called me last night and asked me to come on time because she and her gang are going to be breaking something out at *davening*. Did she call you, too, Ella?"

I shrugged. "Yeah, she did."

"I think she just likes to be in charge of things," Naomi said darkly.

"Well, I've always thought that zis Ruti Reuben was nice," Nana said.

"So, Ella," Chaiky said, trying to get my attention again, "what are you doing next Shabbos?"

"Oh, we have Shabbos *sheva brachos* for Michal's younger sister. She's getting married next Wednesday," I rattled off unconsciously. Then, I realized what I'd just said. Next Shabbos was Michal's younger sister's Shabbos *sheva brachos*. The wedding was next Wednesday. Oh, no! How could I have forgotten about this? I would have to wear that hideous gown that Tova had picked out for me, and I would have to smile at everyone and pretend to be so, so happy when really I'd rather be anywhere else in the world. Anywhere. Even hanging out with Chaiky Cukier.

"Oh, maybe you can come to my house *this* week for Shabbos then?" Chaiky said brightly.

"Maybe," I muttered. This week was getting so much better already.

"You know," Tzippa said, "it's been a long time since you've come to my house!"

"Zis iz true, Ella," Nana said. "You must come visit us! It has been too long!"

"Maybe this week we can all get together," Naomi said, jolting out of her sullen reverie. "You, me, Tzippa, Nana, hey, maybe we can even invite Heidi Brown and run through a few scenes of the play."

"Sounds good." I smiled. But only because I wanted Naomi to be in a good mood. Promise.

"Hey, why don't we sing a song!" Chaiky said. I noticed her cheeks were a weird shade of pink. Maybe she had choked on her daisy or something. She had been coughing before, and the daisy was no longer in her hair.

"Sing? A song? Like in zee choirs?" Nana said with a confused expression.

"Yeah!" Chaiky said, growing excited. "Like in a choir! Okay, let's sing 'Hey Dum Diddlee Dum'!" She immediately began singing in a completely off-key soprano. "Come on, Ells! Sing with me!"

"It's Ella," I said sharply. I had more than enough nicknames. I so did not need or want another one.

"Hey dum diddlee, hey dum diddlee, hey dum diddlee dum!" Chaiky sang.

"Could you please keep it down?" Naomi said. "It's only eight o'clock in the morning and some of us here have delicate ear drums."

Nana opened her window, "so zat it shouldn't shatter."

"Oh, come on! This is seriously the best song ever!" Chaiky said excitedly.

"Chaiky," Naomi said in an extremely serious voice. "Are you feeling okay?"

Chaiky immediately quieted down.

"Why don't we listen to music instead of singing it," Tzippa said. She slipped a CD into the CD player and the sweet strains of the Yeshiva Boys Choir's "*V'ahavta*" filled the car.

When we got to school, there was totally something going on. Our lockers on the third floor were covered in pink streamers and shiny green ribbons. On each girl's locker was a little frog key chain. Whatever they were breaking out, it didn't look like something I would like. Yeah, I know, real positive attitude.

I dumped my stuff into my locker and headed down to the auditorium with Tzippa and Rivky Rhein, who were talking about the play. We took our seats quickly because Rebbetzin Greenwald was already at the podium, making this morning's announcements.

"And, the eleventh grade is invited to stay after *davening* for a very special announcement," Rebbetzin Greenwald said. I saw Ruti Reuben smiling at her best friend Chani Sanders, who sits right next to me (we sit in alphabetical order). Then, I caught Rivky Rhein's eye (she sits right next to Ruti) and wiggled my left eyebrow. She gave me a cross-eyed grin. Unfortunately, Morah Bluestein, who was taking attendance, saw and gave us both angry looks.

"Okay, girls," Rebbetzin Greenwald said. "Let's take out our *sifrei Tehillim* and say a *kapittel*. Ready? *Mizmor shir l'assaf...*"

After *davening*, a large group of girls from my grade congregated outside the auditorium, waiting for those who always took a little more time to *daven* with *kavanah* to finish up, so that Ruti and her gang could break out whatever they had obviously kept in for too long.

Some girls standing around the water fountain were discussing what it could possibly be. Obviously it wasn't color war, because who has color war for just one grade? And it couldn't be Shabbaton, thank Hashem, because it was too early in the year for that. It could be a mini-concert, but why would they do that when we already had a school play going on?

"Well," said Nana, "I think it iz a choir! After all, did zey not put those little *grenouilles* on our lockers?"

"Uh, Nana?" Faiga Hartman said with a confused expression on her face. "What's a grenonilly, or whatever you just said?"

"A frog," said Ricki Klein, our resident French whiz.

"That does make sense," I said slowly.

"Yeah," Naomi said wryly. "But as we realized this morning, not everyone in our grade was blessed with an angel-like voice."

"Too true," Nana agreed with a laugh.

Just then, Chaiky Cukier came to get a drink from the water fountain, so we all moved away.

"Well, it could still be that we're making a concert," Faiga said, not willing to give up her idea. "And the girls in the play will be in drama, and the ones who have nice voices will be in choir, and the ones who can dance well will be dance, and everyone else will work backstage."

"That doesn't explain why this is only for our grade," Tzippa said. "I mean, girls from all grades are in the play. Why narrow everything else to just our grade?"

Faiga shrugged. "Well, I guess we won't have to wait much longer to find out."

The auditorium doors were wide open and the Miami Boys

Choir's "*Shirah Chadasha*" was blaring from the speakers. Almost everyone was sitting down already, so we quickly ran in and sat down on one of the benches. Chaiky Cukier smushed herself right next to me.

"So," Morah Bluestein, our *mechaneches*, said, twiddling the microphone. "I'm sure you're all wondering what we have in store for you! Right?"

"Right!" the girls screamed back. I smiled back cynically. I knew this was totally not something I wanted to be, or was going to be, excited about. I mean, last time we had one of these big assemblies, it was to break out color war. And although I know that some girls are totally in love with the idea of screaming until their lungs get hoarse, staying up all night to work on a silly art project, and running stupid egg races, the idea has never appealed to me. I mean, I told them that I didn't want to run in the egg race, but did they listen to me? Does anyone ever listen to me? No. Everyone was just like, "Oh, no, Ella, you should do it, you really should." And poor little me, under so much peer pressure, was forced to run in the egg race. Well, of course, I slipped and hello, that egg was not even boiled! I had sticky, gooey yolk on me for the rest of the day. This would have been bad enough, but it was a hundred times worse because I had stayed up until six the previous night working on the banner, because everyone was so sure I was an artist and everything, since I — and this is a direct quote from Ruti Reuben — "seem to have that temperament". And even though I wasn't screaming with the rest of them, I can assure you that my ears will never again be the same, not even if I live ten more lives. So, honestly, do you blame me for my lack of school spirit? I mean, it's like asking me to torture myself.

There was a whole group of girls on stage, and I noticed that

Tova was part of them. Goody. This was sure going to be interesting. They were all dressed up as different types of animals. Tova was a leopard, Mimi Grossman was a lion, Zahava Frank was a bird, and then, when the dance music started, they all began moving rhythmically in their own dance, every so often returning to the middle, holding hands and pointing upwards.

Okay, this was really deep. Whatever it was about, I didn't get it.

And then, at the end of the dance, they all began singing *Perek Shirah*. And between every animal, they would sing, "Shabbaton!" Like this was something I was supposed to understand. The girls around me were murmuring excitedly and Chaiky kept nudging me.

Ruti Reuben took the microphone. "Thank you, Tova, Mimi, Zahava, Rivi, Leah, Chani, and Shani, our fabulous Shabbaton heads, for that beautiful dance," she said, this huge smile on her face, all her perfect white teeth gleaming against her tan skin. "For those of you who haven't quite *chapped* yet, Shabbaton is here!"

Tova was a Shabbaton head and she hadn't told me? What else was new?

The girls broke into a rendition of, "Shabbaton is here, Shabbaton is here! If you are lazy, you are crazy!" I could feel my stomach churning. I was going to be sick. This was…this was not happening. No, this was some horrible dream that I had inflicted upon myself, and in a few moments I would wake up and suck some more lemons.

"Now," Ruti Reuben continued, oblivious to the fact that I was pinching my hand and trying to wake myself up. Chaiky pinched my hand, too, giving me an elfish smile. "Our theme is *shira*, song, in particular, *shirah* to *Hakadosh Baruch Hu*, and I'm sure that everyone is going to have a super-amazing time!" Then she flipped her perfect sunshine-colored hair and gave the microphone back to Morah Bluestein.

"Girls," Morah Bluestein said, "this year, Shabbaton is a little earlier than usual because we have our drama club putting on a play when we would usually have Shabbaton. So, this Shabbos, we will be going to Le Château Hotel in the Catskills Mountains for a very inspiring weekend, which I'm sure you'll all enjoy. If someone cannot come, she must let me know immediately. As you see, Zahava and Rivi are handing out the sheets with the information.

Everyone must bring in one hundred and fifty dollars by tomorrow to cover the expenses."

"What about the rooming sheets?" Chaiky called out.

"There aren't any rooming sheets," Morah Bluestein said. "You girls are in eleventh grade now, and I think you can handle not socializing with the same group of girls that you always socialize with for one weekend."

How did she know what I could handle?

"Anyway, girls, your first-period teachers are waiting for you, so hurry back to class!"

For some reason, as I sat in *Navi* class, I knew this day was so not going to be getting better. I mean, my *Navi* teacher, Morah Herman, seriously hates me. And she likes to pick on me. And no, I am so not being paranoid about this. I mean, one time, she even asked me to switch from the honors class into the modified class. I mean, hello, that's a really big jump. I can totally handle honors. Really, I can. I mean, they wouldn't have just put me in there because Tova was in there. And anyway, when she said that, the entire class just like sort of gasped and became quiet, and it was like me and her were in a wrestling ring, and I just like stared at her and I really thought I was going to start to bawl or something. Then, very clearly I said, "Just because I didn't understand the Malbim we had to prepare doesn't mean that I don't belong in this class. Does Morah Herman deny that the Malbim is a very deep *meforash*? Does Morah Herman deny that it is her job to teach me the Malbim, and that she gets paid for it? Is it my fault that I don't understand something I was not taught?"

Morah Herman gave me this long, cool look and said, "I see you have a future in the *tumah-dike* halls of law school." Then she kicked me out and sent me to the principal because I had a lot of chutzpah in me, and someone had to boil it out.

I think she was hoping that I wouldn't be allowed back into her class, but Rebbetzin Greenwald, who is possibly the only person who has ever even attempted to understand me, had a long chat with me about why I felt the need to say something like that to Morah Herman. Just because I was still angry about my mother's *petirah* and my father's remarriage, I shouldn't take it out in school, but maybe I could take a kickboxing class (an all-women one, of course), where I could let out my anger in a physical means. A lot have people have said that. That I'm angry at the world because of my mother's death and my father's remarriage.

But if there's one person who has honestly tried to help me through this never-ending, dark and stormy era, it has got to be Rebbetzin Greenwald.

It's people like Morah Herman who make everything worse, you know? They just aren't understanding. It's like they don't want to understand. They're just sticklers for rules and if you put one toe out of line, it's like, "*Oy vey*, she's a *shiksah*, so we have to get rid of her before she takes the rest of the girls down with her." That's all. It's like Morah Herman and people like her just immediately freak out when they see girls like me. They don't want the other girls to be *exposed* to girls like me. I don't really mean to rant, but people like Morah Herman just see me as a problem that has to be fixed, a screw that's out of place. They don't see me as a person who has emotions, a person who is just, put simply, hurting.

That's all. I'm hurting inside. But as long as everyone is focused on my outside and my "bad attitude", there's nothing I can do. Because that's just my outside, you know? That's just the show I put on to cover the pain I feel inside, the betrayal, the shame, the aloneness, the nights I spend just staring at the walls in my room, wondering what exactly my purpose in this world is and why I was even born. Then there are the days when I walk through the school halls wondering whether or not I'm the worst girl in the entire school, the one who does the most *aveiros*.

People like Morah Herman think that if they rehabilitate my bad attitude, then, then I would be perfect. They don't realize that once they wash away my scowls and sarcasm, they'll be greeted with a horrible monster. A monster that cries and throws tantrums just because she has no other way to express herself; a scary, furry ball of red, black, and orange anger blazing around. Me. They don't realize that they can't fix my outside without fixing my inside first. Because the outside is just a frail covering for the inside.

They make me angrier, people like Morah Herman. They make me want to do something that'll make their eyebrows rise even higher — until I won't even see them anymore. It's like this because they don't even want to know my world; they just want to fix it. It's not like I don't believe in Hashem. I mean, I'm a smart girl, I know that, and I've picked up an English translation of the *Kuzari* and learned it, and the entire thing makes sense. There can't be a true religion other than Judaism.

I mean, think of it this way: There are the Christians, whose religion doesn't even make one iota of sense, because, for the first and foremost reason, Hashem is One, *Echad*, and why should one have to split a god into three parts? Doesn't that undermine a god's divinity? (Besides for a whole bunch of other weird stuff.) Then there's Islam, which is a whole circus in and of itself, because if G-d was giving a religion, why would He just give it to one epileptic person on a mountain? If anyone learns the history of Islam, they'll know that it was just made up, because the Arabs had no religion and needed one so that they could be more cultured.

Matan Torah was witnessed by at least three million people. I mean, how can one argue with the eyewitness account of three million people?

It's just so obvious.

So, thank Hashem, it's not like I'm some heretic roaming the land, waiting for the end of days. It's just that sometimes I can't go one more step, you know? It's like I'm a train, and I just stop. Except that I stop a lot before other people do. And people like Morah Herman, they don't try to build more tracks for me so I can go on further. They just criticize and condemn, like that helps at all. They just like to take things apart, like checking my engine to make sure it works or something. That just makes me want to totally stop. To scream in their faces, "You thought something was wrong? Well, guess what, something is really, really wrong, and it's not going to get better, so just leave me alone!"

It's people like Rebbetzin Greenwald who help me build tracks and make me want to become a better person. I mean, someone might have wondered by now why exactly no one was reaching out and helping me. I mean, I don't expect my father and Michal to, because they're both too busy building their own new little world, and they can't be bothered with mine. And that's okay, really. Because I'm not all that sure that my father knows how to handle me, and it would make me even angrier if Michal tried to meddle.

But one person who tries to help me is Rebbetzin Greenwald. I mean, when I go to her office, she doesn't just try to give me constructive instructions for how I can improve my life and make the world a better place; she actually listens to me. I mean, she listens, you know? She tells her secretary to take all her calls for the next hour, closes the door, and she sits down at her desk in front of me, and just looks at me for a minute and then says, "What's going on in your life, Ella?"

To tell you the truth, I could be a complete sourpuss and say, "Nothing." But the thing is, hello, I do want help, because I don't really enjoy being like this. I don't know why people think I do. So, I tell her. I tell her everything. And the entire time, she doesn't jump in and say anything; she just nods, like she's really, actually listening to me. To tell you the truth, I think that's why she started the drama club. Not only because I asked her for it, but because she felt I needed it.

So, yeah, there is someone who recognizes my agony. But first of all, it's not like I want to be one of those crybabies, so it's not like I go running to Rebbetzin Greenwald every time I have a problem. Also, she's a pretty busy lady, so it's not like she's available for a chat at every moment. I mean, I think she tries to speak to me once a month, and she usually gets that opportunity when I'm sent to her office by teachers like Morah Herman. During those times, she really helps me, sometimes, just by listening, and other times, by asking me to step out of the box and view the situation through another's eyes, but I still feel like something inside me has to click. It's like there's this barrier that's in front of me, this memory that I'm suppressing, something that I can't get through, but once I do, I'll be a speeding train, racing like the wind down the tracks.

Anyway, I couldn't sign up for the kickboxing classes because the instructor had just had a baby and was taking some time off. But my relationship with Morah Herman has been totally downhill since that incident in her class. I mean, the woman seriously has a thing for torturing me.

Now, as I sat in her first-period *Navi* class, I tried to put a focused look on my face as Morah Herman expounded on how *pnei hador*, the face of the generation, is like *pnei hakelev*, the face of a dog, but it was really, really hard. Of course, every other one of her sentences was, "Miss Sender, are you paying attention? Do you *understand*?" Everyone knew she wasn't talking to Tova. So every time she would say that, I would give a quick, little nod and then begin to scribble my name in my notebook over and over and over again, so she would think I was taking notes.

I'm a bad girl. No, seriously. I'm one of those girls who are, like, branded as "a bad influence". It's because people think I have a bad attitude. Well, if they lived my life, trust me, their attitudes would be a whole lot worse.

Anyway, it was a good thing the bell rang right then, because if I had to keep up this charade any longer, I knew I would probably do something really, really bad. Like call out or something. Horrors.

Okay, honestly, I know I sound obnoxious. I know most people think I am. Obnoxious, cynical, sarcastic, and a little bit indifferent. Like I'm not *sensitive*. Most people don't realize that I'm the most sensitive person of all. I hurt, you know.

All over.

Especially, when I'm lying in middle of the floor, my loose-leaf practically going up my nose and Ruti Reuben on my left leg.

Uh-oh. A *klutz* is born every second. For me, it's every millisecond, though.

17

T HIS HAD TO HAPPEN, DIDN'T it? I mean, I knew I was somewhat cursed when it came to Mondays, but this was taking things to a whole new level.

I had to fall, didn't I?

And the person I had to pull down with me had to be Ruti Reuben.

I know that I'm not supposed to space out in the halls, because the last time that happened, Naomi's latte grande ended up all over my shirt — ice cream, coffee, and all. Naomi wasn't too happy about that, and neither was I. But I mean, why was Ruti Reuben walking near me, anyway? Okay, that sounded totally mean, but I really don't like her. Ruti Reuben thinks I'm this big *nebbach* case and everything. You know, the type of person who just needs someone to help her get through today and tomorrow and ease the strain of the past. And Ruti is more than happy to volunteer her services as that "someone" for me. When she talks to me, I can practically see her take out a labeler in her mind and stick *"Chessed Case #43932* — completed" on my forehead. And yes, I'm being totally serious.

Ruti quickly stood up and grabbed my hand, pulling me up with her. "Ella," she said in this voice that was oozing with sticky concern, "are you okay?"

"I'm fine. Sorry that you fell," I muttered. *Had to get to class. Had to get to class. Now.*

"No, no, it's totally fine," Ruti said, brushing a strand of sunshine hair out of her face. Her bright green eyes were glowing really brightly and she had this huge smile plastered on her face, her pearly teeth straight as soldiers in her mouth, as if saluting me with the grin.

Had to get to class. Had to get away. Now.

"You know, Ella, I really want to get to know you better," Ruti said, cocking her head. She looked like some kind of deranged doll, and she was seriously scaring me.

"Uh, yeah," I said. "Yeah, me, too."

"I think you're my type. Like, we can be friends. You know, I'm going to work something out for Shabbaton since I have pull." She laughed. "Heads aren't really supposed to, but…"

"Um, that sounds great," I muttered. So great, that I just might have to find a hole to hide in for the next few months.

"Good!" She smiled again, her eyelashes fluttering. "Well, I'll see you around, won't I?"

"Yeah," I muttered. *Chessed* Case #43932 — completed. Now I could get to class. Well, looking at the bright side, at least I hadn't bumped into Rochel Black. She might have, you know, had to kill me for doing that.

The rest of my classes weren't too great, which I suppose is a good thing, because that means that they weren't too bad either. I mean, I never really have high hopes for math, but my teacher, Mrs. Roberts, is an absolute doll, and she's really understanding. I mean,

I know it's not really her fault that she loves a subject as gruesome as math, but what can you do? She's a really good teacher. Then, it was time for English.

I mean, English is my favorite subject. I love to write, and most of the time I like to read (unless we have to read a classic by Dickens or Bronte or someone. Those authors really, like, put me to bed. Every time I read anything by them, I get this pounding headache and I feel an urge to lie down. So that's what I do. Then I read the CliffsNotes which are, thank Hashem, written by someone from the twenty-first century), and really, grammar isn't so bad. Once you know why you have to know what a gerund is, anyway.

Well, English is supposed to be my easy breezy class, you know? The time when I can just listen and participate and not have to over-work my brain. Yeah, sweet dreams.

Because this year, Mrs. Martin is my English teacher.

There's another Junior English teacher, too — Mrs. Schwartz. I hear about her all the time from Tova, who totally lucked out this year and got her. Mrs. Schwartz likes to read poetry in her class and write essays like, "What I Would Do if I Suddenly Discovered I Could Only See in Black and White". Mrs. Martin makes us read poetry and passages on our own and analyze them. Then, before we even discuss them or anything, we have to write an essay on what we read. Then we get a grade. She said she's preparing us for the English Regent, but I'd really rather she just be easier and not prepare us.

Today was an essay day in English. I'd really rather not talk about it. It was so horrible that I wasn't even in the mood of practice for the play, which is not really saying much, because I wasn't in the mood of the play anymore to begin with. I mean, I know it sounds so childish and everything, and you're probably rolling your eyes, but you don't get it. I really, really wanted that main part.

When I got to the auditorium, my backpack slung over my shoulder, the place was in a state of utter chaos.

"I cannot believe you're taking this week away from us!" Ahuva was screaming. Her brown hair was in a bun right on the top of her head and she was holding the script tightly to her chest. "This is totally ridiculous! I mean, we're putting on a play here!"

"I know," Ruti said. What was she doing here? Did she have to be everywhere? "And I'm really sorry. But I spoke to Rebbetzin Greenwald, and we need this week to prepare for Shabbaton. It's this week, you know!"

"But that's taking away a major part of our cast and our main character!" Chanie cried. "That's crazy!"

"I'm really sorry," Ruti said, "but we need to work on our Shabbaton."

Ahuva threw the script she had been holding on the floor and I honestly thought she would begin stomping on it in a second. "Fine!" she said, throwing her hands up into the air. "But if this play doesn't happen, no one has the right to blame me!" She stomped out of the auditorium.

Chanie was being comforted by a group of Freshies.

"And all the Juniors here!" Ruti said, very officially making a little check on the clipboard she was holding. "We're working on the Shabbaton now and every night this week! So let's get to the lounge, where there's a meeting."

Some girls were happy to get out of practice, and to tell you the truth, I kind of would have been happy, too, if I could have gone home like the Freshies, Sophies and Seniors. But, no. I had to go work on the Shabbaton, where they would probably be making centerpieces and cheering on the top of their lungs. So it would probably be just like color war. Except without the eggs.

We headed to the lounge, Chaiky chattering nonsensically in my ear all the while about how granite counters were not actually made of granite, but were really made out of igneous rocks or something. Like, I had waited my entire life to know that. I smiled and nodded. That works sometimes, you know.

The lounge was a busy wreck of activity. All one hundred and two girls in my grade were there, hustling and bustling around. In one corner, there were girls making long lists and calling out things like, "Jelly fish!" and "Harmonicas!" I assumed they were working on welcoming kits. In another corner, girls were taking Styrofoam pieces out of a big box and there was paint there, too; they were probably making the centerpieces. Another group of girls had millions and millions of bags of chocolate chips, flour, sugar, and, you guessed it, eggs. They probably were the baking committee, and as much as I love baking, I vowed to stay away from them because the last time I encountered eggs in school, the results were not pretty. Some things just aren't meant to mix together. Like oil and water, if you know what I mean.

"Okay!" said a familiar voice. "To the girls who have just come in!" It was Tova. Chaiky jabbed me with her elbow and gave me a smile, like we were sharing some kind of private joke or something. I smiled wanly at her.

"If every girl could please join whatever group she wants, that would be great! The group in the left corner of the room is working on the welcoming kits; in the right corner, they're working on baking; and right here next to me, they're working on centerpieces. Oh, and the girls who are in charge of entertainment are in Morah Herman's room, and the girls who are in choir are in Morah Benjamin's room. So if you could please join a group, that would be great!" She sounded kind of nervous to me. But maybe that was just my imagination.

"I'm going to join the choir," Chaiky said, poking me again.

"Ow, Chaiky, stop poking me!" I said. "And I don't really feel like singing, so no, I'm not joining the choir."

"Come on, just for your best friend, would ya?" Chaiky pleaded, getting on her knees and raising her eyes upward.

"Stop it, Chaiky," I said. This was so embarrassing. Why did Chaiky always make herself into such a show? It was like she was dying for a drop of attention. "This isn't a personal thing. I don't like singing."

"Please, please, please, please, please, please, please — "

"No!" I said. I walked away to find Tzippa and Naomi. I was not allowed to be left alone with Chaiky Cukier ever again.

My friends were by the welcoming kits table, which I suppose is a good thing, because it doesn't take much intelligence or thought to fill a basket with food and trinkets, does it?

"Hey, guys," I muttered.

"Where were you?" Naomi said accusingly. "Tzippa and I were looking for you."

"We were worried," Tzippa said.

"Sorry, Chaiky Cukier kidnapped me and then she tried to brainwash me to the dark side."

Naomi rolled her eyes. "Why won't that girl leave you alone?"

"Naomi!" Tzippa gasped.

"What?" Naomi said. "She follows Ella around like a puppy. I mean, is there a reason for this? It's not normal behavior. And that's in addition to the fact that she's not normal. You know? Like today in the car, that was so weird. I'm really serious — is she, like, mentally okay?"

"I think she just wants attention," Tzippa said.

"And Ella's the only one who can give it to her?" Naomi guf-
fawed. "Don't be ridiculous. I don't know why she just doesn't hang
out with her own friends and leave us alone!"

"Naomi!" Tzippa gasped again.

"Would you gossipmongers like to tell us what you think is a
good idea for the package?" Ruti asked, coming over to us. Great,
she was the head of this group? Like, it just couldn't be anyone else?
"Ella, how about you? Any ideas?"

"I don't have any ideas," I muttered. Wrong thing to say. Now
she would try to psychoanalyze me. I just knew it.

"You must have some idea," Ruti said, giving me a green-eyed
gaze.

"I really don't know," I said. Why wouldn't she just leave me
alone? Or at least start a little fan club or something, where they
could all talk about how they wanted to help me and befriend me,
just as long as it didn't involve me being there.

"Nothing? Nothing at all? Come on, Ella, I expect more from
you!"

"Okay," I muttered, just to get her away. "Maybe give out those
CDs where someone sings *Perek Shirah* on them. Or better yet, the
Yehuda! *Perek Shirah* CD which I've been dying to get."

"That is such a good idea!" Ruti squealed. "Hey, everyone, wanna
hear Ella Sender's idea?" Everyone turned around and looked at me
expectantly. Oh, great.

"No, you tell them, Ruti," I muttered. I was about to walk away,
when Ruti actually grabbed my arm and made me face everyone.

"No, you tell them, Ella. It was *your* idea."

This was lovely. I bet she thought she was racking up some serious *mitzvos*.

"Okay," I said as quickly as I could. "My idea is to give out *Perek Shirah* CDs, like the Yehuda! ones. That's it!"

"Isn't that such a wonderful idea!" Ruti gushed.

Tova, who had appeared out of nowhere, gave me a proud look.

Gag me with a spoon.

I had to get out of this place now. I mean, I had done my civic duty and thought of a wonderful idea, which I was so sure everyone loved, but no, I could not stay. I had to get out. Before I went stir crazy. There were way too many people here, in this small space, and no offense, but I felt really tired. This day had been too long.

"Hey, Tzippa," I whispered, staying as far away as I could from Ruti Reuben. "Still got your car here?"

Tzippa nodded.

"Let's ditch this place," I said.

Naomi beamed at me. "I was waiting for you to say that," she said, grabbing my hand and Tzippa's hand. "Let's go!"

18

IT WAS A LITTLE BIT drizzly outside, but I honestly felt like I was escaping from jail. The millions of girls screaming and laughing, the disgusting smell of paint, Chaiky, Ruti — it was enough to make anyone go mad. I mean, it's not that I don't love my grade and everything. Well, actually, I don't *love* them; that would be a bit too extreme and totally mushy. I mean, the best way to say it is that I can stand them, you know? But some days are bad. Like today. I just like to be alone sometimes, you know? It's not that I don't like to socialize and like I'm anti-social; it's just that I need a little quiet time sometimes, or else I feel totally drained.

I took a Jung typology test once, just for fun, and not because I honestly think that a bunch of questions in a book (*Please Understand Me*, just in case you're wondering) are enough to place me in a little, labeled box (yeah, I know I'm complex), because labels are for shirts, and the last time I fit into a box was when I was two. Anyway, I'm an introvert. Most people don't understand me. They think I'm shy, or snobby, or anti-social, but the thing is, I'm just tired. I need time alone to rejuvenate. I don't like being put in the limelight. I don't like everyone staring at me, and it's not because I'm insecure.

It's just because I'm introverted. It explains a lot of things about me, really. But unfortunately, only twenty-five percent of the population is introverted, so not too many people understand why I don't like color war, and why I don't like Shabbatons, and why I sometimes don't even like recess. Thank Hashem that Naomi and Tzippa are introverted, too. I think that's why we ended up together; we are really different, but then, at the same time, we're very alike.

"Singin' in the rain!" Naomi sang under her breath as we headed to Tzippa's car. *Baruch Hashem*, we had made a clean getaway (read, no interference).

"It's a glorious feeling, isn't it, Naomi?" Tzippa said, raising her eyebrow.

"You don't even know," I said. "Anyone else felt stifled there?"

"Stifled?" Naomi laughed as we got into the car. She sat in the front near Tzippa, and I sat in the back. "I was practically being strangled!"

"Come on," Tzippa said, as she started the engine. "It wasn't that bad!"

Naomi and I both laughed. We sometimes joke that Tzippa is going to head to the extraverted side of life, but we both know that she's too nice for that.

"So, where to?" Tzippa asked, drumming the steering wheel as we waited at a red light.

Chinese. Definitely Chinese. I hadn't had it in the longest time.

"And don't," Tzippa said, giving me a look in the mirror, "say Chinese, Ella! Because I can practically see it spelled out on your face."

"Awww, come on!" I kvetched. "We haven't gone to Chinn's Kitchen in such a long time! And Shanghai Wok — we haven't gone there for, like, forever!"

"No Chinese," Naomi said. "Just the thought of all those fried vegetables makes me gag. How do you eat that stuff without gaining weight, Ella?"

"I have lemons for breakfast," I said with a smirk.

"Mhmm," Naomi said smirking back. "Healthy diet."

"I know."

"So, what's it gonna be? Are you guys just gonna sit there and bicker? Should I turn this car around and go back home?" Tzippa said playfully.

"Nooooo," I said. "Don't take me home!"

"Are things really that bad?" Tzippa asked, again catching my eye in the rear-view mirror.

"Nightmarish. Last night, Yaffa and Margalit barged into my room. Yaffa broke my computer and Margalit, the book thief, got her goo all over my bed."

"She still has that goo?" Naomi asked with a confused look on her face.

"Don't ask."

"Wait, which book did she steal?" Tzippa said.

I fiddled with my bag. "The one you wanted to read. I was wondering where it went and then I see it in her hands. And she was all, like, casual about it."

Tzippa groaned. "Naomi, maybe we should just take Ella to Chinese. You can get a salad or something."

"I always do that anyway, don't I?" Naomi said.

That meant yes! Yay! I loved my friends.

I smelled egg rolls and soy sauce and yummy chicken frying as we walked into Chinn's Kitchen. We sat at one of the little tables in the back of the restaurant, near the window, and the waiter gave us menus and water and said he'd be back soon.

"So, what are you ordering?" Tzippa asked me with a wry smile.

"Oh, everything. Beef sticks, hot and sour soup, General Tsao's Chicken, Schezuan Chicken — I think I'll take the works!"

"Glutton," Naomi said with a sigh.

"You just want to eat it, too!" I said. "Just splurge, this once! We'll order one order of everything so we get only a third of all the calories."

Naomi closed her eyes. "I wish…"

"Wishes come true!" I proclaimed. "Eh, garçon!" I motioned to our waiter.

"What does that mean?" Naomi asked.

"Waiter," Tzippa said. "And I know because I've gone out to lunch with Nana before, and she's asked me what we call the garçon, the man wearing the black pants and white shirt. It took me a few times to catch on."

We all laughed.

"Can I help you ladies?" the waiter said, returning to our table.

"Yes," I said. "We want to share, so could you please bring three bowls of hot and sour soup, three beef sticks, and one General Tsao's Chicken and one Schezuan Chicken?"

"Sure," he said, scribbling it all down on his pad. "It'll probably take around fifteen minutes."

We nodded and he left.

"So, who's excited about this Shabbaton?" Naomi said with a dry laugh as she sat back on her chair.

I noticed that there were large bags under her blue eyes. She looked tired. Of course, I didn't blame her. Her long blonde hair was in a loose braid that wasn't tied at the bottom — it just ended, and she was wearing the navy school sweater.

"I'm sorry to say this," Tzippa said in an apologetic voice, "but I'm really not. I just need a break, you know?"

Tzippa is naturally petite, but for some reason, she seemed to look even tinier today. Her face was pale, and her huge brown eyes seemed to take up half her face. Her dark brown hair was held back from her face with a slender black clip. She pursed her thin cherry lips. "I mean, I don't want anyone to think I'm a party pooper or anything, but don't you just wish we could stay home?"

"Even I wish I could stay home and lock myself up in my room," I said, brushing my dark hair away from my face. "I mean, next Shabbos is step-auntie Adele's Shabbos *sheva brachos*, and I need to save all my energy for then. I don't know how I'm gonna deal with it."

"Well, you're lucky," Naomi said. "At least Michal won't order you to do this and that for her, because she's not your mother. But whatever I do for my mom, she still always makes me feel like I'm at fault. It's all like, 'Naomi, why didn't you do this, and why didn't you do that?' And I'm like, 'Hello, Ma, I have a life, and I'm a slave here!' And then there's that speech about my attitude and how I have to set an example for my ten little siblings. Well, I didn't ask to be the oldest — that's all I can say!" Naomi's cheeks were flushed and she started playing with the glass of water in front of her.

I got what she was saying about the example part. I mean, in the beginning, Tova used to tell me that I had to set a good example for Margalit and Yaffa, and honestly, that was the most irritating thing in the world. But Naomi was wrong about the mother part. I was so not lucky to have Michal. I would much rather have my own mother, even if she gave me a million chores to do. I couldn't say that, of course, because then Tzippa would shoot Naomi a look and they'd both be really quiet for a minute, and then Naomi would say she was sorry in this uncharacteristic, so not 'her,' apologetic voice. And for the rest of the evening, everyone would be kind of avoiding any particular subject.

So, I didn't say anything; I just nodded sympathetically. Sometimes silence speaks a great deal more than words do.

"Well," Tzippa said, clicking her clip open and letting her hair fall softly around her face, "I just don't know what to do anymore. Everyone is so worried about Chana, because she didn't come home last night and everything. She has this new friend, Sheva, who I don't think is exactly the best person in the world, if you know what I mean. Two nights ago, when she came home, she smelled weird, you know? And she and my father got into this huge, huge fight and then she just left and — " Tzippa stopped, put her hair back in its clip, and looked at us. "Sorry, guys, I don't mean to burden you with my problems."

We just stared at her. Tzippa is the nicest person I know, but she's just kind of closed when it comes to her problems — you know what I mean? She never rants like Naomi and I usually do. She takes everything in such stride that Naomi and I sometimes wonder if she's real. Then, at a moment like this, when she's finally getting something off her chest, she immediately clams up because she doesn't want to burden us. I'm sorry, but Tzippa is just not real. She's amazing.

"What do you mean?" Naomi asked.

"I don't want to burden anyone."

"So you're saying that when Ella and I kvetch, and we do it a lot, we're burdening you?" Naomi said pointedly. She's never been one to soft-edge words, you know? Naomi just like throws them.

Tzippa flushed. "No, no, not at all," she protested. She sat up a little straighter in her chair. "It's just that, well, I don't know. No one at home wants to hear, you know? Chana's the one in her own crazy world, Ayalah's busy with her own family, and poor Shana, she's going crazy with *shidduchim* and school, and Eli's always in yeshivah except for Shabbos, so I don't want to burden any of them, and well…"

"Tzippa, we're your friends," I said softly. "We're here for you."

"You mean it?" Tzippa said meekly.

"Always and forever," Naomi said.

Then the waiter came with our delicious food and totally ruined the moment.

W HEN I GOT HOME THAT night, it was pretty late. Okay, really late. Chinn's Kitchen is in Manhattan, and there had been a ton of traffic coming back to Flatbush. I mean, I knew curfew on school nights was ten, but it was only eleven now. And this had not been my fault, because since when do I control New York's highways?

I had tried to call home. But the line was busy. All night. I supposed Michal was talking to Adele about last-minute wedding preparations, like she always seemed to be doing these past few days. Adele had asked Michal to host her *chassan's* brother and his wife who were coming in from Eretz Yisrael for the wedding. Adele was all into the fact that it was the first time they were leaving Eretz Yisrael in like eleven years, and how exciting it all was for everyone.

Well, when I got home, Father Doom and Sister Gloom were waiting for me by the door. Michal, I am pleased to say, was not there.

My father was standing by the door, his arms crossed. Tova's face was a picture of complete shock. I knew — since we're twins and we have this telepathic thing going for us — that she was thinking about the talk she'd had with me, and she was probably wondering how I could still misbehave after it. Well, Tova didn't realize that the sweet words she'd spoken to me during our talk — they didn't mean anything at all, not if they weren't backed by some action on her part. Perfect Goodness had been so busy trying to prove to Yaffa and Margalit that even though I didn't love them, *she* still thought they were the cutest little dolls that ever walked this planet, that she had forgotten about loving her real sister — me. Why didn't my family realize that even though I was a big girl, I still needed love?

"Explain!" my father thundered as soon as I walked into the house. No "Good evening" or "Hi, Ella, how're you doing?" Just an angry command, as if I was in court or something. The sad part was that even though there was a prosecutor and a judge, I had neither a jury nor a lawyer.

"There was traffic!" I said. "I can't control traffic!"

"But you can control the time you leave, and you can tell Tova where you're going, can't you?"

"We left almost two hours ago, but there was so much traffic! And is Tova my babysitter?"

"You're acting like you need a babysitter."

"That's because you're treating me like a baby. I'm only an hour late. You don't trust me."

My father took a deep breath. "This is not a matter of trust, Yellie — "

"Don't call me that!" I shrieked. "I can't believe my own father would call me that abhorrent name!"

"Don't be a drama queen."

"I am not a drama queen!"

"Oh, yes, you are!" Tova interfered. "Everything is about you, Ayelet. You, you, you. You never stop and think about other people. Do you realize how worried we all were about you just now? You never stop to think if other people are worrying about you. You just care about yourself. And you are a drama queen. Everything is blown up into huge proportions, and it's always about how miserable your life is, and how horrible everything is, and you're really nothing but a big kvetch!"

Which was so not true! And besides, who did she think she was, butting in like this?

"I'm not interested in what you have to say! You're not my mother!"

"Oh, go cry now, Ayelet, because you don't have a mom. That's how it always is for you. One big sob story. Well, guess what! My mother's dead, too, and you don't see me acting like a total psychopath, do you?"

"Oh, you're acting real calm now!" I yelled back, tears streaming down my face. "Maybe because you're an ice princess, and you don't feel anything, and you like to keep everything all bottled up inside of you, you're as hard as a rock. Well, get over it, Tova — just because we're identical twins does not mean I'm you and that I always have to act like you and be as perfect as you. I don't want to be perfect! Perfect is boring! And I told you to butt out! Daddy doesn't need your help disciplining me, do you, Daddy?"

My father looked confused about our little catfight. Tova and I rarely fight, but when we do, hoo-boy. "No, Tova, that's enough. You can go upstairs."

A mixture of shock and anger flashed on Tova's face and then she headed upstairs with an obedient, "Yes, Daddy."

When Tova left, my father stared at me. Like he honestly didn't know where I had come from and he didn't know what to do with me. I've gotten that look from him a lot before. It's a look of anger, amazement, shock, and confusion all in one.

"Why don't we sit down on the couch and talk about this?" my father said, pointing to the comfy purple couches in the living room.

"Okay," I muttered.

We sat down and my father took another deep breath, like he was trying to think of what to say.

"Why were you late?"

"I told you," I said, trying to keep my voice even. I would respect my father. I would respect my father. I. Would. Respect. My. Father. "There was a lot of traffic. Honestly, I didn't mean to disregard the curfew, but there was nothing I could do. We left the restaurant a drop after nine. We didn't think it would take so long to get back home. Really."

"Why didn't you tell Tova you left?"

"I thought she saw me leaving," I said. And honestly, I did. She was standing right near Ruti Reuben when Tzippa, Naomi, and I left. Couldn't she have figured it out? "Plus, I tried to call home like a trillion times, but the phone was busy, busy, busy."

I knew my father didn't know what to do. He could punish me, but it wasn't really my fault, and he knew it. On the other hand, he wasn't used to just dropping charges against me.

My father stared at me again.

"Please, Daddy," I said in my meekest voice ever. "I promise to leave even earlier next time." An idea began to form in my head. "And you know what? If you want, just to make sure I learned my lesson, you can ground me. Until Adele's wedding."

"You want to be grounded?" my father said with a confused expression on his face.

"I think it's time I realize that there are consequences for my actions," I said in a serious voice. The words sounded familiar for some reason, and I figured they fit well in this context.

My father smiled broadly. "Wow, Ella," he said. "That's a very mature thing to say. I must say, I'm proud you've realized this!"

He looked at me for a moment, and then his smile disappeared.

"You're having a Shabbaton this week, aren't you?"

Busted.

"Um, yeah," I said.

"Forget it," my father said. He sighed. Then he looked into my eyes. "Ella, I want you to go to this Shabbaton, and to have a positive attitude about it and not give Tova a hard time. She's working really hard on this."

"Yeah, I know," I muttered.

Why were my best plans always ruined?

"And I want you to behave towards our guests next week, and to have a good attitude at Adele's wedding, too."

"I'll try, Daddy," I muttered.

"Now, go to bed."

"Okay," I said. I gave my father a quick peck on the cheek and headed to my room. On my desk was a letter in a crude, first-grader's handwriting. Great, Yaffa and Margalit had been in my room again. I picked up the letter and began to read it.

"Dear Ella," it said. All at once I was gratified that they hadn't called me Yellie. "We are sorry we came into your room without permission last night. We did not mean to break your computer, take your book, or get your bed messy. We hope you won't scream at us again, because that makes us feel sad. We want you to forgive us. Love, your sisters, Yaffa and Margalit."

I did deserve that apology. Ever single word of it. So why did I feel like I was going to cry?

20

THE REST OF THE WEEK passed by pretty quickly. Tova wasn't speaking to me, and to tell you the truth, I wasn't really speaking to her, either, so the warm, sisterly feeling between us was totally mutual. Every afternoon was another meeting with the welcoming kit committee girls, who were seriously starting to irritate me. Ever since I had regaled them with my ah-may-zing idea, they just wouldn't leave me alone. It was like I was their wunderkind and I was bursting with oodles and oodles of ideas. All I had to do was use my noodle, right? Please. My brain was so tired. I mean, there were only so many things I could come up with, and after the CD, musical note stickers, honey (because it's good for your voice), lily-pad candles (continuing the frog theme), gushers (just because I like them), and benchers with Shabbos *zemiros*, my brain was seriously overworked. On Wednesday, when all we did was fill the little bags they had gotten (covered with smiley faces that had their eyes closed and mouths open, like they were all singing), I felt like I was on vacation.

And so, Thursday afternoon, they let us out early from school because we were leaving bright and early Friday morning. After hanging out in The Coffee Room with Naomi and Tzippa for about an hour, I headed home to pack. I was really not at all excited for this. I mean, I hate packing, because it takes me hours and hours to put everything in a teeny little suitcase, or two teeny little suitcases (they're never big enough for me), depending on the occasion. What's worse is that when I get home, I have to unpack everything, put my clean clothes back in the drawers and sort between my clean socks and dirty socks, put all the dirty stuff in the laundry, and my room always ends up being the biggest mess, so I have to clean it up, too. It's all very annoying and tedious. At least we were going to a hotel. Every year, our school goes to a camp for Retreat, and it's just horrible. I have to pack my entire life, linen, towels, pillows, everything. And it's for four days. When I come back, everything goes in the laundry.

The house was pretty quiet because Michal was out shopping with her little girls, getting some stuff for our guests. I mean, why couldn't they have at least offered to take me shopping with them? They were going to Bed, Bath and Beyond, which was right near a lot of great clothing stores. And Tova was invited to join their little outing.

Maybe it was actually better that I hadn't gone. I opened up my closet and stared at the clothes in it. I had nothing to wear. I mean, if I would tell my father that, he would probably hit the roof and be like, "What are you talking about; you have a closet full of clothes!" But no one understands that having a closet full of clothes doesn't mean you have something to wear. I mean, I do thank Hashem for providing clothes for the unclothed every morning, and I know I'm really lucky to have so many nice outfits, but the thing is, Tova's picked out half of them, so I completely abhor them because they're so nerdy and everything. As far as the rest of them, I've probably worn a million times or else they're probably out of style now. As much as I advocate not following the styles and groupthink and everything, and the importance of being an individual, who wants to look like a dweeb at their school Shabbaton?

Definitely not me.

I mean, honestly, it's nothing more than one big fashion show, and when people see you, they give you this long up-down and then they're like, "Good Shabbos", like, oh, I wasn't just staring at you. It's completely ridiculous, and I'm totally a part of it, so what would I wear? I could always wear my black suit again. That was classic. But it was sooo boring. I mean, it's the boringest suit you'll ever see in your entire life. There's nothing wrong with it, but there's nothing right about it, either. Oh, it looks nice on me. And yeah, it never goes out of style. Which is good in a sense. But bad in another sense.

Then I could wear a black cashmere turtleneck and black skirt with box pleats during the day. People would definitely be like, "Whoa, Ella, that's a whole lot of black," but the thing is, I happen to like the color black. After all, black *is* the queen of all colors.

Then again, I could always wear that long, tiered mocha-brown skirt that I had picked up on sale a few weeks ago, with my brown shirt that was almost exactly the same color. And then, on top, I could wear that sweater with the huge collar and the gold studs. That was cool. And I had never worn that before. And... and... I had the amber and gold necklace that my grandmother had given me for my fourteenth birthday; that would match perfectly. I sighed contentedly to myself. It was nice when these things worked out. I was totally wearing that; it would be perfect for Shabbos day.

But what would I wear Friday night? I knew I could always wear black, if worse came to worst, but which black outfit? (Understandably, a large chunk of my closet is black.) I lay on my back and stared at my closet from my upside-down angle.

This was hard. And it was hurting my neck. I stood up, rubbed my neck, and heard footsteps pounding in the hall. "Hello, everyone! We're home!" It was Michal.

All of a sudden, Yaffa and Margalit came stampeding into my room. What did they think? That this place was Grand Central Station or something?

"What are you doing?" Yaffa asked.

"I'm trying to find something to wear," I said distractedly, as I searched through my closet. I was so not wearing that nauseating pink outfit that Tova had bought for me. I mean, it had flowers on it! How last spring was that?

"How come you didn't come shopping with us?" Yaffa asked. I glanced at them. They looked quite cozy on my bed, even though I had replaced my beautiful silk comforter with this polyester blend one that I had found in the closet. Margalit was sitting in front of Yaffa, her almond brown eyes looking straight ahead as Yaffa expertly braided her auburn hair. Yaffa, who looks more like Michal, had her yellow hair in a neat pony, and although she was interrogating me, her dove gray eyes were completely focused on her sister's hair.

"Because I wasn't invited," I muttered, trying to block them out of my mind. I could always wear my purple and black outfit, but the question was, was it too purple? I didn't want anyone to get the wrong impression of me, you know?

"Tova came," Yaffa said, looking up. "And she got such pretty outfits, right, Margo?"

Margalit nodded, causing Yaffa to scream because she was messing up her hair. "Such pretty clothes," she said. "One was pink and had a little pretty bow, and the other one was purple and the skirt was so long and nice and Tovi got this little nice flower she's gonna wear on it!"

"How come Tovi came and you didn't come?" Yaffa asked.

Why all these questions? How was I supposed to know the answers? Why couldn't they just leave me alone?

"I don't know," I muttered.

"I know," Margalit said brightly, looking up. "It's because Tovi likes us and you don't, so you didn't wanna come!"

I blinked. Whatever I had been expecting her to say, it hadn't been this. How was I supposed to answer that?

I just grunted. Non-answers are really good sometimes.

"Why don't you like us, Yellie?" Yaffa asked conversationally. I noticed that she had stopped braiding Margalit's hair, and they were both looking at me curiously, like I was some kind of interesting alien or something, bringing news to them about my own planet.

I could feel my ears burn. They always do when I'm embarrassed, but I couldn't really figure out what I was embarrassed about. I mean, if they would stop calling me Yellie and only come into my room when invited, they would be a lot more likeable.

"You know," Yaffa said, coming to hold my hand, "when my Ima married your Daddy, she told me that you were going to be my best friend."

I stared at her. I could feel my eyes widening. Okay, this was seriously starting to scare me. They had to leave. Now. I had to pack.

"So," Yaffa continued, "even though you don't like me, we're still best friends, right? Because yesterday, Gila didn't want to share her snack with me, so we're not best friends anymore."

"Yeah!" Margalit said, coming to hold my other hand. "Be my best friend, too!"

My tongue seriously felt like a dentist had injected it with Novocain and it was all heavy and yucky. I couldn't speak.

Yaffa wrapped her arms around my waist and gave me a big hug. Margalit looked at her and then threw her arms around me, too. I stood there for a moment, completely confounded. I wasn't sure what had just happened, but I figured that if any of the neighbors were watching through the gaps in their blind shades, it would look kind of weird if I didn't hug my stepsisters back. So, somewhat reluctantly, I put one arm around Yaffa and the other one around Margalit.

"Best friends forever!" Yaffa sighed happily.

"Yeah!" Margalit said.

I could almost hear the narrator of my life say in a contented voice, "Ella, I think this is the beginning of a beautiful friendship."

Well, that was lovely and all, and I guess I couldn't be upset about it, unless they thought this gave them an open invitation to come into my room at all hours and a new reason to call me Yellie. It was actually pretty nice, I suppose.

But that didn't solve my other problem.

What was I going to wear to this Shabbaton?

ICE WAS IN MY NOSE. It was too early and it was too cold out-side. I mean, it was five in the morning and there I was, stand-ing outside of the school building with Tzippa and Naomi. (I had gotten a ride with Tzippa.) I didn't know where Tova was. She had disappeared with her luggage last night around one. Ruti Reuben and the other heads weren't there, either.

"Hello!" Chaiky Cukier said, bouncing up to me. All she was holding was a sports bag. You know. The type you take to the gym with you. I had three suitcases and one suit-bag with me. "You know, I heard it's supposed to snow this weekend!"

"Well, I wouldn't doubt that, since it's January and we do live in New York," Tzippa said, tightening the polka-dot scarf around her neck.

Naomi didn't say anything. She hadn't had her morning coffee yet. It wasn't like we could just go to Starbucks and pick something up for her. No. We had a four-hour drive to the mountains. I didn't know how she was going to manage. Some of us are not morning people.

"Ella, wanna sit with me on the bus?" Chaiky said, poking me.

I was lucky if I didn't have a black and blue mark by the end of the weekend.

I didn't know what to answer her. It wasn't like I could say no. And it wasn't like I could lie and say that I had promised Tzippa I would sit with her or something. So, I just stared at her, and then Morah Bluestein came and yelled about how she was going to read off the bus lists to us, and would everyone please stop talking and listen up. Because, yes, there were three buses and she had split us up completely randomly.

I had never loved that woman more in my life.

Chaiky wasn't on my bus. Neither was Tzippa. Nor Naomi.

This was not a very promising beginning. Actually, it was quite an ominous premonition. I could feel my stomach doing a little cartwheel. Who was I going to sit with on the bus? Was I going to have to sit near some chatty girl who would want to go on and on and on about her life and last month's vacation to Los Angeles? I didn't think I could handle that. I probably would die.

"Okay, girls," Morah Bluestein said. "You all have to put your luggage under the buses yourselves. A good idea would be to put it under the bus that you're on. Like, if you're on bus number one, you should put your luggage on bus one."

I was on bus three, and I headed to the end of the block where my bus was parked. Unfortunately, everyone else who was on my bus was already there, sticking her Louis Vuittons under the bus, and there I stood, waiting for someone to move. There were like a thousand girls with little hats and scarves in every color of the rainbow milling around, and my head was starting to hurt. I was not going to be able to deal with a whole weekend of this. I was not.

Finally, the area cleared up and everyone went on the bus, and then I stared at the space under the bus. Only, there wasn't any space left there anymore. Every inch of it was already filled to the brim with luggage. How was I going to get all my stuff under the bus?

"Ayelet Sender!" Morah Bluestein said, coming up to me. I was standing there staring at the bus. "Why aren't you on the bus yet? We have to take attendance. It's very late and we should have left twenty minutes ago."

"Well, there's no space for my luggage!" I protested.

It was as if she had just realized the small sea of luggage surrounding me. She bent over and looked under the bus.

"Oh," she said.

Oh.

We stood there for a moment, staring at each other (I had a bad feeling that there would be a lot of staring going on this weekend), and then her face lit up, like she had just had a wonderful idea.

"I know!" she said. "You can put your luggage in my car! I'm driving up with you girls." She smiled at me.

That was actually a really good idea, because my luggage was so not going to get crushed or thrown into the icy mud if it was in her car. So, I smiled back.

"My car is right there," she said, pointing to a silver sedan. "And," she smiled again, "the trunk is totally empty because my husband and kids are coming later and bringing my stuff."

"I really appreciate this, Morah Bluestein," I said.

"No problem," she said as she helped me lift my suitcases into her car. Finally, everything was secure. "Now, go get on your bus, because I have to take attendance!"

I got on the bus, but every single seat was full. I gulped. I walked down the aisle and finally found an empty seat. Okay, that was the pro. The con was that the girl sitting in the seat right next to it was Rochel Black. Rochel looked at me for a second, her eyes all icy. Then, she picked up the little bag that was on her lap and put in on the empty seat. Then, she stuck her headphones into her ears and stared out the window so she wouldn't see my shocked expression.

Excuse me! Who did she think she was? Did her father own this bus or something? Where was I supposed to sit?

I headed to the back of the bus and then saw another empty seat. It was right in front of the bathroom, and right across the aisle from the only three-seat row, where Suri Greenberger, Elana Moscovitz, and Shiffi Epstein were sitting, heads together, giggling about something. Random, indeed. How did those three best friends end up together? Why couldn't I end up with Naomi and Tzippa? Why did I end up alone?

I sat in the lone seat. This would only happen to me. I took my iPod out of my bag and stuck Shwekey's *Yedid* into my ears. Something told me that this was going to be a loooong ride. I get lucky with these things, you see.

Everyone around me was chattering happily, so I turned my iPod up to its highest volume until all I could hear was, "*Shema, Shema Yisrael...when you feel pain, when you rejoice, know how He longs to hear your voice...*" And all I could think was, "Hashem, get me out of here!"

Music has that quality sometimes. It makes you think what it "feels," you know what I mean? I mean, I used to listen to secular music until a while ago, but then I realized that when the composers were making their music up, they probably were so not thinking the type of things I want in my mind. But Shwekey and Yehuda! probably were. So, that's why I listen to them and singers like them from now on. I mean, if I'm going to let someone scream into my head for four hours, it might as well be someone whose ideals I agree with. Yeah, I know that sounds sanctimonious, kind of, and I know I'm not perfect. But neither is anyone.

I stared out the window. We were leaving the city, and soon we were in the country. Before I knew it, we were pulling up in front of this grand hotel that looked like a big castle. Everyone was all excited and everything and they were gathering their stuff and getting off the bus, except that I wasn't really too excited.

I was the last one off the bus. Morah Bluestein was standing in front of everyone, giving orders.

"Okay, everyone is going to dump their things in the hotel lobby for now and then we're going to go for brunch. After brunch, the folders that say what room and workshop everyone is in will be handed out, and then you girls can go snow-tubing or ice-skating on the hotel grounds for an hour. Then, you're all welcome back for a snack, and then it's time for Shabbos preparations! Shabbos starts at four-thirty!"

I went up to her. "Morah Bluestein, where should I get my luggage from?"

"Oh, don't worry," she said with a laugh. "The hotel staff already put it in your room for you! They thought it was mine, because it was in my car, so they took it out for me, and I just sent them to your room with it!"

Well, that was a relief. I thanked her and went off to find Naomi and Tzippa. But I was kind of nervous now. I mean, who would be in my room? What if it was someone who completely ignored me? Or what if it was someone like Chaiky Cukier? I took a deep breath. I was going to be placed with Naomi and Tzippa. I had to be placed with them.

Naomi and Tzippa were standing by the coffee bar in the dining room, and Naomi looked like she was going to die if she didn't get a French vanilla blend soon.

"What's up, guys?" I asked, sliding onto the stool next to them.

"Don't ask!" Naomi said, rubbing her temples. "You don't want to know!"

Tzippa clucked sympathetically. "She had to sit with Chaiky Cukier on the bus, because they were both on bus number two, and I was on bus one."

"It's like, you know, she can't stop talking," Naomi said as she filled a cup with hot water and then mixed in the coffee. "I'm drinking this black, by the way." She took a huge gulp, grimaced for a second, and then exhaled deeply. "The whole time it was about this and that and about how pearls melt in vinegar, and that ants don't sleep, and that fish don't have eyelids, and gosh, I don't know, like one quarter of the human brain is used to control the eyes, and all this stuff that I just didn't want to know. And my brain was screaming, 'Overload, overload!' but gosh, she just wouldn't stop, you know?"

"Whoa," I said. "And I thought sitting alone was bad."

Tzippa shook her head sadly at me. "You, too? The seat near the bathroom?"

I nodded.

"Oh, and it gets worse," Naomi said with a bitter laugh as she gulped down some more coffee. "Then, she asked me how I make my hair like that. You know, my bump with the clips? And she told me she's going to always wear her hair like that from now on! I'm never wearing my hair like that again!"

All of a sudden, I noticed that Chaiky was hanging around and her face was this weird shade of pink. She saw me looking at her, gave me this huge smile and waved madly, and then walked over to me, holding a plate full of bonbons and éclairs.

"Hi!" she gushed, as if I was her long-lost sister or someone whom she hadn't seen in months and months.

"Hi," I muttered.

Naomi practically growled, and Tzippa looked at Chaiky and said, "I don't think this is really the best time."

"Okay!" Chaiky said brightly. "Ellaloo, wanna come with me to get more cookies?"

"No," I said. Why didn't she get it? "I'm on a diet."

"Oh, they have the sugar-free type, too. They have these scrumptious blueberry turnovers! You'll never guess they weren't made with sugar!"

"No," I said again. "I want to have a coffee now." I didn't really, but I took a cup anyway and started filling it with hot water.

"Okay," Chaiky said. She sounded a little bit meeker than before and she kept blinking her eyes rapidly, but she still had that big smile on her face. "I guess I'll see you later, then."

"Later," I muttered.

"See!" Naomi said the second Chaiky had turned away. "She just won't leave us alone! It's like she's some kind of gnat or something."

"Naomi!" Tzippa gasped.

"What! It's true!"

"Guys, I'm really scared," I said.

"Yeah, I'm scared, too," Naomi fumed. "I'm going to end up in the loony bin if someone does not keep that kid away from me!"

"That's just the point! They're not putting us with friends by this thing," I said.

"What do you mean?" Tzippa asked.

"I mean, they're splitting us up randomly, so we can make new friends and meet other people!"

"No way," Naomi said angrily. She banged her cup of coffee on the counter. "That's ridiculous! I came here to spend time with my friends, not some snobby JAPs!"

Tzippa looked like she was going to cry. "I don't think I can handle an entire weekend of sitting in the one seat by the bathroom."

My heart went out to her. As hard as these things are for me, it's probably even worse for shy Tzippa.

I knew there were totally some girls who wouldn't have a problem with smiling at new people and pretending to love people they really didn't care a stitch about. But for me, and for Tzippa and Naomi, it's really not that easy. Besides for the fact that we're introverts, and besides for the fact that everyone thinks we're these bad girls (Naomi and I brought this shame upon ourselves, but for Tzippa, it's really because of her sister) — even though technically, we've never done anything wrong — Naomi was right. We came here to spend time with our friends. Why were we going to be divided up? Plus, I'm just not one of those smiley people, you know? It's just not me. People think I'm all sullen and everything. Or snobby. So that doesn't help the image.

"Girls," Morah Bluestein said, passing by us, "please help yourselves to sandwiches! This is your last meal until our Shabbos *seudah*."

Tzippa, who can practically pass as an anorexic, took two tuna sandwiches. "You guys want?" she said.

"Diet," Naomi and I said together.

Tzippa shrugged and laughed.

I ate an apple (I really wanted a lemon, but there were none in sight), Naomi drank three more cups of coffee and began to look a little more alive, and Tzippa ate her two sandwiches. Then, our folders came. Ruti Reuben was handing them out, going from group to group. She was taking an abnormally slow time, chatting with everyone merrily as she handed them their folders, and I could feel my stomach doing handstands, cartwheels and flips and practically begging me to go to the bathroom so I could throw up.

Finally, she got to us.

"Hi, Naomi! Hi, Tzippa! Hi, Ella!" she said, her tanned skin practically glowing. "You guys are going to have such an awesome time!" She handed Naomi, Tzippa and me these pink folders and flipped her golden hair. Then she winked at me.

Okay, I was going to throw up. Where was the bathroom?

As soon as she left, we all flipped over our folders and looked at the stickers on the other side that said which rooms and workshops we were in.

"I'm in room 302," Naomi announced.

Tzippa gulped. "I'm in 205."

"We're not even on the same floor!" Naomi yelled. "What am I going to do? This is like murder!"

"What about you, Ella?" Tzippa asked hopefully. "Which room are you in?"

"204," I muttered.

Tzippa sighed. "Okay, good, we're next door to each other. And Naomi, you can just hang out in our rooms the entire time."

"Good," Naomi said, taking a deep breath. "Maybe I'll just put my sleeping bag in your room, too."

"Ella," Tzippa said softly. "What's wrong?"

"I cannot handle this!" I said angrily. "I'm in the same room as Ruti Reuben, I just know it. On Monday she was all like, 'I'm going to make sure we're in the same room,' and right now she winked at me!"

Naomi groaned. "Who does Miss Perfect Golden Sunshine think she is, anyway?"

"I don't know," I muttered. "But I can't even handle one minute of her stupid smile."

"You can hang out in my room, too," Tzippa said. "Hopefully, there will be nice people there."

"Thanks, Tzippa," I said.

"Okay," Tzippa said, smiling weakly. "Let's go get our stuff."

"I don't have to." I smirked. "The bellboy already took my stuff to my room."

"Lucky girl," Naomi muttered. "You can help me with my stuff. I have to go all the way to the third floor."

I helped Naomi take her stuff to her room. We stood in front of the door and Naomi slowly turned the handle. "Well, this is it," she said slowly. "The moment of truth."

Her room wasn't so bad. The walls were soft yellow with a border of sunflowers. The four beds were made out of cherry wood and had bright yellow bedspreads. The carpeting was a cheery green color and on each bed was a welcoming package.

"Okay," Naomi said. "I pick this bed." She threw some of her stuff on the bed closest to the door. "For a quick escape, you know?"

I laughed.

Other people's stuff were already in the room. Some fancy luggage with a pink and white trim that looked pretty new, a sports bag, and a huge black suitcase.

Funny. Chaiky had brought a sports bag with her. I didn't think it would be best to mention this to Naomi, but just then, the bathroom door opened and out came Chaiky Cukier.

"No way!" she screeched happily. "Don't tell me you two are also in this room!"

"Um, no," I said. Which wasn't really lying if you thought about it. Because I really wasn't in this room. Naomi clutched my arm tightly.

"Oh, 'cuz it would be so cool if you were!" Chaiky said. "Sara Medetsky and Tehilla Summers are in this room, too!" Sara and Tehilla are the two girls in our grade whom I can best classify as "screaming girls". You know, they're color war captains and they just love to cheer at any time.

Naomi clutched my arm harder and I vaguely wondered if it was possible for my blood vessels to burst.

"Oh, wait, Naomi," Chaiky said, her eyes lighting up. "I think you're in this room. See," she said, walking to the wall where a white piece of paper was posted. "The heads stuck a sign in each room, so that if any girl got lost, she'd know where to go, and hey, look, you're supposed to be in here! Isn't that funny?" Chaiky laughed and Naomi practically squeezed my arm.

"Well, we have to go now," I said lightly. "See you later, Chaiks."

"Wait, where are you going?" Chaiky asked. "Hey," she said happily, "did you just call me Chaiks? Is that like a nickname?"

Naomi and I ran.

22

"**I** THINK SHE THINKS YOU'RE REALLY her best friend now!" Naomi said as we pounded down the stairs. "You know, with that whole nickname thing and everything."

"It was a slip of the tongue!" I muttered.

"All I can say," Naomi said, "is that I am so not staying in that room. You and Tzippa better have good roomies, or else I'll have to sleep in the bathroom."

"Okay." I sighed. "Let's check out my room now." We were standing in front of room 204. I felt my heart sink into my stomach. If it didn't get a breath of fresh air soon, it would totally drown. But it couldn't be so bad, could it?

I quickly opened the door. Ruti Reuben was sitting on one of the beds, chatting with Rochel Black. Next to Rochel was Esti Waldman, who was reading a book.

Yes. It could.

They all stared at me for a moment and then Esti went back to her book.

"Hi!" Ruti Reuben gushed.

I didn't answer her. This was all her fault. Not only was I stuck with her, I was actually also stuck with Rochel Black, who practically wants to kill me, and Esti Waldman who is super-quiet and only opens her mouth when it's with her own tight circle of friends. I had a feeling Esti would be pulling a "Naomi" on us and wouldn't be hanging out with her roommates much this weekend.

I blessed the bellboy who had put my stuff on the bed closest to the door. What a doll.

"Why don't we go check out Tzippa's room?" I said to Naomi.

Naomi, her eyes wide, nodded.

Tzippa's room was Heaven. Seriously. She had normal people there. Like Heidi Brown and Faiga Hartman and Nana. It was like a haven in a stormy world.

Naomi and I looked at each other. "We are so staying here," I told Tzippa.

She shrugged happily. "What's mine is yours..." she intoned.

"You guys want to go snow-tubing?" Heidi said. "It's a great way to burn calories!"

"Really?" Naomi and I said together.

Tzippa groaned. "Don't tell me you're in the calorie conspiracy, too, Heidi!"

"Are you kidding?" Heidi laughed. "I practically founded it! So, who wants to go?"

"I do!" Faiga said. She immediately jumped off her bed and started rummaging through her suitcase on the floor. Faiga reminds me of a fairy. She has these big, clear blue eyes that sometimes look purplish (depending on the lighting and what she is wearing — no, not her mood) and that are fringed with white-blonde lashes. Her hair is white-blonde and straight, and her skin is also whitish, with an assortment of silvery freckles sprinkled across her nose. She is as lithe and tiny as one of those little ballerina figurines, and I can just imagine her doing a pirouette. Also, she has this cute, squeaky little voice.

Faiga took out a pink, silky scarf that I did not think would keep her warm and tied it around her neck. Then she put on a huge, pink, down coat and headed for the door. "I'm ready!"

"Wow, Faiga," Heidi said. "That was fast."

Faiga shrugged. "Well, I was already wearing my boots.".

Heidi got up and started to get ready to go, too. So did Nana. "Are you coming?" Nana asked, looking at us as she tied a multicolored striped scarf around her neck.

I looked at Tzippa and Naomi. They looked at me. "Why not?" I shrugged.

"Let's go!" Naomi said. "I'm already wearing my coat and boots, and so are you, Ella. It only takes Tzippa a second to get ready, anyway."

"Well, okay," Tzippa said. "But only one time down the mountain, because I want to blow-dry my hair for Shabbos and you know how long that takes!"

Okay. This was really going to be okay. I was not going to have to spend any time in my room. I mean, that really wasn't rude or anything, right? It was just that I wanted to spend time with other people. This was what this Shabbaton was all about, wasn't it? Spending time with other people. And those people were Heidi, Faiga, and Nana, whom I didn't really know as well as I'd have liked. As for my best friends — I wasn't purposely spending time with them; they were just coming along for…the company.

I sighed. I had never been too good at rationalizing.

"Don't you feel a little bad?" I said to Naomi as we headed to the mountain. The sky was gray and the air was crisp. Sometimes,

I actually like the winter better than the summer. The summer can get so humid. During the winter, you can always breathe. It's like the world isn't hiding anything. The trees' black branches stand starkly against the gray sky, and the ground is cold and muddy. Not covered in leaves, not covered in grass. Just free.

"What are you talking about?" Naomi asked.

"You know, leaving the girls in our room and everything."

Naomi stared at me like I had just told her I liked to eat paper in my free time. "Why should I feel bad about that? I came here to have a good time, Ayelet. Not to chat with two girls whom I've never spoken to before, and another girl whom I can barely stand."

"I guess you're right," I said as we trudged up the mountain. There was no ski lift. We had to walk up to get down.

Naomi laughed. "Aren't I always?"

A big-boned woman with frizzy red hair was standing at the top of the mountain. She gave us each a tube. "Now," she said, "don't try any fancy tricks!"

"We won't," Heidi said sweetly.

"Okay," she said gruffly. "Get into your tubes and I'll push you down."

I sat in that orange rubber tube and suddenly felt a charge of energy as the lady pushed the tube down the hill. The world was ice and I was riding on it! The cool air swished against my face and I could see the people who looked so small from on top of the mountain growing bigger and bigger and bigger. It was thrilling to slide down the mountain! For a moment, I felt as if I was the only being in the entire white world, just falling down a hill with all my might. With nothing in my way to stop me. Oh, there were some rocks, of course, and my snow-tube went bumpity-bump on them, but I could just tumble out of my snow-tube if I wanted, and what would that big lady at the top do anyway? Except, when I was done, I had to take my snow-tube back to the top of the mountain to her, so that didn't really seem like such a good idea. I just soared down the mountain, without any fancy, forbidden tricks, exhilaration in my breath.

Tzippa ended up in the same location as me and we lugged our snow-tubes up together. Tzippa's cheeks were as red as cherry Popsicles and her hair was wind-whipped and crazy.

"What happened to your clip?" I asked.

"Well, I was just about to fix my hair when that lady pushed me down the mountain and my clip fell. Who knows where it is now!"

I stuck out my tongue sympathetically. It was hard to walk up that mountain. Much harder than going down. We gave our snow-tubes back to the lady, and then started walking back to the hotel. Naomi was with Nana, Heidi, and Faiga, and she was telling them about something that sounded like it had to do with Chaiky. They were all laughing.

"What do you think is Chaiky's deal?" I whispered to Tzippa.

"Honestly," she said, "I don't know. I think she might be a little lonely."

That made sense. But it didn't explain everything. I mean, who hasn't felt lonely? The thing was, though, I don't feel lonely when I'm alone. In fact, at those times I feel great and the most creative. I feel lonely when I'm in a room full of people and they're all talking, talking, talking, and even if they try to pull me into a conversation, I just can't converse with them, you know? I'd actually rather be by myself, staring into space, while everyone else talked and laughed, than try to participate in a conversation when I didn't want to or when the others didn't want me to. And according to that logic,

Chaiky Cukier should have been lonelier than ever! She was making herself lonely!

But then again, I didn't know how Chaiky Cukier's mind worked.

I'm still having trouble figuring out how my own does.

23

THE HOTEL WAS A FLURRY of Shabbos activity when we got back. Thankfully, though, no one was in the shower in my room. I figured Esti Waldman was already with her own friends, Ruti Reuben was setting up for something, and Rochel Black had already gotten ready (she didn't really strike me as the snow-tubing type) and was off playing ping-pong or something. Or talking to Mommy on her Motorolla, telling her that this was an absolutely horrible Shabbaton! Because not only was she not placed with one of her snobby friends, she was stuck with me, Queen of the Garbage Dump, Ella Sender. I mean, she thinks she's so cool and everything, flipping her shiny brown hair all around the place, but she doesn't realize that being so cool makes a person totally cold. Rochel Black walks in this, like, little balloon that I like to call Miss Ego.

I took a quick shower and began blow-drying my hair when Naomi came in.

"Good," she said. "Your room is empty. You wouldn't believe my room. Sara and Tehilla invited, like, half their friends and they're having a *kumzitz*. Forget that it's Erev Shabbos or anything, you know? They want to sing!"

"Chaiky must be in her element!" I said wryly.

"You don't even know." Naomi shook her head. "So, I'm taking a shower here."

"Go ahead," I said as I continued to work with my hair. See, it's a whole process, this making my hair business. Because when I blow-dry my hair, I have to straighten it, too. Or else it's puffy.

"Thanks," she said.

I nodded and continued blowing my hair. See, the thing about being alone is that you can think. Most of the time, I just like to contemplate things; life, you know? And you know what they say, that one's high school years are the best years of her life? Well, I have some news: That's just a whole load of junk. Because, why would being a teenager be the best years of one's life? I mean, it's not like I'm one of those depressed maniacs who walk around all day reporting the death statistics in Arkansas or something, it's just that, hello, I have my whole life ahead of me — why would these four years be the best? I am supposed to believe that my wedding day is not going to be as wonderful as these four years of high school?

Honestly, I cannot for the life of me understand why someone would say that high school years are the best years of a person's life. High school years are the worst years of someone's life! And it's not like I hate school. It's just that everything and everyone is so awk-ward. The high school years are like the thread hanging between childhood and the real world, and sometimes that thread swerves so fast between the two of them, that you don't know if you'll end up flat on your face the next second.

No one is really secure about who they are. It's not like I'm *in-secure* or like I have zilch self-confidence. But the thing is, I don't think I have fully actualized my capabilities. Then again, how can I fully realize my capabilities if I don't know who I am yet? And really, who does know who they are at this stage? I mean, we're only in high school.

When I was younger, I believed in myself so much more. I thought that I could do it all. My life was like a blank sheet of paper and I had a whole box of Crayola crayons in blue, pink, green, and all the other pretty colors, and I could have drawn whatever I wanted. But it seems as if at one point, someone took a black crayon, or one of those horribly awful colors that no one ever uses like maize or cyan, and scribbled all over my beautiful blank tablet. And now, in this ugly mess, I am somehow supposed to create beauty. This ugly mess is high school and my life right now, and the beauty, the beauty is what I want it to be.

Story of my life.

"Ella!" Naomi said, waving her hand in front of my face. "Hello?"

"Oh, sorry," I muttered. "I just spaced out for a sec."

Naomi laughed. "I called your name like three times. Anyway, what do you think I should do with my hair? Curl or straighten it?"

"Curls," I said. Naomi looks awesome in curls.

"Good, that's what I wanted to do, too. I'll go get my curl cream and be right back."

"Sure," I said, taking out my iron. It was now time to tame the frizzies. Doesn't that sound like it could be the name of an epic battle? It *could* be an epic battle.

When the door opened, I thought it was Naomi. You know, with her curl cream and everything. So, I put a huge smile on my face, one that could be reminiscent of Ruti Reuben.

Speaking of the devil.

I saw her before she saw me. Her head was bent over just a little bit and her honey hair was pulled back in a tight pony. She was not smiling, which was a big thing for Ruti Reuben. In fact, she looked like she was going to cry. Then she saw me smiling at her, and she immediately flashed me two neat rows of ivory teeth.

"Hi, Ella!" she said in this real peppy voice. "What's up?"

"Nothing much," I said. Except this time, I didn't try to look away from her eyes like I always did. She still had that big smile on her face and I figured out instantly why I thought she looked so much like a lifeless doll.

That smile was totally fake. There was no substance behind it. The thing was, that behind her California tan and her sparkling emerald eyes, she actually looked kind of sad, you know? Like this was all some kind of mask she had put on and didn't want to take off. I knew there was something bugging her, just because there were so many times that I had put on that fake smile myself, my mask, hoping that everyone would think that everything was just fine, that I was cool, calm, and collected, when really inside, a hurricane was raging within my heart. And the raindrops were the millions and millions of tears that no one would ever see I cried. And the howling winds were the screams that no one would ever hear, because, quite frankly, no one could hear them! And that was just what I wanted. For no one to know that I was silently breaking down.

Was Ruti Reuben, Miss Perfect, breaking down inside? Was her big smile and sprightly attitude just some big front she put on, so the world couldn't see what was really going on inside her heart? I looked at her.

She opened up her mouth, like she was about to say something. Then Naomi walked in holding a container of Garnier Fructis soft curl cream and a basket full of clips.

Ruti took one look at her, and then at me. To tell you the truth,

I think she looked just a drop disappointed. But I could have been, you know, dreaming or something. Because I only saw her green eyes spark for a second, and then she muttered something about having to take a shower and headed to the bathroom.

"What's wrong with her?" Naomi asked as she placed the basket on the vanity table mirror.

I shrugged. So, I wasn't the only one who noticed it. Something was most definitely not normal. I mean, this was Ruti Reuben we were talking about, Queen of Enthusiasm and Over-Cheery Hellos.

Naomi shrugged, too. "So, Ella, what do you think? Headband? Clip? Just plain down?"

"Wow, Naomi, this is complicated," I said as I stared at the basket. There were probably three hundred assorted hair accessories there. "Where did you buy all this stuff? It doesn't seem like your type."

Naomi laughed, putting a brown headband in her hair. "My younger sisters all chipped in and bought it last year for my birthday for only five dollars. It was a really big thing for them. You know, five bucks and everything. This is the first time I'm using it, and they are soooo excited! They want me to take a picture of myself using it and then show it to them when I get home."

I laughed. Naomi didn't realize how cute her younger sisters were. "What are you wearing?" I asked. "You might want to make everything match."

"Oh, I'm wearing this brown outfit," Naomi said. "My mother's all like, 'Brown's the new black!' or something like that."

"Brown can never replace black!" I gasped. "Black's the queen of all colors."

Naomi stared at me. "Where do you get this stuff from, Ella?"

"Matisse," I muttered. "Anyway, don't worry; I love brown, too, and I'm wearing a brown outfit tomorrow."

"I'm *really* worried about this, Ella," Naomi said wryly, stroking her chin. "I think we might have to check it out."

I sighed. "Just go with the brown headband. It looks nice on you."

"Really?" Naomi said with a smile. "Thanks!" She opened the container of curl cream and put a gloop of cream on the palm of her hand, rubbed it between her fingers, spread it across her hair, and began scrunching.

I went back to ironing my hair.

Then Rochel Black walked into the room, giving Naomi and me a look. She was already dressed in her Shabbos attire: A lacy pink outfit that for some reason reminded me of dress-up parties I used to have when I was three. She grabbed her brush from her bed and then promptly walked out of the room.

"What's her deal?" Naomi asked as she continued scrunching.

"I think she just can't stand me," I said. I still couldn't believe what she had done to me that morning. "Anyway, on to happier discussions. I think I'm going to wear my hair down tonight, Naomi. What do you think?"

Naomi eyed me and smiled. "Good idea."

I didn't know the hotel had a PA system, but apparently it did. Because just then, I heard Morah Bluestein announcing that we should be in the main lobby for *Kabbalas Shabbos* in an hour.

"Okay," Naomi said, giving her hair a final scrunch. "I have to go get dressed. I'll be back soon, Ella, so don't go anywhere without me."

"I won't," I said. "Trust me, I ain't going anywhere without you and Tzippa."

Naomi laughed. After she left, I opened up my suit-bag to take out the black suit I was wearing tonight. Plain, simple, elegant. I was snazzing it up with some of a girl's best friends, so I wasn't too worried. And I was wearing these awesome, awesome pointy shoes. I mean, I know some girls can't stand pointy shoes, because they think they look like witches' shoes or something, but I absolutely adore them! I mean, I can't stand round-toe, and square-toe just makes me think of the '90s when those grossly chunky platforms that everyone had were in style (gag me with a spoon), and pointy shoes are just so delicate and wonderful. So, I had these slingback BCBGs that had rhinestones on the side. I mean, yeah, I know they weren't diamonds (Chaiky told me that diamonds are really hard and never break, but still, who'd be silly enough to wear diamonds on their shoes!), but they totally went with my outfit, so it was just perfect! Plus, they had really high heels, which is always a plus in my book, because flat shoes make my calves look fat for some reason.

I'd look fine. I wouldn't stand out. I wouldn't fit in. Just the way I liked it.

I quickly got dressed and then, ah, the diamonds. I love my diamonds and I usually don't wear them, because, hello, they're diamonds, and if you wore them every day, then they wouldn't be special anymore and make your heart skip a little beat when you saw them glistening in the mirror. I slowly clasped the necklace around my neck, and put on the bracelet and ring. My father had bought Tova and me diamonds right before his wedding. Because, as he'd said, we still were the girls in his life. That was sweet, wasn't it? Too bad I was in such a rotten mood that I couldn't really enjoy the way they sparkled with my shimmery gown.

Then Ruti Reuben came out of the shower and gave me a big

smile. "Wow, you look really pretty, Ella," she said. "I totally love your suit."

"Thanks," I said.

She started blow-drying her hair and I sat on my bed and began flipping through the novel I had brought with me for situations like these. You know, when I was dying of boredom. I knew I could always go to Tzippa's room, but firstly, it seemed kind of rude to just leave Ruti Reuben, even though I didn't really like her, because that would be like practically spelling it out before her eyes. And you know, I don't really like spelling things out for people. They should learn how to read themselves, right? Also, I just knew Tzippa's room would be a frenzied mess. I mean, I've seen Nana get ready for Shabbos before. And as easy-going and funny as she is, when she's getting ready for a party or Shabbos or something, she's like a tornado, flying from here to there in a whirlwind of activity. Blowing her hair, then buckling one shoe, then putting on her earrings. And I could just imagine Heidi. She seemed like the real prima-donna type. Not like that was a bad thing. I mean, we all have our prima-donna moments. Some more than others.

"Ella?" Ruti Reuben spoke up in a quiet voice. She had stopped blowing her glossy hair. She was wearing a white suit with a fur collar that made her skin and hair glow even more than ever. "Can I ask you something?"

I looked at her for a moment, and suddenly it struck me that I didn't know who Ruti Reuben's friends were. I mean, she's a pretty popular girl, but in terms of friendship, that doesn't really mean anything. I mean, I had never seen her hang out with a specific *chevra*, just flitting around from group to group, never staying too long with one. I didn't really know what to say to her, so I just slowly nodded. I mean, what could she want to ask me already?

To help set up for the *kiddush* tomorrow or something?

"I—" Ruti started to say, and then Naomi walked into our room, decked out in her finest. She wore a long, brown, A-line dress, with an empire waistline that made her look even taller, dangling sapphire earrings, a very pretty sapphire necklace, and brown flats. Her blue eyes were practically shimmering under the effect of all those sapphires.

"Come on, Ella," Naomi said. "Let's go! I hope Tzippa is ready, too."

I dumped my book under the bed and looked at Ruti Reuben. She didn't even seem remotely perturbed or interested. In fact, she was busy with her hair again, and I wondered if I had just hallucinated or something.

"Well, bye," I said as I followed Naomi out of the room.

It was only until after I closed the door behind me that I realized: Ruti Reuben hadn't given me another one of her hundred-watt smiles and told me in a perky voice that she'd see me later.

Weird.

Whatever. I had my own problems to deal with; I didn't have to deal with Ruti Reuben's, too. I didn't want to. Well, mostly, anyway.

Tzippa's room was actually pretty calm. The girls were all sitting on the beds, involved in an animated discussion. Lucky ducks.

"Hi!" Tzippa said, motioning to Naomi and me to come sit on her bed. She was wearing a hunter-green, silky-looking suit with zippers all over it. Her shoes were pointy sling-backs with kitten heels and a zipper opening in the front. Her brown hair was glossy and fell softly around her face.

"I love your outfit!" Naomi gushed to Tzippa. "Just don't let Chaiky see you or else she'll be calling you Zipper for the rest of her life."

A snort escaped from my nose before I could even control it.

"Ella, I love your outfit!" Faiga Hartman said, looking more like a fairy than ever. She was wearing a lavender dress that had silver sparkles running through it, and these lace-looking lavender shoes that ribboned up. Sort of like wintery espadrilles.

"Thanks!" I smiled.

Heidi was wearing a black turtleneck sweater and a long black pleated skirt with a wide gold belt and lots of golden pearl necklaces. Her side bangs were pulled back with two crisscrossed bobby pins and pushed back, so there was a huge bump.

Nana, as usual, had pulled off something I could never even dream of wearing, because I didn't have her tall, svelte frame. She was a ballerina. Seriously. She had put her blonde hair into a French twist and was wearing a cotton candy-pink shirt with tiny pearly buttons running down the back. Her skirt was made out of this pink, tulle material, and yes, she was wearing ballet slippers. And fingerless, lacy, pink gloves. Only Nana.

"So," Faiga said, "did anyone look at this schedule?" She was holding up a pink sheet of paper that had been in the folder they had given out. "The curfew for tonight is at eleven. And I am not joking. After the meal, there's a workshop and then a speech and then it's time for bed!"

"Who follows schedules?" Naomi shrugged. "Rules are meant to be broken."

Faiga looked horrified. "It's obvious you haven't read this, Naomi. Because in big, bold letters it says: 'All girls must follow the schedule at all times. Any girl who is in the incorrect place will spend the rest of the weekend with Morah Bluestein.'"

"Does this mean they're *patrolling*?" Heidi asked, disbelief in her voice.

171

"Sounds like it," Naomi said, rolling her eyes.

This was really bad. It meant that I had to be in my room, when I'd really rather not be there. Sort of like jail or something.

Tzippa glanced at her watch. "Well," she said, "we'd better get to the lobby. It's almost time for *Kabbalas Shabbos.*"

"And if we're late, we might have to spend the rest of Shabbos with Morah Bluestein," I said.

Which wouldn't really be so bad, if you thought about it.

CAN YOU BELIEVE THEY ACTUALLY assigned tables for all the meals? So I couldn't even sit with my friends then. I had to sit alone, stuffing my face with this soggy gefilte fish, as I thought about why exactly Yaffa and Margalit weren't being so annoying anymore, and everyone else discussed whether or not we were going to have a Senior *kallah* in our grade. Then, I slurped on oily soup while thinking about whether or not I should go to seminary in Eretz Yisrael next year. It would provide a great escape, but the thing was, I didn't know if I could handle being stuck in a dorm with another hundred girls, twenty-four-seven. The girls at my table were now discussing funny *shidduch* stories.

Kugel and chicken proved to be a time for me to contemplate whether Chaiky was really nuts or not. If she was not, then why did she act like she was? And if she was, then why didn't she get help? Like, she could always speak to the guidance counselor or something. The girls at my table were discussing babysitting stories.

Dessert, thank Hashem, was set up on a long buffet table. We could get up and socialize with other people, so this was really big. I met Naomi and Tzippa by the fruits while I ate a chocolate-covered pineapple. Unfortunately, there were no lemons in sight.

"One meal down," Naomi said in a bored voice. "Two more to go."

"Plus *kiddush*," I said.

"*Kiddush* doesn't count, because we're not *barred* behind tables," Naomi shot back.

"Come on," Tzippa said. "Let's just *bentch* and get back to our rooms."

"Tzippa?" Naomi said in a mock-horrified voice. "Breaking rules? Not following the schedule? This is bad, ladies and gentlemen. This is very bad."

"Oh, knock it off," I told Naomi. "Let's just get out of this place."

"Gladly," Naomi said.

We *bentched* and left the dining room, but lo and behold, Morah Adelman (who had come up with her family for the Shabbaton, in addition to Morah Bluestein and Morah Reich), was standing by the door.

"Where are you girls going?" she asked in an accusing voice.

"To get some fresh air," Naomi said boldly. Sometimes, I wonder if Naomi is afraid of anyone. Morah Adelman is the tallest woman I have ever seen my life. Plus, she has these dark eyes that always seem to be boring into you. Plus, she has ruddy cheeks, which makes it seem like she's always angry. She scares me, you know? She doesn't seem like the type of person with whom one should mess around.

Morah Adelman just looked at her. Then she looked at Tzippa. Then she looked at me.

"It's kind of stuffy in there," I said. I wasn't lying, because it really was.

"We'll be back in time for the workshop," Tzippa said.

This seemed to win over Morah Adelman, because she reluctantly nodded her head, adding, "If you're not, you know who you'll be spending the rest of your Shabbos with."

"What is this?" Naomi asked as soon as we got into Tzippa's room. "Some kind of boot camp or something? Do this, do that, be here, be there, and if you're not, whoa, big time punishment."

Tzippa and I just groaned.

"Okay," Naomi said, sprawling out on Heidi's bed, which was right next to Tzippa's. "How many minutes of freedom do we have left?"

Tzippa stared at her watch. "Twelve. And thirty-nine seconds."

Naomi groaned. "Too short. It's always too short."

"Well, let's at least do something fun!" I said.

"Why?" Naomi said in a dry voice. "To make the time go by faster?"

Tzippa laughed.

"Naomi!" I said, scrunching a pinch of Tzippa's bedspread into my hand. "Do you want to just sit here?"

"Yes," Naomi said, staring at the ceiling.

Silence filled the air for a moment. Tzippa began zipping and unzipping one of the zippers on her suit jacket and I played with my necklace absentmindedly.

"You know what really bugs me?" Naomi said suddenly, sitting straight up.

"What?" Tzippa said softly, playing with her hair.

"Hypocrites," Naomi said as she sank back into the bed. "Everyone's all like, do *chessed*, do *chessed*, do *chessed*, and I'm sitting there at the table with these three girls, and they're all gossiping about how Rochi Reindenhammer or something from somewhere in the middle of nowhere is going to get married any day now, and how they have to go to her wedding and everything. And do you think they even looked at me? I mean, hello, how disgusting. Your sister was there, too, Ella. At least she said hello, but that was it. Are you guys in a fight again? I thought you made up on Sunday."

"Don't ask." I sighed. "I thought we made up, but all she wants to do is preach at me like she's some kind of *rebbetzin* and I'm some poor, poor girl that needs to be reformed, you know?" I took a deep breath. "I don't think she even cares about me, you know, how *I* feel. The only thing that seems to be on her mind is that there should be *shalom bayis* and whatever. Me — I'm just this frustrating person standing in the way of that. You should have seen the way she was screaming at me on Monday."

Naomi sighed. "Sisters. Can't live with them, can't live without them."

"*That's* profound," Tzippa said with a laugh.

"I'm serious," Naomi said. "You don't get it, Tzippa, because you're the youngest and everything, but younger sisters aren't exactly easy."

"Hey," Tzippa protested. "I was an easy kid."

"Well, Shana and Ayala were lucky then," I said. "I mean, even though Tova is three minutes older than me and everything, she honestly thinks she has to lord over me."

"I don't know," Tzippa said. "Tova always seemed so nice to me, like she wouldn't want to hurt anyone, you know?"

I snorted. "That's because you don't live with her."

Tzippa was quiet for a moment, brushing her hair away from her face. "No," she said. "I don't live with Tova. I live with Chana instead."

Chana. That's right, Tzippa had told us about her sister's downward spiral, how she'd started hanging out with the wrong crowd, coming home late, and acting "crunk". It wasn't as if there was anything wrong with Chana. I mean, she never seemed like a bad person to me. She was more on the quiet, serious, contemplative side; she always seemed to be thinking about something. Sometimes that could be the problem. Thinking, I mean. She was a little sarcastic — not at all like Tzippa. But you know, I just thought that was part of her personality. Some people are just like that.

I think Chana had always been labeled "at-risk," the type of person who was liable to fall through the cracks, because she didn't have many friends (I always suspected she was introverted, too), and she just didn't accept things easily. I guess because she thought about everything so much.

Actually, she reminded me a bit of myself. I know some people definitely labeled me an "at-risk teen," like I was some kind of bomb that was going to explode any second.

A lot of times, when I tried to judge Tova favorably, I kind of imagined that she was dealing with me the way Tzippa deals with Chana. I know that even though Tzippa's sister is OTD ("off the *derech*"), she still loves her. She's just hurt. I hoped that Tova still loved me and that she was just…hurt by my attitude. Because when you love someone and you care about your relationship with that person, you are willing to stick it through the hard times. You're willing to forget about the hurt; you're willing to be patient with the person. But when you don't love someone, all you want to do is get away from that person whom you no longer recognize and no longer want to know. I don't think I'd be able to bear it if Tova was like that with me. Now, all I muttered was, "Consider yourself lucky." Even though I didn't really think that was the most appropriate thing to say.

Tzippa looked at me. I knew she wanted to say something,

but Tzippa's the sensitive type, you know, the type of person who actually thinks before she speaks. But it's okay, because she's friends with Naomi, who doesn't.

"No, you consider yourself lucky, Ella," Naomi said. "I think that once and for all, you should make up with Tova. For good."

I groaned. Oh, great. Them, too? It wasn't like I didn't get enough of it at home — people telling me how I should live my life and what I should do and how I should do it — now, Naomi had to write her own little book on how Ella Sender should live her life? Why couldn't everyone just leave me alone?

"Don't start," I said, holding up my hand. "Do not even start."

Tzippa shook her head and gave Naomi a look. Naomi shrugged. "Whatever," she said. "I was just saying it for your own good."

"Well," I said, "I'm a big girl now. I don't need you to hold my hand. I can decide for my own good."

"Ella — " Naomi started to say, and then she just shook her head to herself, like she didn't think whatever she'd been about to say was worth saying. "Whatever, never mind. Let's get back to the dining room."

"Yeah," Tzippa said. "Workshops are going to be starting soon. What are you guys in? I'm in workshop F."

"L," Naomi said with a sigh.

"B," I said. I hadn't really expected them to put us together. But it would have been nice. Then again, a lot of other things would have been nice, too, such as not being in a fight with my sister, and not having two bratty younger stepsisters, and if my mother were still alive, that would be pretty nice, too. Oh, well. I just hoped there would be lemons there. I needed something to suck on. Yeah, sort of like a pacifier.

We headed to the dining room, where Ruti Reuben was pointing out the various tables with letters on them. I gave Naomi and Tzippa a reluctant grin and headed to table B, which was full already, besides for one seat which I assumed was mine. There was a sheet of paper on the table in front of me.

"Hi, Ella!" Kochava Weingarten said as I sat down at the table. Kochava's really friendly. Her family moved to Eretz Yisrael last year, but she stayed behind and boards here. I'm not really friends with her — she hangs out more with the Sara Medetsky and Tehilla Summers crowd — but she's nice. You can just see it in her clear brown eyes. Her wavy blonde hair was brushed away from her face with a clip.

"Hi," I said, sitting down. It was then that I noticed that everyone at the table was staring at me, and I wondered if I had a smear of chicken fat on my face. But no, it couldn't be; Tzippa and Naomi would have told me if I did. "Um, okay," I said.

"Don't be shy!" Kochava said, patting me on the back. "I'm sure you'll do a great job!"

While I was grateful for her vote of confidence, I had no clue what she was talking about. "Um, thanks," I managed to mutter. "What will I do a great job at, though?"

Kochava let out a high-pitched peal of laughter. A few of the other girls, like Yona Hertzberg and Penina Goldenberg, whom I had never really liked anyway, started to giggle.

"You're our workshop leader!" Kochava said. "Didn't you read the folder? Gila Auerbach is in my room and she's a workshop leader, too. Her folder was like twice as fat as mine."

"Um," I said slowly, my mouth turning dry and my mind going blank. Oh, it wasn't like things were bad; now they had to turn nightmarish? Whose idea was it to make me a workshop leader? Why hadn't they told me about this beforehand? And what was I

SHADOWS ON THE MOON

going to do now? Was I actually going to have to conduct a workshop? I could feel my palms getting clammy and my neck stiffening as I read the paper before me, which gaily welcomed the workshop leaders and told us that they hoped that we had read the entire booklet very thoroughly. Below was a sample of some questions we could use, but, the sheet said, we workshop leaders should made sure that the conversation did not stray from the list in the booklet.

I quickly glanced at the questions. Maybe it wouldn't be so hard. Maybe they'd ask some question like "What do you think is the best way to improve your *middos*?" Then we could all just give any answer and get out of here as soon as possible.

No such luck.

How do you feel incorporating song into your life will help you reach greater heights?

How has the power of shirah *previously affected you?*

Discuss the metaphysical aspects of song and its deeper meaning in life.

Oh, my. This was really heavy stuff. I could feel my face flushing, especially when I read the last line. It said, very strongly, that as workshop leaders, it was our responsibility to make sure that everyone (this was capitalized) participated. And that was followed by what looked like a thousand exclamation points.

I gulped. Hard. This was going to be difficult, especially considering the fact that I didn't really want to participate myself. But I would be fine. I would survive. I'd been through much harder things. I'd practically swam with sharks in an icy, raging sea. So this would be fine; it would be like wading through a kiddie pool. Right?

Everyone was staring at me. Honestly, I felt like I was in some cellar in a police department, sitting under a dingy light that was making me sweat profusely, with all the lawyers and authorities staring at me.

"Okay," I said, laughing nervously. "Why don't we start? Well, um, we're supposed to answers these, um, questions, and I think it would be really great if we went around the table and, um, everyone would contribute a little. Kochava, why don't you start?"

"Okay!" Kochava said brightly. She stared at me. I cleared my throat; why wasn't she starting?

Then, Kochava cleared her throat. "Ella, are you going to read the question?"

I laughed again. To tell you the truth, I was frightened by the sound of my own giggle. It was high-pitched and anxious, like it belonged to someone else. "Yeah, sure," I said. "Sorry about that; I just spaced out for a sec."

Kochava nodded. Her lips were turned upwards in a grin, her eyes were sparkling, and her right eyebrow was raised.

"Um," I said, staring at the wretched paper. "How do you feel incorporating song into your life will help you reach greater heights?"

She stared at me. "You aren't serious, are you?"

"I wish I wasn't."

"Okay," Kochava said, taking a deep breath and twirling a strand of hair around her finger. She stopped suddenly and looked at me. "You know, it's not fair, because everyone else gets time to think about this, and I have to answer right now. Why don't you go first?"

"The workshop leaders go last," I said, even though I wasn't sure about that at all. Hey, I was in authority. I might as well make good use of it.

She sighed. "Okay, okay," she said. "I'll go. But no one is allowed to laugh if I sound stupid." Kochava stared off into the distance for a moment and then her cheeks reddened ever so slightly. I think only I could have seen this because I was sitting next to her. "Well, everyone here knows that even though I sound like a frog on good days, I love singing. And, when I was in first grade, we had a *chazzanis* who led the *davening* each day; does everyone remember that?"

A few girls nodded and laughed.

"Well," Kochava continued, "I remember that one day when Morah Shoshana — do you all remember her? — picked me to be the *chazzanis* and I was the one who got to sing all the songs out loud! Well," she said, then paused and took a deep breath, "I don't think I've had a better *davening* since then." Then she turned red. "Okay, that's it. I'm done."

"Come on, Kochi!" Ariella Moradi said. "That was nice."

Kochava shrugged. "Thanks."

"Okay," I said, nodding at Yona. "What about you?"

Yona stared at me. "This is kind of a hard question, you know?" she said, crossing her arms. With much wheedling and cajoling, Yona, Penina, Ariella, and Miriam all answered the question. I wasn't really listening though. I mean, I did hear Penina, our resident genius, talk about how Elisha had asked for a *menagen*, a musician, when he was depressed, so that he could receive *nevuah*, because "*Ein haShechinah shorah ela mitoch simchah* — The Shechinah only rests where there is happiness," and therefore, *shirah* brought *simchah*, which brought us closer to Hashem,

But the thing was, I was hearing, but I wasn't really listening. All I could think about was what I would answer. My question was, what was the *shirah* I was going to be incorporating, and what greater heights would I be reaching? I mean, I totally admire those people who live on some kind of spiritual high and are constantly talking about Hashem and marveling at the world around them, and even though I think that is a beautiful, beautiful, mystical thing, I just can't imagine myself like that. I'm no *rebbetzin*. And this isn't a matter of whether or not I wish I was one; it's just that I can't imagine being on a spiritual high. Yeah, a few years ago, there were these bumper stickers given out that said "High on Torah" and everything, but the thing is, I've never been high on Torah. I've never been high on *Yiddishkeit*.

Thinking about it, I got a dreadful feeling in my stomach — almost as if someone was punching me repeatedly. Because, unfortunately, I couldn't remember the last time I "grew". I couldn't remember the last time I had reached greater spiritual heights. Even though everyone is always all like, "You'll grow in seminary," for some reason, I just couldn't imagine myself instantly transforming overnight, or even over two months, from the near-*shiksah* I was now to some kind of super-*frum* Hadar girl. And I was practically a *shiksah*. I mean, okay, it's bad to put yourself down, and it could be that was my *yetzer hara* speaking and everything, but honestly, besides for the fact that I already had a label branded on my forehead, I didn't feel like I was growing. I could have been in a six-year-old body and no one would have known the difference — and that was bad. I didn't do anything with my heart or soul.

For some reason, I wanted to open up my *siddur* right now and just pour everything out to Hashem. I hadn't done that in a long time. Maybe never.

I always saw other girls doing it, standing with their *siddurim* wrapped around their faces as their bodies shook with sobs. Why couldn't I do that? Tomorrow. Tomorrow I would. There was always tomorrow to start fresh. Because as cynical as I was, I did want to reach greater heights. I mean, I didn't want to be this sullen teenager forever.

"It's your turn," Kochava sang, smiling at me.

I gulped. "Okay," I said. I really didn't know what to say, but I supposed honesty would be the best route and everything. Everyone probably saw me as this hard, cold girl who didn't really smile much; maybe I could show them another side of me. Maybe I could show myself another side of me. "I, um…well…" I looked at my fingernails as I stumbled over my words. "At this point, I think incorporating anything into my life will help me reach greater heights," I said with a little laugh. I didn't think anyone was really listening to me, and to tell you the truth, I kind of hoped that they weren't. Because if this was a book, it would have been called *Confessions.*

"But song," I said, my voice growing stronger. I knew where I was going with this now. I took a deep breath, "song not only affects one's mood, it also affects one's soul. That's why I've stopped listening to secular music." I took a deep breath. I wasn't all bad, was I? After all, I had stopped listening to the radio. Which was a big step for now. "And I really hope that helps me reach greater heights. Because right now, I'm kind of crawling on the ground."

Then, before anyone could question or comment on what I'd said, I quickly looked at the paper and read aloud the second question. "How has the power of *shirah* previously affected you?"

Kochava was quiet for a second, and I think she was looking at me, wanting to meet my eye, but I kept staring at the paper, like it was filled with some fascinating news about the price of tea in China. Then she laughed. "I'm not doing this one again. The *chazzanis* example from first grade was enough!"

I tried to think of my answer while Yona told us how she always started crying when the band played *Od Yishama* at weddings and the *chassan* and *kallah* headed out from the *chuppah* in a pink cloud of wedded bliss. Penina told us that her mother liked to play the piano, and that her earliest memory was of standing near the piano, barely reaching the keys, as she watched her mother's fingers dance on them.

And then, I was transported into a world of my own.

My mother. I remembered her soft, almost musical laugh, and the way she would drape one arm around Tova's shoulder and the other one around mine, and tell us that we were her little girls, her precious little girls.

Tova and I were miracle children. We were born in the sixth month and the doctors didn't think we would survive. If we did survive, they predicted that we would be mentally and developmentally delayed. But we were fine. By the time we were two years old, we had caught up with the rest of our peers.

When we were little, we loved to go to the park. My mother would hold my hand and Tova's hand and we would walk to a certain park not far from our home that had open fields of lush green grass. Tova and I would run and chase each other on the grass under the endless blue sky. In the summer, the sprinkler system there created countless waterfalls, each one shooting clear spurts of wet magic into the air, and I would dance under the water. My mother always stood close by, watching me while holding Tova's hand (Tova had never wanted to get wet or dirty). As my jelly sandals moved swiftly on the ground and my mother smiled at me from afar, the world had never been more perfect.

One afternoon, on the way home from one of my water dances in the park, my legs were blue and my lips were purple and I remember shivering, the teeth in my mouth hitting against each other again and again. Right there, in the middle of the street, my mother wrapped me in her big blue jacket, the one with the happy yellow daisies scattered on it, and promised to make me chicken soup for dinner, and again everything was okay, because I was warm now and my mommy was going to make me soup. And so, I was the happiest girl in the world.

Until late that night, when I awoke, burning up with fever. I thought a monster had come and turned on all the sprinklers from the park in my room, because I was freezing cold and yet dripping with sweat at the same time. So, I screamed. Tova only turned over in her bed, but my mother came running into my room. Even after she had given me Motrin and tea and promised me that I would feel better soon, I still couldn't stop crying. Because I was scared.

"Mommy, am I going to die?" I whispered. I was only a child and I had no idea what death was, but I had heard my parents discussing it in hushed tones and I knew it was something bad. Possibly something that had to do with a monster.

I still remember my mother's soft, cool hands caressing my sweaty cheeks. "No, Ella. You're going to be fine," she said. Then, she sat on the big wooden rocking chair and I sat in her lap, a soft, silky comforter wrapped around me.

"Mommy, sing the little girl song," I said. I loved the little girl song. I loved the fact that there was a song about a little girl when so many songs were about big people. This song was a lullaby my mother would sing to me whenever I was sad or scared. It was her way of telling me that despite the pain and fear, it was still possible to be happy.

My mother began to sing the song to me. I still remember her voice, a soft, sweet soprano, filling my ears, filling the room, filling the night and surrounding me. I snuggled up closer as my mother sang. She stroked my hair gently, her cold wedding band touching my warm scalp every so often. When she began singing the song, it was like there was no beginning or end to time, just a wonderful, safe place in between. My world was calm and serene, like a peace-ful lake. I remember the words, sung to a slow, haunting tune, even though it was so long ago:

Rosy cheeks and bright eyes
Wild ebony curls
How I love you with my whole heart
My precious little girl.

I watch you always
dancing in the sun
spinning round and round
sparkling for everyone

I will catch you
when you fall
I'll hold your hands
so frail and small

Though this world is full
of cold December days
of blue, bruised, knobby knees,
I will make the pain go away.

I love to see you smile
How you shine, you glow,
From deep within.
Hold my hand and don't let go.

Hold my hand for now, for now,
One day you will let go,
One day I'll be far
and you'll be on your own.

Little girl, my little girl,
remember — I am always holding your hand tight.
Even when the night is dark
The moon will always shine bright.

I remember a full and silvery moon shining in the window as my mother sang this song that I didn't really understand, but I still loved. I remember being wrapped in a blanket of love and feeling incredibly good, even though I was sick. I remember thinking the world would stay this perfect forever. But that's all I remember.

"Ella!" a voice said suddenly. It was Miriam. She looked partially confused and partially concerned. "Where are you? It's your turn!"

"My turn for what?" I said blankly. I wanted to be four years old again and sit wrapped in my mother's arms.

"How music has affected your life," Yona said slowly. She gave me a weird look.

"Oh," I said. "I like music. That's all."

"Is everything okay?" Kochava whispered.

I nodded, but everything really wasn't. Suddenly, I felt very hot and cold, and I wanted to leave the room and go somewhere. Where I could be alone, preferably.

Kochava looked at me and then took the sheet of paper from in front of me and read, "Discuss the metaphysical aspects of song and its deeper meaning in life." She looked around at everyone at the table, and I could feel her eyes lingering on me for an extra second. "I think we covered this, guys, didn't we?"

Everyone nodded.

"Okay," Kochava said. "I'm pretty sure we can go back to our rooms until the speech. It doesn't start for another half hour anyway."

I noticed that all the other groups were still in session, but I was too busy shivering to care. I didn't get up. I would. Soon. In a matter of seconds, the entire table was empty, but Kochava was still there. She put her arm around my shoulder.

"Ella, is everything okay?" she asked. Her eyes were a warm brown color, I noticed.

I nodded. "Yeah," I said. I wanted to say that I supposed I was a bit tired, but I couldn't get the words out.

"You know," Kochava said, "if you ever want to talk, I'm always here."

Before this workshop, I would have definitely thought that Kochava just wanted to adopt me as her new *chessed* project, but she did look very concerned. And besides, Kochava had once been a little girl, too. She, too, had a mother who had sung her to sleep while rocking her gently. She couldn't be bad. I mean, was everyone really bad? Why would the whole world with little girls and caring mothers who sang to them, be out to get me? Why would everyone want to hurt me and preach to me? Maybe some people genuinely cared about me? Even though they didn't really know me so well? Could that be?

"Thanks," I said. "I appreciate that."

She nodded.

"Right now, though," I managed to say, "all I want to do is lie down."

Kochava nodded again. "You know where to find me if you need me," she said.

I got up and left the table. And as I was walking out of the dining room, I looked out the window. The moon was full and silvery.

And I realized that even though the moon appeared different during different times of the month, changing from a sharp sliver to a lonely half to a grand, beautiful full moon, it was really always the same grand and beautiful moon. I just couldn't see this because for a while, I had been living in my own lunar eclipse.

25

I WALKED DOWN THE EMPTY CORRIDOR to my room. All I wanted to do was to sit on my bed and contemplate — everything in general, really. I was still haunted by my mother's song, which was replaying itself in my mind a thousand times over and over again. How long had it been since I'd last thought of that song? How long had it been since my world was perfect?

An awful smell hit my nose as soon as I entered my room. The room was empty, but I could hear a soft sobbing coming from somewhere. Was I hallucinating? I looked around the room and checked the bathroom, but there was nothing and no one to be found. Who was crying?

I sat on my bed in the dark, cool room, my heart pounding in my ears, and it was then that I noticed it. The lump on Ruti Reuben's bed, under the blankets.

Who could it be? Surely it wasn't Ruti Reuben in her bed during a school Shabbaton that she had organized. And crying?

But it was. There were her perfect little patent-leather pumps strewn on the floor near her bed. This was Ruti Reuben we were talking about. This was the girl who always blow-dried her sunshine hair, always had a glowing tan and a pearly smile, was one of the most popular girls in our grade, and was in charge of close to everything. Plus, she had a perfect little family, as if to accessorize her perfect little life. I honestly didn't understand what a girl like her would cry about.

"Ruti?" I whispered. I was kind of scared, to tell you the truth.

The sobs grew harder.

"Ruti, what's wrong?" I managed to say. I twisted my ring around my finger. Talk about having one's world shatter in a day. Here I was, the girl with the messed up life and attitude, trying to figure out why the girl who flipped her hair as perfectly as she did everything else in life, was crying hysterically. It seemed like it should be the other way around.

"Just go away!" Ruti Reuben howled. "Leave me alone."

For some reason, right then, "*CHESSED CASE*" flashed in big, bold, neon letters in my head. I wanted to ask if "everything was okay," but that seemed like a silly, superfluous question that would make her cry even harder.

"Please tell me," I said very softly. I did want to know what was wrong, and not just from curiosity either, but to tell you the truth, I didn't expect her to tell me.

But she did. She threw the blanket off and sat up, facing me.

"You really want to know?" she said, a turbulent edge in her voice. "You really want to know why I'm crying?"

I nodded. I couldn't say anything because I was too busy staring at her. Her hair was tousled around her face, her cheeks were pale, and her eyes were big and green, protruding slightly. I had never noticed this before, but her face was so…gaunt. I had never noticed how skinny she was.

"Because I'm just sick of it!"

"Oh," I said in the most sympathetic voice I could muster. I wasn't really so sure what she would be sick of, but I was pretty sure that she would tell me.

"I know what people call me behind my back," she said with a hollow, bitter laugh. "Everyone thinks I'm 'Perfect Ruti Reuben,' the girl who gets perfect grades and who always looks perfect and who always has this perfect life!" She took a deep breath, like she was almost choking on her words because she needed to get them out so fast.

"No one realizes that I'm tired of being perfect. No one. For G-d's sake, everyone thinks it just comes effortlessly. No one even thinks I'm under any pressure. No one knows that I'm going to pop any second now. Sometimes, I don't want to smile, Ella, do you know what I mean? Sometimes, I just want to scream at everyone, but I just don't!"

I nodded. I knew what she meant. I knew what she meant all too well. Who would ever think that Ruti Reuben and I had something in common?

"No one realizes that when I go home, I have to work on my entire cover, because my parents will kill me if I don't. I have an image to keep up, you know." She stared at me expectantly, as if waiting for some kind of answer.

"What do you mean?" I said.

Ruti laughed. "Ha!" she said. "You think I *want* to get a hundred on every single one of those tests? You think I *like* staying up until four every night to study? Ha! No way. I can never relax, you know, because I have to be perfect. And if I don't get into BJJ, well then, that's the end of the world and my parents will throw a fit!"

Her parents? Why did her parents care?

"Oh, sure," Ruti continued. "You know, they say they want the best for me, but all they really want is the best for their image. You know, they say they love me, but, ha, I know they don't really love *me*. They love the me I've built for them. It's always pressure, pressure, pressure, you know?" She took another deep breath. "The calories! I can't control anything, not even what I eat! I can't get fat, you know?"

"But you're so skinny!" I gasped.

She began laughing hysterically and suddenly I felt very scared. The awful smell in the room. I wanted to get up and run out, but I was glued onto the bed and I couldn't move. My heart was palpitating and I was desperately hoping, praying with every fiber of my being, that she wouldn't say what I thought she was saying. My hands were shaking and suddenly I was shivering again, and I hoped that this was all some kind of sick, warped dream that I would wake up from in a second.

"That's because I throw it all up!" she said with another hysterical bark of laughter. "Every single one of my meals. You don't understand how much I love cake and cookies and ice cream and even steak, but I can't get fat, you know? So, no one sees how much I eat anymore, because nothing stays with me. Nothing. I just eat and eat and eat and eat and then throw it all up, so it shouldn't stick to me and make me fat. Because if I get fat, then I won't get a good *shidduch*, and then my parents' lives are ruined, and who's going to be the one who's going to pay if that happens? Me, hello!"

I felt ill suddenly.

"And I have no one to talk to," she said angrily. "I used to be such good friends with Esti Waldman, but my parents don't let me talk to her anymore because her family is not my family's type. It's just not fair!" she burst out. "It's just not *fair*! I'm under so much pressure, I just might pop!"

My head was pounding. Not only was her life completely messed up. She had bulimia.

"I knew you would understand, Ella," she said. "That's why I'm telling you all this, things that I never told anyone. I really look up to you, you know? You don't care what other people think. You don't smile just because it's Monday morning and you should, technically, greet a new week with a stupid, sunny smile."

I smiled wanly, but really I felt sick to my stomach. Who was this girl? What was I supposed to do? She was ill and was desperately begging for some form of help, but I couldn't just be like, "Oh, why don't we go talk to Morah Bluestein about this?" She trusted me. Only me. I was the only one who knew.

"I can't handle this anymore, Ella," she said.

I looked at her and gulped and nodded. There were tears running down my face and every part of my body was shaking. If people like Ruti Reuben, whom everyone thought was so perfect, really had all these horrible problems, then who really did have a good life? People like me, who had half their problems in their head?

I felt like *I* would throw up.

And then, the door swung wide open, and in came Morah Bluestein with an angry look on her face.

"Why aren't you girls at the speech?" she hissed, oblivious to the tears on our faces. "Ruti Reuben, I am especially disappointed in you. From Ella, I would expect it, but from our star student? You were supposed to introduce Rabbi Myers. What will he think?"

Ruti didn't answer.

"I'm *waiting*, Ruti!"

Talk about being harsh! And she was always so nice to me. Now I knew it was all because of low expectations. Guess that's what they have for all "at-risk" kids like me.

"You girls better take your things and come with me to where I'm staying," Morah Bluestein said, crossing her arms. "You'll be spending the rest of Shabbos there."

Without even protesting, Ruti took her suitcase and stood up. I grabbed my bag with the pajamas and suit-bag. I tried to judge favorably and think that the only reason Morah Bluestein was being so hard on us was because she couldn't see our tears in the dark room, but she didn't even look at us as we walked solemnly to her suite on the first floor.

Her suite was actually more like an apartment, with one big bedroom, two smaller ones, a living room, and even a small kitchenette. Her husband was sitting and learning in the living room.

He gasped when we came in. "Chaya, what's wrong with your students?"

Morah Bluestein turned around and it was like it was the first time she saw us. Her eyes widened and her mouth dropped open. "Girls," she whispered, "I'm so sorry. What's wrong?"

I looked at Ruti, expecting her to say something. She didn't. Finally, Morah Bluestein said again, "Girls?"

Ruti started sobbing again. "I'm tired of keeping this in for so long, Ella! Tell her, tell her everything!"

And so I did. Morah Bluestein started crying, too, and her husband brought us some tea, which Ruti didn't want to drink.

"You'll be spending the rest of Shabbos here," Morah Bluestein said, but this time, it was more softly, more tenderly, as if she wanted to take care of us. She promised she wouldn't tell anyone what had happened and about Ruti's problem, but she assured us that she would get help. I felt as if a burden had been lifted off my shoulders.

Everyone thought Ruti and I had gotten in trouble, which was why we spent the rest of Shabbos with Morah Bluestein. No one knew the real reason; no one ever would. On Sunday, once we got back home, I made up with Tova. She was surprised, but the whole fight just wasn't worth it for me anymore. In a sense, I felt defeated, like I had been fighting my own invisible battle for too long against something that was only imaginary.

Ruti didn't come to school on Monday. Everyone just thought she had gotten the flu from one of Morah Bluestein's kids. I called her, but she wasn't in the mood of talking. She told me a little bit about a counselor she had met with.

I felt broken inside; my illusions had been shattered.

But no matter how many emotions I had experienced that Shabbos, and no matter how many changes I vowed to make because of it all, I still screamed when Michal told me on Tuesday morning that she was giving my room to the guests.

26

"WHAT DO YOU MEAN, I have to give up my room?" I yelled. "That's like an invasion of personal space!"

I could see Michal take a deep breath.

"Why don't Yaffa and Margalit have to give up their room? Why doesn't Tova have to give up her room? Why doesn't Ari have to give up his room?" I continued. This was a blatant display of favoritism, and I was so not going to sit here and tolerate it!

"Ella," Michal said softy. "I was going to give the Shenkers the little girls' room and have Yaffa and Margalit move in with Tova. But then I heard that they are bringing along their little daughter, so I'll have to put her in Yaffa and Margalit's room. Your room is the next choice for the Mr. and Mrs. Shenker, because it is bigger than Tova's or Ari's rooms."

"So?"

"Ella, please, just this once, could you let it go and not make a big deal about it? I have to go pick them up from the airport soon. Oh, and if you could, please change the linen on the beds in your room and make up the extra bed in Tova's room for yourself."

Anything else? This was so unfair! Whatever happened to democracy? And in the confines of my own home, too! "No one ever gives me a choice around here!" I muttered as I stomped off. At least Tova wasn't interfering; that was all I could say. And she did whisper that she'd take care of setting up my bed for me.

After I'd gotten home from school, I went upstairs to Tova's room and basically stayed there the whole evening, even when I heard happy voices from downstairs. That meant our guests were there. Well, whatever. They'd see me soon enough, wouldn't they?

I was so not in the mood of socializing. I mean, who were these people anyway? Michal's sister's *chassan's* brother and his wife and kid? Puh-leeze. I had much better things to do. Like sleep. Tomorrow, the wedding day, was going to be one of those abnormally long days that required a whole lot of unnecessary smiling, and I needed every ounce of energy possible for it.

Tova shook me awake at seven the next morning. "Ella!" she yelled. "Come on, get up!"

I groaned and rolled over.

I got out of bed soon enough. Tova drove Margalit, Yaffa, and me to the hairdresser and then the make-up artist. By the time we got home, it was already noon. Our guests had left, and although Michal's nails and makeup were perfect, she looked like she was going to have a meltdown.

"We have to be at the hall in an hour!" she said. "Adele is marrying into a *yekkishe* family and they're going to start pictures right on time! Girls, get into your gowns."

I had to wear that wretched gold gown that Tova picked out for me when I was in exile, and I was so not happy about it. Tova gave me a sympathetic look, but this really had been her fault, if you thought about it. Well, mostly, anyway.

After smiling like some kind of deranged plastic doll for like three hours while the photographer took all the family pictures, I went to the lounge in the bathroom, because that was the only place that was semi-private. Most of the guests were arriving now for the smorgasbord and *kabbalas panim*, and I needed a few minutes alone before socializing with the world.

Unfortunately, I only got a moment.

Then, two women walked in and began fixing their *sheitels* in front of the mirror. They had their backs turned to me and were so involved in their conversation that they didn't even notice that they weren't alone in the room.

Huddled in a chair in the corner of the room and nearly obscured by all the bags of *shtick* that were strewn around, I tried to mind my own business. Still, I couldn't help but overhear what they were saying. Especially when they began talking about…me.

"So, Zahava," said the one who had gold buckles on her shoes, "did you see Michal's new stepdaughter? You know, the scowling one."

"Uh-huh. I find it hilarious really," Zahava answered.

Well, excuse me for not being Miss Susie Sunshine! As if they had even *tried* seeing things from my point of view. That's all they could say about me — that I was some kind of scowling teenager? Okay, maybe I wasn't all rainbows and unicorns, but they didn't even *know* me! They had no right to talk about me.

"Well, I'm glad I'm not the only one who noticed!" Buckles giggled like a little girl.

What did they notice? Did I have a stain on my gown or something? That would be so embarrassing.

"I remember Michal so well from when she was that age. The look on that girl's face — what's her name again? Ayelet? — is practically identical to the one Michal used to walk around wearing!"

What?! I was like Michal? Well, she had said so herself, but to hear it from someone else was different. Oh, this was news. News that I suddenly didn't feel so comfortable hearing. I squirmed.

Buckles tsk-tsked. "Yes, that cynical, bitter, cold personality. Am I glad Michal worked on herself to get over it. No one likes a person who walks around in a self-absorbed, dark world like that. I pity this Ayelet's family."

I wanted to scream. Who asked this lady for her pity? I felt like calling out, "You know, I'm right here!" I wanted their faces to mirror some of the shame that I felt. How dare these women talk like this about me! This was none of their business. Instead of feeling sorry for my family or me, they should've felt sorry for themselves. Talking about people they didn't even know behind their backs. Assessing other peoples' lives as if they knew better. Like they knew what I was going through. Like they knew what it was like to lose someone you love and then have to replace that person with someone else.

And these women — they thought they were sooo perfect and sooo wonderful. Well, it might have surprised them to know that what they were speaking was pure *lashon hara*. Who did they think they were helping? In whose life were they making a difference by talking...about me?

"Hey, there's hope for her," Zahava said. "If Michal could change, anyone could!"

Wow, so sweet of them. I was so glad that they thought there was hope for me. Really and truly, I was touched.

The two finished tweaking their *sheitels* and left the bathroom, still talking.

My head was reeling. Emotions swirled and charged within me — anger, hurt, shame, and...hope. Anger and hurt at being the target of their ugly *lashon hara* conversation. Shame for the way people were perceiving me. And that tiny spark of hope for the wisp of a dream that, like Zahava had said, if Michal could change, then maybe, just maybe, so could I…

Three minutes after they left the bathroom, I left, too. Just then, the band started playing and the *chassan* entered with an entire crew of men for the *badeken*. The floor shook as the men danced in and Adele's *chassan* covered her face. I could feel my eyes tearing. Weddings always do that to me.

The *chuppah* was beautiful! Which *chuppah* isn't, after all? As Adele marched down the aisle, her parents proudly holding her hands, I couldn't help but feel the familiar lump in my throat I always get before tears. I glanced at the *chassan* swaying with concentration under the canopy, and my eyes began to water. I was so not going to cry.

But, like I said, I always do at weddings, and Tova just smiled and handed me a tissue.

After the first round of dancing, I went back to the lounge in the bathroom to catch my breath. Suddenly, I saw an unfamiliar woman, who had been there before I came in, staring at me.

Oh, no, not again. Was she also noticing my scowl and thinking how comical it was that I was so *similar* to my stepmother because of it? Was she going to go *yent* to all her friends about it, too?

Before I had a chance to turn away, the woman began hesitantly approaching me. At this point, it would've been plainly and simply rude to walk away, so I just stood where I was, staring back at her.

"You know, you look so much like someone I once knew," the woman said to me. She appeared to be in her mid-forties and had a heart-shaped, friendly face and dancing brown eyes. For some reason, I immediately took a liking to her.

"Oh?" I said. "I mean, my name is Ella Sender. I don't know if that helps you at all, though."

The woman paled. "*Sender?* Any relation to Rena Goldsmith who married a Sender?"

My mouth dropped open and for a few seconds I couldn't speak. Finally I whispered, "She was my mother."

"*What?!* You're Rena's daughter?" For a second, I thought the woman was going to faint. Then she took a deep breath and composed herself. "I-I...your mother and I were best friends all throughout high school and beyond. She was like a sister to me. Closer, even. And now, after all these years, to meet up with her own daughter, who looks so much like her...!"

Without warning, the woman reached out and hugged me. Tightly. I stood there stupidly for a moment, and then awkwardly returned the hug.

Then she pulled away and looked at me. "I don't think I even introduced myself to you yet! My name is Shoshana Shenker."

Shenker, Shenker. "Wait a minute! Are you by any chance staying at our house?"

Mrs. Shenker stared at me. "Hey, that's right. We're staying with David and Michal Sender. That's your father and...?"

"Stepmother," I finished briefly for her. "Michal married my father a few months ago."

"I can't believe this!" She shook her head in amazement. "Sender is a common last name, you know. I had no idea I would be staying with my best friend Rena's kids... None of you were around yesterday when we came, and if I hadn't seen you now, I wonder if I'd have ever known... Hey, I think I'm even staying in your room!"

So she was our guest! Her husband was Adele's *chassan's* brother!

All at once, I was gratified I hadn't put up a fuss with Michal and refused to give up my room for the Shenkers.

"And," she continued, "if I remember correctly, you have a twin sister, right?"

I nodded. "Yeah, Tova. And a brother, too — his name is Ari."

Mrs. Shenker gazed off into space. "That's right. Ari. I don't remember him too well, though. He was the baby when…when — "

"When my mother died," I finished off for her again. For a moment, there was silence.

"Oh, and this is my little girl," Mrs. Shenker said, introducing the little girl who was standing shlyly next to her. "Chaya Rena."

I gulped hard. "Named after my mom."

Mrs. Shenker nodded.

"Mrs. Shenker — " I began.

"Call me Auntie Shoshana," she interrupted me. "That's what I told your mother I wanted her kids to call me."

"O-okay. Auntie Shoshana, how come you never contacted us after my mother died?" I asked.

Auntie Shoshana looked away, and all of a sudden, I regretted being so blunt. "I'm sorry," I said. "I didn't mean to — "

"No," Auntie Shoshana said. "You have a right to ask. When Rena died," she said softly, "it was like my whole world came to an end. Your mother and I were so close, Ella. So, so close. She was the best person in the world." Auntie Shoshana sniffed loudly. "And I know people just say that about everybody, but about Rena it was true. She never let anything bother her, you know? She was just so serene and accepting, and when…when she…when she died, I couldn't believe it. It hurt so much, Ella. I went through a really hard time and well…" She looked at me apologetically.

"Some people like to talk about everything, you know? I'm just one of those people who like to pretend my problems don't exist. It's just easier to block everything out. And that's what I did." She hugged me again. "I'm so sorry. Your mom would be so proud to see how much you grew up. She loved you kids more than anything in the world."

"I...I don't think my mom would be so proud of me," I blubbered. "I think she'd hate me."

"Why do you think that?" Auntie Shoshana said, grabbing me by my shoulder and looking me in the eye.

"Because I'm nothing like her! I don't accept anything, and I'm just bad," I managed to say through my tears.

"No one's perfect, Ella," Auntie Shoshana said.

"I know," I said. "But no one's like me either."

"Ella," Auntie Shoshana said, holding both my shoulders. "Your mom would have had faith in you. She would have known that you would do your best to be the best person you could be. All you have to do is have a little faith in yourself."

IT WAS TWO WEEKS AFTER the wedding and I had just finished talking to Auntie Shoshana on the phone. She and I had
already grown amazingly close, and since she'd returned
home to Eretz Yisrael, we'd spoken on the phone almost every day.
This time I had called her to share my exciting news: I was done
writing my play! It was three in the morning for me and ten a.m.
for her — a perfect time for a celebratory chat.

After I put down the phone, I fondled the papers on my desk and
added a little flourish with my pen under the last words. I couldn't
believe it! I had actually finished writing my first play!

The next morning when I woke up (after a scant four hours
of sleep!), I felt invigorated. The past few weeks, particularly the
Shabbaton and wedding, had just been so…stressful. My head had
consistently felt like it was going to burst or spontaneously combust,
but now…I finally felt like everything could calm down, could relax,
even if just a little bit.

I hummed as I got dressed. Maybe Tzippa would come with
me to The Coffee Room after school, and who knows, maybe even
Naomi would find some time to hang out with the rest of us lowly

folk who didn't have major parts in the play. It was going to be a good day. I could just feel it. I could hear the birds chirping, the sun was shining on this winter morning, and even though the trees were stark and black against a whitish-silvery sky, they seemed to hold the promise of spring. *Soon,* they seemed to be telling me, *little green leaves will begin to bud. Soon the world will be electrified with color.*

For some reason, I decided to take the bus to school instead of getting a ride with Tzippa as usual. It was still rather early, so I didn't have to worry at all about being late. I walked, breakfast-less, to the bus stop a few blocks away. As I waited for the bus, I noticed how alive the whole world seemed, even at this early hour. Cars sped. People walked. Motion swirled and colors blurred around me.

The blue and white city bus pulled up to the bus stop and I rummaged through my bag for my Metrocard. Marching up the three steps of the bus, I was startled to see how crowded it was so early in the morning. There were *frum* men with long *payos* sitting in the front of the bus, their Gemaras open and their eyes slowly scanning the pages. Rowdy high school teenagers jostled each other and laughed, the neon yellows, pinks, and greens of their sneakers creating a stark contrast with the black floor and the blue seats of the bus. All around me was more noise and more color, all of it glimmering, pulsating with this thing I could almost taste: life.

As my eyes continued roving over the crowd of people, they suddenly caught sight of a familiar flash of orange-red at the back of the bus. The long, long hair in a braid, the usually inquisitive, lively green eyes, for some reason now looking rather downcast, almost... dulled. Chaiky Cukier. From where I stood, squashed between two big black teens, I knew that she could not see me. But I had an excellent view of her, and for a moment, I just watched her. To tell you the truth, I was rather curious about her now. After that whole crazy

Shabbaton, where I'd seen all too clearly that the facades people put on are sometimes the complete opposite of who they really are, the thought gnawed at me: Was all this, all this pomp and craziness of Chaiky Cukier, only some kind of...show?

From my vantage point, Chaiky looked rather small and vulnerable — her shoulders rounded, her arms held close to her chest, as if she was trying to protect herself. Her eyes were not darting wildly as they usually did, as if trying to capture the entire world. Instead, they were fixed on some point in the distance, some point outside, far away. It seemed as if she was completely oblivious to the whizzing traffic and commotion going on around her.

What was Chaiky Cukier thinking about? What could possibly concern the girl whose greatest joy was in telling us that pearls did not melt in vinegar? Yes, every once in a while I would wonder, were all the screws one hundred percent tight in Chaiky's mind? Every once in a while I would catch myself thinking, *What is* wrong *with that girl?* But now, I could only think about how sad she looked. How her skin looked whiter than usual. How every freckle on her face seemed to be screaming, *Look at me! Look at me!* How, with her red braid unraveling, she was holding so tightly onto that metal pole.

I got off a few stops before I had to. Firstly, because I had time to walk, and secondly, because I didn't want Chaiky to see me. For once, she looked normal. Why was it only when she was around me that she became totally crazy?

When I got to school, the halls were emptier than usual. I didn't remember having ever arrived at school that early! I almost expected one of the teachers to come marching out and yell at me, "Miss Sender, what are you doing here so early?" But the halls were quiet. I liked that.

As I stood at my locker, I couldn't help but take my play out of my schoolbag (yes! I had brought it to school with me! Go laugh all you want, but I had been working on this thing for months!) and read through parts of it. I couldn't believe that I had actually written this play. I was so comfortable in my own little world, a world which I myself had created, that a locker banging shut startled me. I looked up.

It was Ruti Reuben. I suddenly realized that I had not seen her since the Shabbaton two weeks ago. At this point, it felt like *years* ago.

"Hi, Ella," she said quietly. Her hair was in a neat pony and her cheeks were rosy.

Cautiously, I asked, "Is this your first day back?"

She nodded silently, her face still closed and wooden-like. I couldn't believe it. This was Ruti Rueben. This was the girl who sang and danced on stage, whom all the teachers adored, whom everyone was secretly just a little bit jealous of. This was Ruti Rueben...and I, Ella Sender, the girl whom everyone felt needed help and *rachmanus*, felt bad for her.

I put my arm around her shoulder. "It's good to have you back, Ruti," I said.

Ruti stiffened. She knew. She knew that I felt bad for her. In this weird world, the tables had been completely turned. And now, Ruti was the one on the other side. She was the object of my pity. And I was the only one who knew who she really was and how she really felt.

I know what it feels like. The glance the girls give you when you walk down the hall; the way they only look at you for a second but you see it in their eyes — that mixture of pity, sadness, and sometimes even a hint of laughter. I know what it's like to have girls come sit down next to you by Shabbatons and ask you, "How are you?" not because they care about how you really are, but because they think they have to be nice, and the object of their kindness happens to be you. I know what it's like to stand outside the circle of dancing girls at *chagigahs*, watching everyone spin around and seeing all their hands so tightly clasped together. And then, some girl, well-meaning, no doubt, with a bounce in her curls and a smile plastered on her face, will come and try to draw you into the circle because she is a kind girl and she doesn't want you to feel like you are left out. But, like everyone else, she doesn't understand. It isn't a feeling that she can erase with her kindness. It is just the way you are — a girl who knows she doesn't belong.

And now, that was what I was doing to Ruti. Because I didn't know how else to treat her. I was being saccharine sweet and all we-missed-you-so-much-come-let-me-stick-a-chessed-sticker-onto-your-head to Ruti. But wasn't the reason she confided in me only because she thought I would understand what it was like to be different, and because she had hoped I wouldn't treat her the way she knew the other girls would?

Now, I had become like the old Ruti Reuben! I could feel the bile in my mouth. No! I would not sugar-coat this for Ruti. She did not come to me because she wanted sugar-coating. She did not want someone to pat her on the shoulder and tell her that sunshine and goodness would return to her life once again. She had oodles of admiring girls who called themselves her friends to do that for her. What Ruti really wanted was someone who would understand.

It was weird for me to have to suddenly play this opposite role. To be the understanding one, the listener, instead of the kvetcher. But, I suddenly realized, I was…lucky. I was lucky because I had people to kvetch to. I had Naomi and Tzippa, real friends who would listen to my kvetching and would not just try to categorize it and make me move on, but who would understand and really care. While Ruti had...no one like that. Except, maybe...*me?*

I looked her right in the eye. "So how is that BJJ application coming along?" I asked.

Ruti looked at me. For a second, her eyes widened with shock. But then she started giggling, laughing so hard that her body was shaking. The wooden expression slid off her face, and she actually looked like a regular girl who was frustrated. "Oh, Ella," she said. "These past two weeks have been so crazy. It's like everyone is on top of me all of a sudden. I mean, I understand that they care, but this has been like a massive, family-wide intervention, you know? With the cousin who's a psychologist, and the brother-in-law's friend's neighbor who's a psychiatrist, and all the married siblings being flown in to discuss what to do with me. And everyone's just been so serious, serious, serious. They walk around with grave faces and everything. And I know, I know that bulimia is a serious thing. But I am so happy that I have someone to joke around with! It was getting depressing! I thought I would never see the sunlight again. I thought they would lock me up in the house until I passed some kind of normalcy test."

"Aha," I said. "Welcome to my world. Seriously, Ruti, I am so happy you are getting better. It all isn't worth making yourself sick. That much I could tell you."

Ruti smiled. "I know. I just don't know how it got so bad. It was like I almost couldn't realize what I was doing to myself."

Then Ruti became her studious self again. "I've missed out on so much schoolwork!" she groaned. "I am so not prepared for class. Ella, would you go over with me the Malbim we're up to in Morah Herman's class?"

"Me?" I stared at her. "Ruti, I am like Morah Herman's least favorite student in the whole world. That woman abhors me!"

Ruti shrugged. "So what? You were in school these past two weeks. I wasn't. I haven't even cracked open any *sefarim*. You must know it better than me."

"We'll see about that!" I said. We opened up our *sefarim*, Ruti Reuben and I, and for a few moments, it felt…normal. Then the bell rang.

When Morah Herman's class began, I immediately felt her beady gaze staring down at me. I felt like a pigeon. What else was new?

"Miss Sender," Morah Herman said in that cool voice of hers. "Would you like to read the Malbim for us?"

I began reading. I never realized what a difference some preparation could make! Really. The words were flowing off my tongue like butter. I was transliterating; I was explaining; I was mixing my own ideas in; I was unstoppable. The classroom was quiet. As I began reading the last paragraph of the Malbim (whew!), I snuck a glance at Morah Herman.

Her eyes were wide and she was smiling. She looked proud.

"I can see that someone really prepared for class today," she said, her voice swelling with some emotion I could not pinpoint. Her eyes were shining. "Good job, Ella."

I smiled. A little voice in the back of my head said, *See? That wasn't so bad, was it?* Well, after putting in preparation beforehand, of course it wasn't! It wasn't like I had woken up brilliant this morning, all perfect and able to recite a Malbim without batting an eyelash. This had taken effort and work on my part.

But then something got me thinking. Ruti, whom I had always thought of as so brilliant and perfect, had *worked* to be that way. Sure, she had taken it to an unhealthy level. But perfection wasn't something one cultivated overnight while getting her beauty sleep. Perfection was something one chased endlessly…almost like Tova did. Tova *worked* to be good. Being good wasn't something that had just stumbled onto her plate.

The bell rang. Was class over already? The girls quickly shuffled out of the room and suddenly it was just me and Morah Herman.

"You really did a beautiful job with that Malbim today, Ella," Morah Herman said.

I couldn't believe what I was hearing. Was she actually…complimenting me? Me, Ella Sender, the child of scorn and trouble? She thought I had done a beautiful job at something! Me!

"Thank you," I said, shuffling some of my papers together.

"You know Ella," Morah Herman said, "I make you girls prepare the *mefarshim* for class not because I am trying to get out of teaching you, but because when you come in having already read the material, you can grasp the concepts more easily and you can participate better in class. Do you understand what I'm saying?"

"Yes," I said. I did understand her point. I also could not believe that we were having a normal conversation, Morah Herman and I. Of all my teachers — Morah Herman! The one who I'd thought was totally out to get me. The one who I'd thought couldn't stand me and couldn't wait till I got out of her classroom. And wonder of wonders! That same Morah Herman seemed to actually be a nice person after all! Her eyes, looking deeply into mine, didn't seem to carry an ounce of hate for me at all. I remembered all the *chutzpadik* comments I'd said to her, and I suddenly felt ashamed.

"Morah Herman," I began to say. "I just…I just want to say that I know I am not always the best and most motivated student in class, and I'm really sorry for all the times that I wasn't respectful."

"Ella," Morah Herman said, "it means a lot for me to hear that from you."

She smiled at me, and I, not knowing what else to do, awkwardly smiled back.

"Now run along to your next class!" she said.

THE REST OF THE DAY passed by in a blurrrrr. Classes, lunch, more classes, drama practice.

"So, Tzippa," I said as we banged our lockers shut at the end of the day, "are you up for a night out?"

"Totally!" Tzippa exclaimed. "I don't know about you, Ella, but drama really drains me! I need fun!"

"Did anyone mention the word fun?" Heidi Brown said, waltzing down the hall, her backpack slung casually over her shoulder. "I need some fun, too! Why don't we go out tonight?"

"Naomi? How about you?" I asked, turning to Naomi who had been sitting on the floor, studying for tomorrow's calculus test.

"I don't know," Naomi said slowly. "There is the big math test, and the play day is rapidly approaching, so…"

"Aw!"

"Come on!"

"A girl needs to have some fun!"

"Well, okay," Naomi said, getting up. "But only if we get fruit smoothies instead of lattes. I'm getting really sick of coffee."

"Great, we can go to Iced Cream Cafe!" Heidi said with a smile. "Let's just forget about the calories for one day!"

"Yeah," Naomi agreed. "I heard they have some great tropical smoothies there! Plus they have some sugar-free stuff!"

"You mean the kiwi-pineapple mixes? Yum!" Tzippa said.

When did everyone try these? "Hey, I want to try this!"

"Okay, so let's do it!" Naomi said.

I smiled. This was going to be fun.

The school was pretty empty, since everyone had already left, besides the drama girls. The four of us grabbed our things and headed to Tzippa's car, chatting about the fun stuff we would do. First, we'd get smoothies, then we'd hit the mall because there were great sales this week, and after that, maybe we'd all study for the calculus test together at Naomi's house.

Could life get any more fun?

"Hey, guys!" said an overeager voice as we left the school building. "Where are you going?"

It was Chaiky, and to tell you the truth, she looked absolutely ridiculous. She had a piece of hot-pink fabric tied around her head, totally clashing with her red hair. And she was wearing a huge yellow smiley-face sweatshirt, and yes, her white espadrilles.

It was Tzippa who answered, because I think the rest of us were reeling from shock.

"Oh, we're just going out. You know, to get some smoothies, then maybe go shopping and — "

"That sounds like so much fun!" Chaiky said, jumping up from the step she was sitting on.

She started to walk with us. "So, where are we getting smoothies from? Smiley's? Choco Roco?"

We?

We got into the car and Chaiky got in with us, too, sliding into the seat right next to me.

"Weren't you waiting for someone?" I said slowly. I mean, she was sitting on the steps, and most people sit there when they are waiting for their rides.

Chaiky's cucumber-colored eyes sparkled. "Yes!" she said.

"Who?"

"You!"

I could feel my eyebrows furrow in confusion.

Chaiky Cukier was *so* weird sometimes.

On the way to Iced Cream Cafe, we practiced a scene in the play which all of us were in, while Chaiky whistled loudly to herself.

Was she even normal?

I took a deep breath. I remembered how "normal," and vulnerable, Chaiky had looked on the bus that morning. Trouble was, the way she was acting now, it was quite hard to think of her as being anything other than weird and sooo annoying...

As soon as we got to Iced Cream Cafe, Chaiky Cukier jumped out of the car. Tzippa hadn't even parked yet. She ran to the door, her hair flying, and held it open for two tall businessmen, who were just leaving the place. They gave her confused looks. Hmm, I couldn't imagine why.

I couldn't help but notice the nervous look that flashed in Chaiky's eyes for a second as we walked into Iced Cream Cafe. Then it was over and she winked at me.

"Welcome to Iced Cream Cafe, madam," she said in this smarmy British announcer's voice. "Do sit down and there will be someone to serve you shortly."

I laughed. Okay, she was kind of funny. I could almost picture her as a fat, little butler.

"Come on, Elz!" Heidi said. She and Naomi and Tzippa were already sitting at a cozy little booth. A booth that only fit four people.

I looked at Chaiky, who for some odd reason had turned that same weird shade of pink that I had noticed on her before. At least that matched her ribbon. She noticed I was looking at her and gave me a prim, little smile. "I'll go get a chair," she said in her new accent.

Uh-oh, did she think I actually *liked* that accent? I'd never hear the end of it, ever. Wherever I'd go, whatever I'd do, that sycophantic little accent would be following me, nagging me about how we should be best friends. No. No way. *Totally* no way. Even though I knew Chaiky was smiling at me, I didn't look at her.

I quickly sat down at the booth with my friends. Tzippa was poring over the glossy menu and Naomi and Heidi were making themselves comfortable in the upholstered seats. The entire place had a hushed and elegant tone, no doubt intended to be as inviting as possible for customers. I sighed with contentment. I had to come here more often.

"I'm here!" Chaiky said happily as she dragged a chair from one of the tables. It screeched against the floor as she brought it over.

We all looked at her. The waiter positively *stared* at her.

"Uh, madam," he said in a voice that was almost identical to the almost-accent Chaiky had been using earlier. "We don't allow customers to move chairs."

"But I want to sit with my friends!" Chaiky protested loudly.

The waiter sniffed. "I'm sorry, but we don't allow customers to move chairs," he repeated.

To tell to you the truth, I almost felt bad for Chaiky. She looked pitiful, the ridiculous headband in her red hair drooping along with her eyes. And people were staring.

"It's okay," I muttered. "We'll squish." I moved over until I was practically sitting in Tzippa's lap. Tzippa gave me a look. Well, what could I do?

"Ow!" Chaiky screeched as she moved in next to me.

Huh? I mean, it was kind of *smooshy*, but that really didn't call for a scream and everything, did it?

I could feel Heidi's eyes boring into my forehead.

Oh. *Oh.*

The waiter primly lifted the chair and carried it away. A few moments later, he was there to take our orders.

"Four tropical smoothies, please!" Naomi said.

"Sugar-free," Heidi cautioned, her face as serious as ever.

The waiter nodded as he scribbled the order furiously onto his notepad.

Yum, I couldn't wait to try it!

"And I will have —" Chaiky started to say.

"A tropical smoothie, as well?" the waiter asked.

"No, no!" Chaiky shook her head emphatically. "I want a strawberry-banana shake with whipped cream and swirls of chocolate and a chunk of vanilla-pineapple ice cream."

I saw the waiter's eyes widen as he scribbled on his little pad. As he scurried away, we all stared.

"Do you *know* how many calories that has?" Heidi managed to say. Her eyes were as round as saucers, and I could see her cheeks getting a little flushed. After Torah and *avodas Hashem*, Weight Watchers ranks on Heidi's most-important-things-in-life list.

"Who cares?" Chaiky shrugged.

Heidi blinked.

I felt my mouth drop open and I could almost see Naomi, who has always been just a tad chubby, stiffen.

"Well," Tzippa said in that delicate voice of hers — the one she always used when she was trying to ease tension. "Calculus sure is getting more challenging these days."

"Yeah," Heidi said, still eyeing Chaiky. "What did everyone get on the last test? My 74 was like the crowning glory of this year's achievements."

"I got a 99," Tzippa offered modestly. "Which is pretty bad for me."

"Tzippa!" We all groaned. Tzippa is a math freak.

"I got an 82," Naomi complained. "After studying like crazy. It just isn't fair!"

Heidi laughed. "I'm totally happy with my fabulous mark. What about you, Ella?"

"Oh, well, that is something you *don't* want to know," I said, dropping my voice to a whisper. "Trust me, you *really don't* want to know what I got!"

"Come on!"

"All right," I said with a sigh. "I got a 65. I suspected I was just passed because she felt bad for me."

Heidi started laughing hysterically. "You're a *riot*! If you ask me, studying is such a waste of time. I mean, like I gain thousands of calories while I'm studying because I'm constantly *fressing* out on double-chocolate-chip cookies, and then I never do well in any case! I bet you didn't even study. "

"I did, too!" I exclaimed. "A little," I added.

Tzippa and Naomi giggled.

The waiter brought us our smoothies and Chaiky's masterpiece. It was a sight, I tell you. I tried not to stare. The biggest glass I had ever seen was filled with a frothy pink liquid and topped with oodles and oodles of soft, cloudlike whipped cream. Wisps of princess-pink cotton candy decorated the border, and on top of it all was a waterfall of chocolate and chunks of pale yellow.

I swallowed. Hard.

I took a sip of my smoothie, which was delicious. "Derivates have never been my thing. I missed that one lesson on functions last year, and since then nothing has ever been the same."

"Well," Heidi said, "I missed that lesson on —"

"*I'm* not taking calculus, guys!" Chaiky Cukier said suddenly, a huge smile on her face. I noticed she was, um, eating her drink with a spoon. Not the ice cream part. She had placed that on a small dish near her glass. No, the pink froth. Like it was soup. Umm... This really wasn't such a big deal, was it?

"Oh, no?" Tzippa said vaguely.

"Nope." Chaiky shook her head. "I'm taking AP Spanish instead. Languages have always been my thing."

"Oh," Naomi muttered.

Tzippa nodded slowly, not fully comprehending what Chaiky was trying to say.

Heidi and I just stared.

We spent the next half-hour listening to Chaiky blab about how hard it was to conjugate some Spanish verbs, and how she was considering taking some courses in Latin and then maybe French. And how after that, she wanted to study Russian and Polish and then maybe take a tour of the entire Europe.

Right.

Right.

Why did Chaiky Cukier confuse me? Why did I feel like there was something different about her? It was like she just didn't care about what anyone else thought.

When we got to the mall, Chaiky insisted that we go to stores that I would never have stepped foot in.

"Oh!" Chaiky said, giving me a dazzlingly white smile. "Why don't we go to Tauber's? They have the nicest shoes there!"

Tauber's is like this grandma store. The shoes they sell there come in three colors: black, navy, and taupe. Needless to say, it isn't really on my list of stores to visit.

"Actually," Heidi said, "I really want to go to Stella Luna."

I sighed with relief. "Me, too!" I said.

"Me three!" Naomi said.

Tzippa quietly sighed.

"Oh, *all* right," she muttered.

"Zipper!" Chaiky squealed. "It's just me and you, then!"

"Yep."

"What is wrong with her?" Heidi asked as soon as Chaiky and Tzippa were out of earshot. Well, I thought they were out of earshot, anyway. Chaiky turned around just a little bit, but then she flipped her thick, carpet-like, braided orange-red hair and kept walking.

I shrugged. "Chaiky's always been that way," I muttered. "You know, annoying, always there when you *don't* need her, and irritatingly oblivious about it, too."

"How about we go there?" Heidi said, pointing at a boutique where mannequins wearing neon orange suits and Miss America sashes had on huge purple hats with lavender feathers in them.

I gave her a confused look.

"Sounds good," said Naomi with a twinkle in her eye.

"Is there something I'm missing here?"

"The play, hello?" Heidi said. "Don't you remember the fancy ballroom scene? Does this, like, not look like the absolute best place to get costumes from?"

Oh, right, that scene. Personally, the *frum* side of me had a lot of problems with that scene, but since I was the only one who seemed to think this, I didn't really think voicing my opinion was the best idea.

"Lez do it!" I said.

As soon as we walked into the store, we were overcome with the odor of mothballs mixed with what smelled like Chanel No. 5. A clashing symphony of drumrolls and wailing instruments was blaring in the background, while a woman in a maroon peasant dress and hot-pink espadrilles was getting her nails painted a garish bluish color by a girl who honestly couldn't have been more than sixteen, but had snow-white hair piled onto her head, held in place with a turquoise clip.

What alternate *universe* had I entered?

"Look at that!" Heidi said, pointing to a hat shaped like a bird's nest. "I wanna try it on! It looks so heavy! Like it would burn twenty calories on the spot."

She placed the hat on her head and I noticed that there was a teeny bluebird in the nest.

"Hey," I said, poking the bird.

"Cuckoo!"

Naomi practically jumped. "What was that?" she asked, her hand clutching her chest. Her eyes were as round as the moon.

Heidi was silently laughing, her shoulders shaking. "The bird," she managed to gasp. "When Ellala poked the bird, it said, 'Cuckoo!'"

"Who's Ellala?" Naomi asked, a bewildered expression on her face. "And why would a bird call me cuckoo?"

I honestly didn't know if she was being serious or not, but it didn't take long before Heidi, Naomi, and I were practically rolling with laughter. I could barely breathe.

"Oh, Ellalalalala!" Heidi gasped in a very Chaiky-like voice. "Knock, knock."

"Who's there?" I managed to sputter.

"Calorie."

"Calorie who?"

"Calorie Cuckookookoo!"

"Excuse me," said a nasal voice. "Would you ladies like to sample the newest color of Franklina Dowager eye shadow? It's called Purple Moonlight."

I turned around. It was the white-haired girl. I noticed that close up, she had teeny wisps of feathery eyebrows.

"Why, yes," Heidi said, waggling her left eyebrow. She was still wearing the crazy bird hat. "My friends and I most definitely would like to try it on." Talk about pomp.

For some reason, when Heidi did her wacko act, it wasn't half as annoying as when Chaiky did it. In fact, it was kind of enjoyable. Okay, *very* enjoyable. I didn't know if my lungs would ever be the same from laughing so hard.

I felt an uneasy buzz in the back of my head, and I knew it was coming from an uncomfortable realization: When the craziness came from Heidi, I tolerated it and even enjoyed it (and so did everyone else, really), but when it came from Chaiky, it was somehow unbearable. Why was that?

It just didn't make sense.

"I'm sorry," the girl with the white hair said in a prissy voice, suddenly gazing upward at Heidi's head. "Customers aren't allowed to try on the merchandise unless they want to buy it. Ma'am, you're going to have to buy that hat."

"Wha- what?" Heidi said in a confused voice. She looked like she had just been caught shoplifting.

"Ma'am, because that hat touched your head, you're going to have to buy it."

"Bu-but — "

"Twenty-five ninety-five."

I was laughing so hard, it seemed like I was underwater and my ears were clogged up from the pool. "Well, at least you'll have something nice for Purim," I managed to gasp.

"No way," Heidi said, still in disbelief. "No way."

"Hey, it'll be great for your costume as Mrs. Mermelstein!" Naomi said brightly.

Heidi took off the hat and stared at it. "You know what?" she said slowly. "It would!"

We looked around the store for more costumes. I got a long polka-dot skirt made out of this flimsy material, and Naomi got a bright-green plaid suit which, she claimed, must have been the fashion during the early nineteen-hundreds (when the story of the play took place) — and if not, it still looked like it was from a thousand years ago, so it was okay.

Our white-haired friend was now manning the cash register, so we took our finds to her, along with Heidi's hat, in order to pay. Suddenly she was all cheerful with us, telling us what great use we'd get from our purchases and how fortunate we were to have such wonderful fashion sense.

"Now, you have yourselves a great day, gals," she said. "And be sure to come back again for some other great outfits!"

Choking on our laughter, we managed to thank her and escape from the store.

Afterward, we got drinks (Diet Coke for Naomi, Diet Coke for Heidi, and Diet Pepsi with a twist of lemon for me) from one of the little vendors in the mall.

"So, then," Heidi continued, recounting to us about the time her cousin had a solo in her school concert, "some girl that we had never seen before in our lives came and told us she wanted to speak with Ruchala."

"So weird," Naomi said, shaking her head and stirring the ice in her Coke. She likes it when the ice melts. I mean, diluted coke — yuck! But, to each her own, I guess.

As Heidi told us how the girl then went and totally embarrassed Ruchala, I vaguely wondered what Tzippa and Chaiky were doing. Just then, one of the waiters brought us a lemon — not cut, of course, because we didn't know if we could use their knives — but Heidi claimed she could peel a lemon with her hands, and then we could twist it into our drinks.

She started to peel the lemon, and then she asked the waiter for a little baggie. Because she wanted to save the peels for a cake she was making at home.

"You are so weird, Heidi," Naomi said in an admiring voice.

"Aren't we all?" Heidi said with a laugh. Suddenly, a squeeze of lemon squirted in her eye, which made Naomi and me burst into another round of laughter.

"All right, all right," Heidi mumbled. "What time is it, anyway? Didn't we tell Tzippa we'd be back soon?"

"It's late," I said with a gulp as I glanced at my watch. Tzippa was gonna kill...

We rushed to the car. Tzippa was sitting stoically in the driver's seat, staring ahead, and Chaiky was blabbering about the price of tea in China versus England versus India, where tea was originally from.

Tzippa didn't look at us as we got into the car, but her shoulders seemed to relax just a little. She turned on the car and started driving.

"So, what's next on the schedule?" Chaiky asked, pronouncing the word schedule as "sezual," in accordance with her new British accent. Once the fun started, Chaiky just wouldn't let it stop.

"We're going to Tzippa's house," Naomi said.

"Fun!" Chaiky said happily. "We can have a slumber party!"

"Actually, we're going there to study," Heidi said. "For our calculus test." There was a long pause. "And you're taking AP Spanish."

"Oh," Chaiky said in that same, ever-happy voice, except her cheeks were that same weird shade of pink again. "Then, take me home, Zipper!"

Tzippa muttered something I couldn't hear.

We dropped Chaiky off at her small, nondescript house. I don't know, but for some odd reason, I had been expecting a zoo with giraffes and zebras doing the *Horah* out in front.

"*Finally!*" Tzippa said, the moment Chaiky got out of the car. She was angrier than I had ever seen her before. And that's saying something, because Tzippa never gets angry and she never gets annoyed. "She is *so* annoying! You guys left me to deal with her for like the entire afternoon! I mean, I try to be nice and everything, but there is only so much a person can handle. And if anyone ever calls me Zipper, I'll…I'll…"

"We totally understand, Tzippa; what you did was harder than running a ten-mile marathon to burn off dinner," Naomi said soothingly. "You're a *tzadekes* for putting up with her for so long. She is *such* a freak."

I noticed that the car window was open, and I wondered if Chaiky had heard the conversation or not. As we drove away, Chaiky stood by her front door, waving furiously at us, wearing the biggest smile I had ever seen on her lips.

Her eyes were shining so brightly, it almost looked like they were glistening with tears.

"Okay, James," Heidi said to Tzippa. "Take me home."

"Aren't you coming to my house to study?" Tzippa asked, wrinkling up her nose.

"Yeah." Heidi laughed. "I was only joking."

About fifteen minutes later, we pulled up in front of Tzippa's house. We wandered in and found the place to be quiet. It was already pretty late.

"Tzip, where's your fam?" Naomi asked as she dumped her bag in the foyer.

Tzippa shrugged. "I don't know. Everyone's probably out doing their own thing. Come on, let's go to my room."

We headed up to Tzippa's room. Everything in Tzippa's room was white — plain white — from the bedspread to the wall, to the bookshelves, to the wicker chair.

"This is blinding," Heidi said, settling herself on Tzippa's bed. "You don't believe in color, Tzippa?"

Tzippa shook her head. "No," she said in a serious voice. "Color is nothing more than an illusion."

"Well, everything is," Naomi said.

Heavy, heavy stuff.

"I'm going to get a drink," I said suddenly. "That okay, Tzippa?"

Tzippa nodded. "There's a pitcher of water in the fridge, and bottles of seltzer and Diet Pepsi and even cranberry juice. I'll have the cranberry juice."

"Well, Diet Pepsi for me," said Heidi. Naomi's order was also Diet Pepsi, and I decided to have water. I went downstairs, and then I noticed something strange. Naomi had dumped her bag right in front of the door — dead center. Now, it was on the side. The only way it could have been moved was if someone had come into the house and moved it. But I hadn't heard anyone come in, and I didn't hear anyone, other than the four of us, anywhere in the house.

My heart started beating a little faster. Was there someone else in Tzippa's house? Had we locked the door? In fact, the entire place smelled kind of funny.

I gulped. Okay, I was here to get drinks, not to fantasize about robbers in the house like I did when I was six. I walked into the kitchen and then stopped short.

Chana was sitting at the kitchen table. It had been a while since I had seen her. She wasn't dressed like a Bais Yaakov girl anymore. She was wearing a big gray Harvard sweatshirt, with the hood on, and she was leaning backward on her chair ever so slightly, an energy drink in front of her. "Hey," she muttered as I walked in.

For some reason, I felt a little nervous. I took a deep breath. This was going to be fine. This girl was just Tzippa's sister, after all. "Hi," I squeaked. I felt my face flush as I opened Tzippa's pantry and took out four plastic cups. My hands were trembling as I took out two cans of Diet Pepsi from the fridge and poured Tzippa a cup of cranberry juice. Then, I poured myself water.

I could feel Chana watching me as I bustled around the kitchen, making myself quite at home, and that made me even more nervous.

"Four?" she said.

"Um…" I managed to say, even though my tongue felt like lead. "What?"

"Why are there four cups?"

"Well, another classmate of ours is here, too," I blabbered. "Heidi Brown."

She nodded, raising her eyebrow.

229

She wasn't a bad person; but I wondered why she was just sitting at the kitchen table. Didn't she have anything better to do?

"Hey, El," she said again to me, just as I was about to leave the kitchen. Her voice was so low that I might have been able to think that I hadn't heard her. But I had. I slowly turned around.

Chana looked at me for a second, but I almost felt like it was forever. "Why'd you do it?" she finally said.

"Do what?" I asked.

"Go all OTD on everyone."

Gosh, I never understood how the pot could call the kettle black, and all of a sudden the Diet Pepsis in my hand felt really cold.

"*Excuse* me?"

She looked very relaxed, which made me even angrier for some reason. "Don't deny it," she said. "You and I, we're made from a different mold than everyone else. They don't understand us. They never will."

"I…I am not! I am not off the *derech*!" I managed to blubber. "I'm very much on the *derech*! I just have some issues that I need to sort out, that's all!"

Chana just laughed. "Issues. Everyone has issues. The biggest rabbis and rebbetzins have issues. You think you have more issues than everyone else? What makes you so special?"

"So, why did *you* do it?" I said defensively. "Why did *you* go off the *derech*?"

She stopped laughing and raised her eyebrows, as if she hadn't been expecting this. Sure, she had probably been asked this question by parents and teachers many times. But this time, it was different. Because this time, I wasn't trying to fix her. She thought that she and I were confidantes, that we were on the same page.

She was silent for a few moments and sat very straight on her chair, almost as if she was being prosecuted for a crime. "Because," she said, her jaw set very straight, "everyone expected me to."

I looked at her.

"Oh, sure," she said to herself, as if she'd forgotten that I was in the room, "when I was really good, they'd tell me I was wonderful and I was a *tzaddeikes*, but we all knew that it wasn't true. Because at the same time, they never stopped letting me know that I was doing this wrong and I was doing that wrong. I thought too much, I asked too many questions, I wasn't acting like a regular Bais Yaakov girl. They'd get this worried look on their faces and ask me why I couldn't just conform. They just didn't let me be *me*, because *me* was different."

That was the way it always was, wasn't it? If someone was different, they were immediately labeled "bad" and put in a little box away from all the rest. People immediately covered the children's eyes, saying that they didn't want to show them the ugly side of life. But who's to say that different means ugly?

And anyway, life has ugly parts in it, too. Perhaps, if people acknowledge the ugliness in life instead of pushing it deep under the floorboards, they'll be able recognize the beauty in life more.

"They just didn't let me breathe," she said. "And now, I'm drowning. I'm free, but I'm drowning."

Suddenly, this entire situation struck me as very odd. "I have to go," I said.

She took a sip of her drink and I walked out of the room as quickly as I could.

Like Chana, I was also "different". But just because I was different didn't mean I was bad, and it didn't mean I had to drown.

And that's why I had to consciously make a change. I had to stop being so angry. And as much as I'd change and try to become better, when I finally got there, there would probably still be a little of the old me clinging onto the new me, like a strong perfume that would never completely fade away, and I'd need people to accept that that was who I was. I hoped that they wouldn't slam doors in my face because of my differences.

To some people, different automatically means ugly. But I would show them that it could be beautiful to be different.

I would change.

I THINK I DID WELL ON the calculus test. I mean, better than a 65, at least. The study session with my friends must have been effective.

Math is my last period of the day. After we took the test, I chatted with Tzippa, Naomi, and Heidi as we made our way to the auditorium for drama practice. Tova met me on the stairwell. She was on her way home, but she promised to get me a latte to celebrate my successful math test.

I almost hummed as I strolled down the stairway. I had been feeling a lot better, about myself and everything in general, really. It was like everything had almost just clicked into place.

"You seem happy," Tzippa said, giving me an amused smile.

"I am," I said. I really was. Okay, so things at home weren't that great yet, and there were some little nuisances marching around my life, but I was kind of happy. Because I wanted to be.

Then I entered the room of doom, gloom, and shrieking baboons.

Havoc. That was the only way to describe what was going on in the auditorium.

"What's going on, Chanie?" Heidi yelled above the din.

"The play is *off*!" Chanie moaned. "All that work, all the practices are down the drain! I can't believe this!"

"But why?" Tzippa gasped.

"Rebbetzin Greenwald doesn't approve of the script!"

"WHAT?!" Naomi screeched.

I didn't think this was the best time to say, "I told you so." But I had told them. If people would only listen to me, life would be a lot easier. Ugh!

"I don't get it!" Heidi said. "You didn't check it with her beforehand?"

Chanie shook her head. "I *assumed* she had gotten it and read it and since she didn't say anything about it afterward, I just *assumed* everything was okay. Now, when the play is a few weeks away, she tells me she never saw the script and how could we start practicing before she approved of it. Well, as soon as I showed the script to her, kaput! The play is cancelled. Everything is down the drain!"

"But we already sold some tickets!" Tzippa said. "I mean, my cousins coming from LA are flying in early just to see this play."

"And what am I going to do with the nauseating hat I bought?" Heidi groaned.

"And that skirt?" I muttered.

"And that horrible, horrible suit!" Naomi rolled her eyes.

"Well," Chanie said, "Rebbetzin Greenwald said that we just have to get a new script, that's all! But where am I supposed to get a new script? It took Ahuva and me months to find that script!"

Suddenly, the auditorium looked very bright. I could feel the fluorescent lights screaming into my eyes and my heart started to beat a little faster.

Then Chanie started to cry. Heidi, Tzippa, and Naomi rushed to comfort her. I stood there, the puzzles in my head clicking together. Would it work?

"Wait," I said slowly. "I might be able to help."

Everyone looked at me. Everyone. Ahuva and Chanie stopped crying and the fighting group in the corner quieted down.

"I may have a script for you."

"Like what?" Ahuva said sarcastically. "Shakespeare's King Lear or something?"

I blushed hard. "No, more like Ella Sender's."

"You *wrote* a play?" Chanie said slowly. "Isn't that, like, really hard?"

I shrugged.

"Everyone!" Ahuva said. "Let's go to Ella's house. I've got to see this play!"

"How are we going to get there?" Rivky Rhein asked.

"I have a car, Chanie has a car, and Tzippa has a car," Ahuva said, grabbing her jacket. "This play is in just a few weeks! We have to make it snappy!"

I noticed that Chaiky Cukier, who always hung around at drama practice (although she was only part of the costumes committee), didn't get into anybody's car, but I assumed she was just going to walk or something.

The silence in Tzippa's car was almost palpable. I could feel the nervousness in the air; it felt as if we were all headed to a courthouse where our future would be decided. I think my heart was beating the fastest. I mean, I had written that play for fun, but imagine if it would come to life! Me as the princess, of course. But what if the girls all thought it was nerdy? What if they laughed when they read it and thought, who in the world would ever have time to sit and write such a piece of junk — something worthy enough to… blow your nose on?

I rang the doorbell when we got to my house.

"Who is it?" Margalit yelled out in that shrill little voice of hers.

"It's Ella and um, some of my friends."

Margalit slowly opened the door, and I could see her little eyes widen. "Mommy…" she called slowly, and Yaffa came running toward the door, too, her mouth dropping open when she saw all the girls behind me.

Michal was yakking on the phone and she had her apron on when she came to the door. She gave me a surprised look. "Ella, what is going on?" she said.

"Um, it's like this," I said nervously. "You know that play I'm part of? Well, the manuscript was just vetoed. So, I wanted to invite my friends over to show them my play."

Michal looked confused for a second, like she didn't know what to do. "Ah, okay," she said. "Come in, girls, come in."

Heidi socked my shoulder as we entered the house. "This is gonna go great," she whispered. "I can just feel it."

Margalit and Yaffa followed everyone to my room and settled themselves comfortably on my bed.

"Come, sit near me," Yaffa told Rivky Rhein. Rivky looked amused and plopped herself on the bed near Yaffa.

Before, I knew it would have bugged me like crazy to have Yaffa and Margalit there, and I probably would have screamed, but right now, I just looked at the two of them. They were actually kind of cute, if you squinted a little.

I gave Chanie a copy of the freshly printed manuscript and then I printed one out for Ahuva also.

My hands were totally shaking as they read the manuscript. We sat there for about an hour as Heidi regaled us with stories about her five years at Camp Leilah.

"This is really good," Ahuva murmured.

I twisted my hair around my finger.

The two of them couldn't put the play down. Heidi was going hoarse, so we started playing *Apples to Apples*. Yaffa and Margalit, too.

"It's amazing!" Chanie said after an hour of reading.

"I'm driving it over to Rebbetzin Greenwald right now!" Ahuva exclaimed gleefully.

I couldn't help but smile as everyone patted me on the back.

Later that night, we got the green light from Rebbetzin Greenwald. It was all set! Our new play was: *The Princess and Delilah*, by Ella Sender. Oh, it had a nice ring to it!

"Girls, would you like to order something for supper?" Michal said, knocking on my door. To tell you the truth, I was kind of impressed. Michal? Fraternizing with my friends? This was big, folks, this was real big. "How about pizza?"

"Pizza sounds great!" I said, and my friends nodded.

"All right," Michal said, sounding quite pleased with herself. "I'll call Benny's Place. Three pies with everything on top, okay? It'll probably be here in about twenty minutes."

"Thanks," I said shyly. It was nice of Michal to do this. For me.

When the pizza arrived, everyone, including Tova, was sitting on the floor of my room having a DMC about being a doormat.

"Anyway," Rivky Rhein said as Yaffa came into the room, unsteadily holding three boxes of pizza. Rivky helped her onto the bed. The two of them had become tight friends, it seemed, "I don't believe in martyrdom at the sake of my sanity, you know. Like, I can be good, but to a certain level. Then, I'll crack."

"Well, I'm already cracked up, so it don't make no difference to me," I said.

Rivky gave me a look. "What are you talking about? You're the most levelheaded person I know!"

"Her?" Tzippa laughed. "Nah, only lately Ella's been normal. Before, she was a total nutcase."

"Yeah, Ellala," Naomi said. "What happened that made you so normal all of a sudden?"

"Oh, this and that," I said, winking at Tova. "So, what's in box number one? Is it anything with broccoli?"

"Hey, no pineapples?" Tova asked as we opened the boxes of pizza.

"Ew, pineapples?" Heidi said, wrinkling up her nose. "The only person who likes that is Chaiky Cukier."

It was then that I realized that Chaiky Cukier had never shown up to my house with the rest of the drama group.

And I actually cared. About not seeing her there, I mean. That was the weird part. But then Ahuva started speaking, and all thoughts of Chaiky Cukier flew out of my head.

"So," Ahuva said, her voice graced with a new ebullience. "Chanie and I are going to re-assign the parts tonight, and I know that everyone'll be really happy when we post the list up tomorrow!"

I knew what part was mine.

The princess, of course. After all, didn't Cinderella become a princess?

THAT NIGHT, I SLEPT BLISSFULLY. No more would I be relegated to the role of Sasha, the annoying little sister! I would be the princess, the main character! I mean, after all, Chanie and Ahuva would have at least a little bit of *hakaras hatov,* right? They'd give me the main role.

They'd have to.

The next day, school seemed to drag out. I couldn't wait for drama club! I couldn't wait. A list was posted on the door of the auditorium, but I didn't even bother looking at it, because I knew what part was mine.

"Congratulations, Ella," Rivky Rhein said to me as I waltzed into the auditorium. "You definitely deserved such a big part."

I gave her a big smile.

"All right!" Chanie said, trying to get everyone's attention. "Ahuva and I went to Office Max last night and we made photocopies of the script for everyone. We are majorly pressured for time, so please, everyone, take a copy and let's start from the beginning. Princess and Delilah, get up on stage."

Naomi and I walked up to the stage, and I thought how nice it was that they gave Naomi the second biggest role. I mean, she had been the main character in the other play, so it was probably kind of hard for her to concede and give me the biggest part.

I stared at the script, even though I didn't really need to, since I basically knew the whole play by heart (and it was a good thing, too, since I had the biggest role), waiting for Naomi to start.

She didn't.

"Ella!" Ahuva said impatiently after a minute. "We're all waiting for you to begin! What's wrong? Don't you know we have a ton to do tonight? The play is in less than four weeks!"

"But Naomi starts!" I protested.

"Come on, Ella!" Chanie sighed. "You can read! You know it says that the first one to speak is Delilah!"

I was Delilah? *I was Delilah?!* This had to be a joke! I was the annoying scullery maid? That was me? That was the role they had given me? I had been so kind and I had given them my play, the play I wrote diligently, lovingly, every single night. I had offered them my magnum opus and this, this was how they were repaying me!

How could they?

There was a snicker from the back of the room, so I slowly, devoid of any real emotion, began to read my part.

Practice did not go well that night, to say the least.

After practice, I went over to Chanie and Ahuva, who were packing up their stuff and getting ready to go home.

"I want to be the princess," I said, my voice sounding immature to my own ears.

"What?"

"I really had my hopes on being the princess," I said. "And I don't think it's fair that you gave that part to Naomi."

"Well," Chanie said slowly, "I don't think it would be fair if we took away the starring role from Naomi just because we switched plays. She really, really worked hard practicing for the other play. You should know that, Ella; you're her best friend."

Best friend, indeed! Suddenly, I felt ashamed.

"And we really did want to give you a big part," Ahuva said. "That's why we gave you Delilah."

I looked down at the floor. "Thanks," I whispered.

"Not everyone can be the princess," Chanie said softly. "There's only one."

I knew I owed someone an apology. A real apology this time, one that was long overdue.

I found Naomi cleaning out her locker.

"Hi," I said.

She looked up. I don't think Naomi and I had had a private conversation since I, um, since the fateful day when I didn't really behave.

"I'm sorry," I offered.

"Ella," Naomi said, her eyes welling up with tears, "why is it so hard for you to be happy when someone else gets something that you wanted for yourself? Especially when that someone else happens to be your best friend."

"I haven't really acted like a good friend, Naomi."

Naomi shook her head. "No, you haven't. I mean, was it important enough to you to have that part that you'd have wanted to take it away from me?"

"No way," I said, and I found that I really meant it. "If it meant you giving up the part, the whole thing loses its importance to me. You know, I know that there are much more important things in life than what role I play in a school production. It's just that it seemed

241

so important to me at that second, and I...I just didn't use my head," I finished lamely.

Naomi laughed. "It's okay, I guess," she said. "I'm just glad you realize that I wasn't trying to steal the part from you or anything."

"I realize," I said.

I realized something else, too. It wasn't *what* part you played that mattered; it was *how* you played it. Profound, no?

And Naomi and I linked arms and walked to Tzippa's car together.

Tzippa took a second look when she saw us laughing together.

"Did I miss something?" she said.

"No, Tzippala," I said. "I was the one who missed it."

When I got home that evening, Michal was in the kitchen cooking something. I dropped down my books and bag and headed to the fridge.

"So, Ayelet," she said, "how was your day?"

I cringed. Did she always have to pry? I knew she was nosy and she just wanted to find out what was going on in my life so she could get me in trouble.

"Good," I mumbled over my shoulder as I rummaged through the fridge for something to eat. I found an orange and closed the fridge door. Then I looked at Michal.

There were laugh lines by her mouth and her eyes were sparkling. She didn't look mean. Why did I think she was?

I sat at the table and started my math homework when Yaffa and Margalit ran into the kitchen.

"Hey, Ma!" Yaffa said with a laugh.

"Hey, Yaffa!" Michal said. "What's doing?"

There she was again, smothering her girls with love and affection and totally ignoring me. I started to brood again about how unfair it was and how she would never love me, when something about Michal's words suddenly struck me.

"How was your day?"

"What's doing?"

She had asked Yaffa and me almost the same question. She *was* treating me like her own daughter! *I* was the one ignoring and snubbing *her*! Could I simply have been projecting my own feelings about her?

The realization was like a dazzling streak of white light. *Michal never really hated me. I was the one who didn't like her,* and because of that, I deluded myself into thinking that she didn't love me. It reminded me of a Rashi we once learned. Bnei Yisrael said that Hashem didn't love them. The question was how Bnei Yisrael could even say such a thing, especially after all the miracles Hashem had performed for them and everything. Rashi explained that it was because Bnei Yisrael really didn't love Hashem. When someone says, "I hate you," he really means, "I think you hate me."

I thought I was so smart and knew everything, but I really didn't know anything at all. *Michal treated me exactly the same way she treated her own daughters.*

It was like I had spent the entire past year staring into one of those funhouse mirrors and all my features had looked so grotesque — fat lips, bulging eyes, bulbous nose. I had been so angry by what I was seeing that I didn't realize that if I'd just move aside, I'd see something very different. And now, was it just me, or was there a rosy glow bouncing off the counter? Was I just dreaming, or was I actually thinking that maybe I *could* love Michal?

Of course, Michal could never take the place of my real mother. But no one was expecting that. And whom was I helping by staying so angry? Whom was I helping by destroying what everyone else in the family was trying so hard to build? The real question was: whom was I hurting? And the answer was: everyone, but most of all, myself.

I could not, as much as I wanted to, go back to the past. I could not remain latched onto what was already gone. But I could carry the past with me in my heart — as I moved forward.

A fragrant whiff of something cooking on the stovetop reached my nostrils. Still caught up in my wondrous thoughts, I asked aloud, "What's for dinner?"

Michal smiled at me. "Chinese," she said.

"That's my favorite," I said slowly.

"I know," Michal said.

I got this warm, bubbly feeling inside me.

Michal gave me a wink. "Did I ever tell you that Chinese is my favorite, too?"

I don't know what overcame me, but right then and there I got up and gave Michal a big hug.

And she hugged me back and whispered in my ear, "I hoped you would be happy."

The words I'd said to Tzippa earlier that day replayed themselves in my head. *I was the one who had missed it.*

I'd had a lunar eclipse, you see. My world had been darkened even though it had really been in broad daylight. But I knew that I wouldn't be having another one of these lunar eclipses for a long time now. Instead, I'd be bathed in a glow. Because now, I could finally see the light.

THE FLOOR VIBRATED FROM ALL the commotion. Girls were running back and forth and dozens of babbling voices filled the air. Today was the big day — the day of our play. Finally. After these past few, frenzied weeks, when whoever was in the play practically *lived* the play 24/7, what with our round-the-clock practice and all, I couldn't believe we had actually reached this point.

I lounged on a chair that had the word "DIRECTOR" emblazoned on the back. It was really Ahuva's chair, but I didn't think she'd mind if I sat there. Only for a few minutes, anyway.

I watched Chaiky pin a sash onto Naomi's gown. When I'd heard that she was the head of costumes, I think my eyebrows had shot up even above my hairline. Chaiky, who looked like she couldn't put herself together if she tried, as *head of costumes*? But, as it turned out, she had once taken up sewing, and, as it was with all the other "knowledge" she'd picked up, she really knew her stuff! Looking at Naomi's shimmery gown, I realized that Chaiky had actually done a great job at it.

"So, Chaiky," I said conversationally, "did you finish fixing the collar on my costume?"

As the scullery maid, I was going to be wearing a black gown with a white apron in front and a white headband thing.

Chaiky nodded, but she didn't smile, which was odd, if you asked me. A few minutes later, she handed me the dress.

"Whoa, it's amazing!" I gushed. "Chaiky, how did you sew all these terrific costumes in such a short amount of time? I would never be able to do it!"

I expected her to say something funny, or odd, or make a little joke that I would find corny and grimace at, but she didn't say anything at all. She didn't even look at me.

And that's when I started to think that something was wrong. It suddenly dawned on me that I hadn't seen Chaiky acting like her crazy self for a few weeks already. Since…maybe since the day we had gone together — she and Tzippa, Naomi, Heidi, and me — to Iced Cream Café. I had been so busy with the play that I hadn't let it enter my consciousness too much, but now I was thinking about it. And…it made me concerned. I mean, where was the Chaiky who was usually doing all kinds of wacky things, the Chaiky who couldn't stop smiling, the Chaiky who couldn't stop laughing? I opened my mouth to say something to Chaiky, but just then Tzippa rushed over to me, begging me to braid her hair. She was playing one of the funny guards.

"What's wrong with Chaiky?" I whispered to Tzippa.

"Huh?" Tzippa said. "Ow, Ella! You're hurting my head!"

"Sorry," I said, not pulling her hair as hard as before.

The hours flew by as all the actresses got dressed and made up. Throughout it all, I watched in amazement as Chaiky, her red braid flying, fixed up costume after costume, all the while issuing orders to the other girls on the costume committee. I had never, ever seen her like this! I mean, there she was, our pesky little Chaiky, actually being a tremendous help! She was hemming, snipping, sewing, and cuffing, in addition to directing others. And the girls were listening to her, following her directions, scurrying around at her every command! I couldn't believe it. I almost didn't recognize her.

Still, though, I was bothered by the fact that she had none of that playfulness to her anymore, none of that funniness. This Chaiky Cukier was all business. Although I had to admit that I was impressed, I was also more than a little worried.

For now, though, I wanted to bask in my own glory! Does that sound conceited? It's just that I couldn't believe the moment was actually here. I couldn't believe that there would be an audience watching *my* play, *my* thoughts, turning into reality. These characters, the ones that I had thought up, they would actualize, on stage, for all to see! It seemed kind of unreal, to tell you the truth.

"Ten more minutes!" Ahuva called out.

Naomi's face was all red and she looked jittery. "It's a full house out there," she said, leaning on me for support. "What if I make a mistake?"

"You won't," I assured her.

"I will," she said. "I know I will."

"Chanie, I think we have a case of performance-phobia, a.k.a. stage fright here! What should we do?" I called out.

That actually made Naomi laugh and calm down.

"Seven more minutes!"

Out of the corner of my eye, I saw Chaiky putting on her yellow coat.

"Hey, Chaiky!" I said.

She looked at me, green eyes blazing with indifference.

"Where are you going?"

"Home," she said. "I'm going home."

"You're not staying for the play?" I said, not fully comprehending what she was saying.

"Nope."

"Five more minutes!" Ahuva blared.

"But why?" I asked.

"Why should I stay?" Chaiky retorted.

"Because it's the school play, that's why you should stay!"

Chaiky turned away. "It's not like anyone will ever care if I stay or not."

Did anyone really care about Chaiky Cukier? Chaiky, who tried so hard to be involved in everything, to act like she was having a good time…when she really wasn't.

"I care," I whispered.

"Don't lie." Tears were rolling down her cheeks.

"Two more minutes!" Ahuva's voice was reaching a feverish pitch.

"Chaiky! You have to stay! You have to!"

Chaiky shook her head. "I've had enough of trying hard."

"One more minute!" came the call.

"Aaaah!" Rivky Rhein rushed over. "Chaiky! Help me! My gown ripped and I'm in the first act!"

Chaiky immediately conjured a needle and swiftly fixed the hem of Rivky's gown.

"Thanks!" Rivky said happily.

"Chaiky, you have to stay — " I started to say again.

"Showtime!"

Chaiky began walking towards the door.

"Please, Chaiky. We need you."

This time she turned back. For a moment, neither of us spoke. We just stood there, looking into each other's eyes. Hers were brimming with tears. I was struck by those green eyes; I had never realized how beautiful they were.

"Okay," she said softy. "If you need me, I'll stay."

I gave her a quick hug, almost unaware of what had actually happened, but then, when I was on stage, reciting my memorized lines, I realized that all Chaiky Cukier ever wanted was simply to be wanted and appreciated. She needed to be needed. That was the reason behind her desperate attempts at getting attention.

Even as the play continued, I could not get Chaiky Cukier out of my head. How different was I from her? Didn't I need to be wanted and loved, as well? Didn't we all, for that matter? So what was so wrong with being friends with Chaiky?

This annoying façade she put on — could it be that it was only because she was afraid people would not see the real her, the amazing her, the Chaiky who could sew with a golden touch and who could manage a whole crew of people effortlessly? Well, she didn't have to be afraid anymore. I had seen the real Chaiky tonight, the one behind all the goofy jokes and smiles. Just as I had seen the real Chaiky on the bus that time. The Chaiky who was not one big joke. The Chaiky who was an introspective girl, who just happened to crave for others' love and attention — maybe a little like me.

The standing ovation at the end of the play was a sure sign that the play was a success. The audience must have been clapping for ten minutes straight!

Tova, Michal, Yaffa, and Margalit ran over to me the minute I got off the stage.

"You were so good!" Margalit squealed.

"I couldn't believe that it was *my* sister on stage!" said Yaffa.

Tova just gave me a bear hug while whispering into my ear, "Wow, wow, and more wow!"

Then Michal held out her arms to me, a bit hesitantly, as if she was unsure what my reaction would be, but I just smiled sheepishly and allowed myself to be hugged by her.

"You were wonderful, Ella!" she said warmly.

Again I felt that warm and bubbly feeling seeping through my body as I soaked up my family's compliments.

Just then, I saw someone waving to me. It was Ruti Reuben. She was standing together with her mother and Esti Waldman, and she was smiling. A real smile, not a fake one.

"Oh, there's Ruti Reuben," I said. "I must go over to her."

"Go, go!" Michal said with a laugh, patting me on the back. "We'll see you later at home!"

After another round of hugs from everyone, I waved goodbye to my family and went over to Ruti.

"Hi!" I said.

"So, you're the girl who was the maid in the play," Ruti's mother said to me.

I nodded. "Something like that."

"I was just telling Ruti," her mother said, "that she should join the play next year. Don't you think it would be a nice, creative outlet for her?"

"Oh, it's a lot of fun," I said. And then, winking at Ruti, I added, "It looks great on applications, too!"

Ruti quickly made a slashing motion and grinned back at me. "Then I have to join," she said. Her eyes sparkled. "But then I won't have time to do G.O. Oh, well, so I won't do G.O. next year!"

Her mother gasped and turned to her. "What, no G.O., Ruti? But all the girls in our family did G.O...."

Ruti just shrugged and laughed. "Well, I guess I'm unique, Ma!"

Once everyone in the audience had left, we had a huge cast party, compliments of Chanie and Ahuva.

On my own, I sat next to Chaiky, and she looked so happy about it, that it was almost worth it. Almost. Sometime during the evening, Chanie gave a little speech thanking Ahuva, and Ahuva gave a little speech thanking Chanie. Of course, the two of them then gave me a whole thank you speech, telling me how much *hakaras hatov* they had to me for saving the day with my play. And then they thanked all of us and gave us these mugs with our pictures plastered on them. After that, a few girls began singing color war songs.

That's when I stood up. "I just want to say — " I began.

"What are you doing?" Naomi, who was sitting on my other side, hissed, kicking me in the shin.

Tzippa just looked confused.

But everyone stopped singing.

"I just want to say, that there is someone else who must be acknowledged, because without her, this play would not have been nearly as wonderful as it was."

Everyone began whispering. Even Chaiky looked rather perturbed. All the thanks had already been given, right?

"That someone," I continued, "is Chaiky Cukier! I don't know if everyone realizes how hard she was working backstage and how much effort went into all of our costumes, even though Chaiky, talented as she is, made it look effortless. Let's hear it for Chaiky!"

I sat down. The girls started cheering and patting Chaiky on the back. Chaiky's ears were pink. Her eyes were glowing. For once, I realized, Chaiky didn't have to work hard to feel good and be happy. This time, like Ruti Reuben, her happiness was real.

It was the perfect evening.

Tzippa drove Naomi and me home.

"You know," I said, feeling warm and cozy in the car with just the three of us there, everyone tired and happy, "I was really surprised by Chaiky Cukier tonight. It was like I had never actually seen the real her before."

"I know," Tzippa said. "That girl is really amazing. When I think back to all those terrible things we said about her, I really feel bad."

"Why?" Naomi said. "She was always *sooo* annoying!"

"That's because she was trying to get our attention," I said quietly. "That was all she ever wanted. And we thought we had her all figured out. Just some crazy girl. We thought we really knew her."

"But how many times do we think we really know a person, and then think that we have the right to go ahead and talk about her?" Tzippa mused, her eyes focused solely on the road ahead of her. "We are always jumping to conclusions."

"You're so right, Tzippa," I said. "I-I've learned that you just need to give people a chance. When you talk about people, you automatically begin judging them, and you convince yourself that you know them, when you really don't at all."

"What are you two tonight, the *mussar* police?" Naomi said. "I mean, come on. It's not like we ruined Chaiky's life or anything. So we said a few not nice things about her behind her back. What's the big deal? Everybody does it."

"Naomi — " I said quietly. I remembered those two women speaking about me at Adele's wedding, as if they knew me and my entire situation and were in the position to judge me. I remembered how awful I'd felt. They didn't know me at all, and there they were, judging me and speaking badly about me behind my back.

But Naomi hadn't heard me. She was still going on. "Pretty soon,

I'll bet you'll start singing, '*Lashon hara lamed hey*, you belong in Pre-1A!' Come on, lighten up. It's normal."

"Naomi," I said again, "what if it was you?"

At first I could see that she was trying to think of a way to refute me. But she couldn't. No one wants to be the girl other girls whisper about. So why should we put others in that position? What had given me the right to judge and speak badly about Chaiky or Ruti or anyone else either, for that matter?

With the three of us sitting so close together in the car, in this rare, deep and pensive mood, I suddenly realized how young and reckless we were. We had hurt so many people with our words. We would never even know all the people we'd hurt. The thought was sobering, to say the least.

The streets were dark and empty, and, as Tzippa drove carefully through them, Naomi, who happens to have a beautiful voice, started humming softly the slow song of *"Mi Ha'ish Hachafetz Chaim."* Tzippa began harmonizing, and before we knew it, the three of us were singing, singing together in that little car in the dark night, singing until all the red lights turned green and we could go, go, go.

When I got home, it was quiet downstairs. Exhausted, I crept straight upstairs to my room — where I found Yaffa and Margalit coloring at my desk. I would scream, really, I would. What were they doing still up and out of bed? And what made them think they could just go into my private property and use it as their recreation center?

But then I thought about my discussion with my friends in the car. And I thought about what Auntie Shoshana had said about my mother, how my mother had never let anything bother her. Then I looked again at at Yaffa and Margalit, and you know what? I suddenly saw how cute they were, and how they could be my sisters if I wanted.

So I took a deep breath and just asked them tiredly, "What are you doing here, girls?"

"We're making you a picture!" Yaffa said, a smile on her face.

"So, you should hang it up on your wall!" Margalit exclaimed.

I approached them and saw a crude picture of a stage with a stick-figure girl — round, boppity, circle head, a bony line for a body, two arms jutting out, and a triangle as a maid's skirt — scribbled in black. It was beautiful. It was me.

"I love it," I said.

Yaffa smiled happily. "We were so proud of you when you were acting on stage, so we decided to make this for you!"

And I was glad I hadn't screamed at them.

Later, after Yaffa and Margalit had left the room, I glanced out the window, where I could see a round moon, like a brilliant, flawless jewel, gleaming in the sky. It was the same moon that had been there when my mother sang to me. I opened my drawer and took out the broken sparkly barrettes. Slowly, I glued each one back together. I placed them in my hair and looked at myself in the mirror.

I felt as if the heavy velvet curtain was slowly, slowly falling onto the floor of the stage. And then I listened for the audience. They were there, wildly clapping and cheering. And all of a sudden, it was as if a thousand cameras had flashed a brilliant dazzle of yellow, and I smiled.